VIRGINTOOTH

by Mark Ivanhoe

for MB

III Publishing
P.O. Box 170363
San Francisco, CA 94117-0363

1st Printing: Halloween, 1991

Cover Illustration by John Borkowski

ISBN 0-9622937-3-3

PRELUDE

She saw a beckoning shadow, which spoke to her without words, and she saw in its embrace destruction, and that which was worse than destruction.

Under the eye of the shadow, she saw revealed her entire life, and its conceits: its causes, faiths, ideologies, lovers... A parade of futility, dreams broken and bleeding on the shards of bottles and needles.

Now that she stood before Evil made manifest, the realization came to her that her life's petty and vulgar impurities had been nothing more than an audition for this moment; her heart, still young in years but burdened with the weight of her sins, leapt to perceive that she had been found acceptable: her tepid blood found worthy for the slaking of the shadow's need...

Without another backwards glance, she went to it.

THE MASTER'S WORDS

1.

In the beginning, there was nothing, and that was good. But ever so slowly, there came to her a flicker of sensation, an awareness below consciousness that her existence continued. That was less good, for the long unknowing sleep had held no dreams, no discomfort. For the essence of this sensation was *pain*: a quiet gnawing that never ceased, like insects worrying at the tissues of her dead brain.

Then, there came to her a gradual awareness of direction. The source of the pain emanated from above her current position. That knowledge produced in her a recognition of spatial relationships: if the sensation came from above, then evidently there was something else which was below, and her entity occupied a certain area which was bounded by these other somethings.

Thus, she came to an awareness that she possessed a body. So her expanding mind sent forth questings of nerve-currents, to seek the bounds of her flesh. Her torso she discovered, and her limbs, and finally sensation reached even to the tips of her fingers and toes. Yes, she possessed a body, and one of human shape, but there was no sensation to it, save only for the continuing experience of its pain, which persisted without dulling.

Up to this point, there had been no sight or sound to interrupt the discovery of her body. Now, softly and faintly, she began to be aware of a distant scuffling sort of noise, muted as if it came from beyond a barrier. The sound rapidly became louder and nearer, until it was just beyond the cubicle or receptacle in which she was contained. Then there was the hard noise of the splintering of wood, and a sound of lifting.

Light shot into her space, piercing, crushing, and the pain became many degrees of magnitude greater. She forced her muscles into their first movement, drawing her arms up to her face to hide it from the light. There came a low, painful whine, which she slowly realized was coming out of her own throat.

A voice came down from above her: "Stop that. You look like a cretin. Come along, get up, the night isn't going to last forever."

She withdrew her hands, opened her eyes, and looked up the shaft of her grave to see a tall figure which stood on its edge. It was male, dressed in black garments from throat to foot. The hurtful moonlight reflected down off his high forehead and hooked nose, but left coal shadows in his eye-sockets, below the hairy brows. She was distressed by that face and tried to shrink back, seeking the safety of her casket. But he reached down, and his arm stretched all the way down to her in an unnatural fashion, and, seizing her in a wrenching grip, brought her up to the level of the ground.

The man looked her over with a distasteful grimace, and then broke into a smile without humor. "You're a mess. In all the days you were conscious down there, didn't it ever occur to you that you had the power to halt the decay processes and keep all the vermin away from you?" he remarked drily. His voice was deep and harsh, but not entirely lacking in melody. His eyes remained hidden in shadow. "Excuse me, I have been remiss," he continued. "I've failed to give you the greeting which my people traditionally offer to those who have joined their ranks." He gave a mock bow, and said, with a note of derision: "*I welcome you, once child of mortal flesh, now heir of the unending mastery, to the brethren of the night-tide, the keepers of the blood-quenched thirst. Spurn the agony of the day and abide with me, until the dark has conquered and ceases not.*" Then he strode to her and struck her across the face so that she collapsed on the ground. "And let that be your very first lesson: I am your Master in everything you say, do and think, and I have a quick and capricious temper."

He smiled again down upon her. "But I am also kind-hearted when I want to be. You're nothing but an empty shell. Fill yourself." He withdrew from somewhere on his person a small furry thing which cried with fear, and handed it to her. She gripped it, turning it over in her hands, listening to its squeaks. After a moment, she clutched it to her breast and looked puzzled. The Master laughed mockingly again. "You *bite* it, girl! Bite it and drain the good things inside it!"

Following his gesture, she did just that. There was a small rush of warm stuff into her throat, which she automatically swallowed. It was bitter, and seemed to burn her a little as it went down, but after she was finished there was a slight alleviation of the gnawing pain. She smiled a little at that.

She wanted more, but had no words in her to ask. She stood there, silent in the moonlight, her entire being filled with supplication to him, the provider. This helplessness in her softened something in him, so that he smiled softly and reached out to give her the slightest of caresses. She flinched at the first contact, but seeing that this was not to be another blow allowed herself to flow into his hands. Then he spoke to her again: "You're still no better than an animal. You can hear what I'm saying but you can't understand anything but the tones of the words I speak.

"Should I keep you like this? Do I want yet another brute blindly following behind me, reminding me of my own hungry lower nature? Or shall I mold you into some exotic form that amuses me? I can do that. When I drained you, it wasn't only the blood that I devoured, but all of your memories with it, all your dreams and motivations. If I wanted to, I could reach into the stock I have inside me, of the uncounted millions who have felt my sharp kiss, and choose a little bit of thought here, another belief there, and make you into a completely new person according to my fancy.

"But that's not what I want tonight. I want you to be free beside me, within the limits I'll impose; for that, I am going to restore to you all your past, a full awareness of your position, and your fate."

He took her face between both hands, brought it close to his, and at last she could see the fierce eyes within his sockets. They seethed and burned, and the fire leapt out towards her, causing a scorching unlike the other pain she felt. It strove against her, the light of his eyes, piercing into and violating her inner being, and planted in her mind the knowledge of what she was and was to be.

"Your name is Elizabeth."

2.

There flooded back into her soul everything, both for good and for evil: the delighted cries of her mother at her first quavering steps, and the tears falling over her father's grave... The secret fire engendered by her first impassioned kiss, and the ache of the endless series of heartbreaks... The charge of the first drag on a smuggled bottle, and the dull throb of the loss of virginity... The frenzied struggle against the bonds of a straightjacket, and the terror of standing alone before the magistrate... The empty contemplation of restored freedom while still enchained in the prison of her own skull... The first nibble of encroaching despair at the finish of another night without rest... The growing feeling like there was a hook in her jaw, and a net ready to take her away from the seas of the living and cast her into the blankness of death... And finally, the opportunity for escape, into the beckoning shadow: the shadow that now stood once more before her.

But Elizabeth turned away from his revealing eyes, and glared down upon the gravemarker, now dirt-encrusted and tottering at an angle from her exhumation, and she began to feel anger. "*Why*?" she demanded. "Why did you have to disturb me? I never knew it was going to be so peaceful there, and so painful back here again. Why couldn't you have let me stay down there?" She might have attacked him, but his eyes still held her will transfixed.

His reply was like the growl of distant thunder: "And how could I have possibly passed you up? Thousands and thousands of humans have died for my nourishment, and every one of them I now contain inside of me, each one crying out for this freedom I've given you. But almost every last one of them has been rife with his commonplace beliefs, rancid with his self-satisfaction, his petty jealousies and passions. They are small and common; how they wept and pleaded when I cut their pallid lives short! Only the tiniest handful through the centuries have I touched who disdained the trivial goals of mortal life, seeking their own path toward an aim outside what the world forces on them, the Zen master, the starving poet, the sex murderer, those are the ones I particularly seek out with hopeful pleasure, and ever so sweet their life tastes when I destroy them...

"You, you are one of the rarest jewels among all mortal lives. You had no purpose to your existence. You rejected the everyday concerns but failed to find comfort in iconoclasm. You were like a blank canvas, untouched by the common, yet also unmoved by uncommon thought, and unable to find even the comfort of madness. It is to you, and the few others like you I have located over the centuries, to whom I give this gift: the second life of the undead. I have given you my will, and a share of my powers, to quench your thirst both for blood and for a reason for existence. And in return, I am your God now, and it's for my service that you exist."

"But the pain, it's so bad," she said, shaking with its spasms.

His laughter was cruel and disdainful. "But what better way could unlife be, but agony? Look up into the sky!" he commanded, and he pointed toward the lowering quarter Moon. "That's the source of your pain! It is the Moon's light which stabs at you, trying to reject you as something which should not exist on the sleeping face of Earth. The light of the Moon will tear at you forever, and you're never going to find rest from it; be aware that this light is nothing more than a reflection of the even more dreadful light of the Sun, which will burn you to ash and destroy you in its deadly power, if you ever make the mistake of venturing into daylight.

"Yet it is this very same agonizing light that gives you your vitality. You *felt* it, didn't you, even while you were lying in your grave? It's what first defined you as a being, as the subject of inflicted pain. At the deepest core of your person it is still the sum of what you are, that which reacts to this pain, and seeks the one way to make it cease, even if only for a moment. The pain gives you the strength to fight it, the cunning to resist it, and the desire for its removal. The only way you will ever free yourself from it is to totally surrender to the agony, and allow your whole soul to collapse into nothingness."

She listened to all he was telling her, and her thoughts swam in wonder and fear. "Do I have any choice?"

"You have the most important choice of all, Elizabeth. I've given you the gift of undeath, and I can take it from you again, and return you to the noisy throng inside my heart. Just tell me, any time, and I'll return you to the endless silent grave. But let me tell you now, the priests are liars and the mystics deluded. There is no life other than this beyond the tomb. Only our way. Will you reject it now?"

"No!" She was surprised at the vigor of her outburst. "I don't know what to think. It's all going too fast. Is any of this really happening? You're my murderer. How can I trust a word of what you're telling me now?

"But I still don't want to die. Not even now. I can see now that I've never really lived, so I'll take this, whatever it is, that you're offering me. It's another opportunity... And the last chance I have left."

His expression was enigmatic. "You accept my gift then, and all the consequences that may come out of it?"

That gave her a moment's pause, but then she replied. "I do. What do I have to do?"

There was a wind beginning to blow, cutting fiercely through the grass, but having no effect on them. "You must bow down to me, on your knees, and acknowledge me, as your God and Master, forevermore."

And she did so.

3.

The Master accepted her worship, and then turned to point again at the sky. "Look, the Moon is starting to set, and our power is reaching its height. Time is passing by, and there is so much that I have to teach you." He drew her gaze down, to the empty grave. "A vampire is the master of appearance and delusion, and controls the elementary powers of the world. Look at what we can do." He gestured, causing the wind to gather around them, and to fill in the dirt of the grave, even setting the marker aright and leaving no sign of their disturbance. He caused the ground to rise up into a great mound below his feet. Upon the crest he held up his hands and conjured in them balls of fire, which he juggled, causing them to dance and encircled him as he spoke further. "Earth and air and fire are under our control, and we can make them do anything within the possibilities of imagination. *Anything.* Only water is outside our power, because water is moved by the Moon, which drives its tides. But outside that one restriction, there is nothing we can't control; this is only one of our powers, and not even the greatest of them."

The Moon had indeed now vanished under the horizon of the distant city, and a weight was lifted from Elizabeth's frame. The pain didn't vanish; it would never wholly depart from her, but it was lessened now to a dull sensation in her gut. She felt as if she could fly, she thought, but then caught herself, realizing that the cliche was now a valid possibility. She stifled a giggle.

The Master perceived this thought, and he smiled. "Yes, that's another of our capabilities. But the legends distort and try to degrade the grandeur of our existence. We don't have to turn into a bat (although we could if we desired it). No, we walk invisibly among the human throng, and they feel nothing, except maybe a faint disquiet as we pass. Take my hand now, and let me show you the path."

And even as he spoke she saw his form commence to fade into a cloud. Elizabeth hesitated. "I'm afraid. If my body disappears, how can I control where I go? Don't leave me, Master!" But as she was saying this, he became wholly insubstantial and her gripping fist lost him and closed on itself.

He was no longer extant, but she heard his voice, in the wind which he commanded to form his words for her to hear: "Be strong, and don't be afraid! Don't you realize that your body is nothing but a shell to enclose your being, your *will* which has refused to surrender to death? It's your concentration, your refusal to allow yourself to diffuse into the atmosphere that will preserve you. Come with me now, and I'll keep you close to myself this first time."

He reached out to seize her will and forcefully stripped her of her bodily self. She quailed, but then suddenly found herself free. Free of the encumbrance of form. She no longer had a boundary between that which was clearly her and that which was other than herself. She flowed into the surrounding night, the laughing wind, the watchful trees. She felt the breath of sleeping birds and mice, the silent stalk of the cat through the underbrush. The hungry pain tempted her; how easy it would be to reach out to snuff those tiny flames of lives. But the Master was impatient and called her to follow him. They flew on, two faint clouds of mist dry as bones, and passed from the cemetery.

4.

They moved into the city, an entirely foreign environment to Elizabeth with her extended sensibility. The sharp verticals of buildings daunted her will, impeding the soft flow of her dissolved body. Life was furtive in the underpinnings of the city. Blades of grass struggled to break free of the sterile concrete, yet sought the safety of corners to escape the decimation of vehicles and feet. Insects hid restlessly in cellar cracks. Rodents scurried among the shadows, seeking food, a quick mating, and then the return to safety.

But the pain had come to life in her once again. A hundred thousand heartbeats surrounded her, and she felt the throbbing of each one, calling out to her, mocking her by their challenge, to come and stifle each one. "You feel them now, don't you," the breath of the Master whispered to her. "Yes, it's out there, a sea of warm fresh blood, just waiting there for us. Don't you wish you had a thousand hungry mouths, to take and devour the last one of them this very night, to still that horrible beating racket, to bring the great silence of the grave to this din, and to fill that emptiness inside you that can never otherwise be satisfied.

"But that's too much for us, on this one short night. Someday, when we have quenched the Sun for all time, they'll scream and quail in the darkness that will never end. And then, then we'll finally take our vengeance on them all, and the pain will cease, in the final thirsty apocalypse of the vampires. Wait just little while longer, hold the pain inside and cherish it, and that way you'll fully relish the night of our wrath.

"For now, you have to concentrate yourself, draw your wide-flung senses together, and seek the one who is looking for us tonight." And together they focused their energy, looking for the one heartbeat among the multitude, one who searched for them as much as they searched for it. Hunters and prey, linked by the chain of causation, a swift motion from the willing to the completion. They coalesced, back into the form of male and female, and found themselves standing in the shadows of a darkened street, hearing quick footsteps moving towards them.

There was a man, walking along the echoing streets of the night city. He was small and shabby. Worn-out shoes. Lines carved in the unshaven face. He walked quickly, but with uncertainty, hesitating for a moment, and then rushing forward again, toward their shadowed meeting place. His voice was harsh, guttural but wheezing as he spoke to them:

"*You!* I know you! You're waiting there. You've been waiting right outside my reach, all my life!" A hacking cough. "Your eyes burn me, every night. I can't sleep, cause I feel them, but can't burn them back! They're so empty... You make me want to fill them, but I'm too smart, too smart to let you pull that trick over me!"

But big dirty tears were running down his ruined face. "But I wanted you so much. Why didn't you understand that? So many years I wanted you. I wanted to give everything to you, and you'd give those hungry eyes to me, and then I'd be strong and silent, like you, and then none of them would've dared what they done to me! I could-a shown her something different then, that night she laughed at me. I'da stepped right down on her face, and then I'da dried her up and squashed her down just like a paper bag!"

He withered to the pavement like a balloon losing air. He drained the last drops from his bottle. "'S all too late now. Don't care no more now. Time's come to get it over with." A pause. "Well, come on! I'm ready now, ready as I'm ever gonna be! Do it, or lemmee go once and for all! I don't care." The Master gestured, and the man arose, not of his own will. He gathered his courage, and met them with dignity, though he trembled a little.

The Master approached him, and softly, perhaps lovingly, took hold of him, in the arm, with the teeth. And Elizabeth moaned when she saw this, unable to withstand the violent craving coursing through her body; she leapt at him like a dog, tearing his throat, feeling the greasy flesh part under her bite. She swallowed the taste of sweat and dirt and hair, and then came the hot blood smashing into her mouth, and forcing its way down her throat like a weapon. The sound of the heart pumping the blood drilled all sensation out of her being, save only for the bitter salt taste, pouring on and on into and through her, an unending fountain. She grew aware that the taste of the blood carried the essence of the victim: birth, love, joy, tears, and the shock of this sudden death. She tasted the galling frustrations, the incomplete satisfactions, the lathe of the years wearing him down past both sorrow and joy, down to the quick of desperation. She ate his personality, and relished its extinction.

And it was delicious.

5.

She regained awareness of herself kneeling on the cold pavement, worrying and gnawing at the throat of the corpse, and she wanted more, *more*! The pain, the pain had vanished during the sweetness of the kill. Now it was returned, and it compelled her, calling on her to find more blood, more sacrifices to assuage its rage within her, but the Master savagely kicked her away from the dead meat. She rolled away into the gutter, and she arose again with a feral stare.

"You fool! Stupid idiot!" He spat red upon her. "You think you're a beast now, to take what you want like an animal?" And he struck her again.

He seized her with a about her throat in a grip almost strong enough to tear her head off. "Think! I'm not going to allow you to get away from me. There are too many mindless crying things in the night. You are greater than they. I gave you back your consciousness. You mustn't let it go again."

"But Master," she moaned, "it's so hard, I can't fight it. I don't deserve to be your servant."

"You must fight it, and you will. I'll drive the beast out of you with these hands, if I have to." He turned to the stiffening body. "And now look at what you did to this meat. You've torn the throat completely to shreds. You've ground his bones to dust under your rage to take every bit of him. The humans are stupid, but not morons! Do you want the city to rise up with a million hunters with their crosses and stakes, poking into every dark corner where one of us might be hiding? No, we have to be subtle, and disguise what we do, until the night of our triumph comes." He ran his finger over the wounded corpse, and made the flesh heal itself. "Look! Our power over the elements has many uses for us. This one will be thought the victim of exposure, maybe, or cardiac arrest. They mustn't suspect us, before our power waxes to its height."

"Am I forgiven, Master?"

He paused. "This time," he said, and then he suddenly smashed her in the belly, so that she had to retch, and vomit forth all the blood she had taken in, black and slimy with the bile of the undead. "But don't forget that I am the Master. I am the first one to feed, always, unless I tell you differently. You take only what I leave you. Remember! Now come on with me again, it's getting late, and we have to get back to our shelter."

Yes, the first glimmerings of impending day were appearing on the horizon, like the first touch of despair. Elizabeth sobbed a little, and stuck out a finger to take up just a tiny bit of her meal now lost, and licked it with sorrowful regret. The Master allowed this, and then caused the blood on the street to vanish from human detection. (There were traces that remained, which only the vampires could still detect. Elizabeth would perceive them there forever, every night when she might pass this corner by, there to mock at her and remind her of her moment of weakness.) Then he returned them to immaterial form, and they passed from that place.

His will took them to an even more deserted portion of the city, a realm of empty warehouses and boarded-up tenements. Into the tiniest of cracks they flowed, where even a cockroach might struggle, to materialize in a dank sub-basement, with no entrances or windows. There were no fixtures or furniture, just a pair of ragged pallets lying on the earthen floor. Elizabeth couldn't help but feel a certain disappointment.

The Master smiled as he explained: "What were you expecting? No, there are no haunted castles or mausoleums for us, you see. Although I could do it, if I really wanted it that way. But this is enough for me, and good enough for you too. We're weak in the daytime, nearly helpless as we lie here. I prefer to have a secure refuge. There isn't a single human now alive who's aware of the existence of this cellar. We'll be safe here, if anywhere." And at that, with no further word or preparation, he laid himself flat on one board.

Elizabeth hesitated, uncertain of the events of the night. She was awash in horror, at the vile thing which they had done, but more so at the terrible reaction which she had experienced. There was nothing in her memory that could match the savagery of the bestial attack she had made, or the hopelessness of being which it had dredged up within her. And now they were here, in filth and degradation, hiding from the innocent light of day. Was there any escape possible from this? Would she take the course of escape even if it was available? The pain lay crouched in her bones, mocking her every thought beyond its own satiation.

And then, the pain was magnified. The Sun, cruel and relentless, had risen, and it proclaimed that she was dead, *dead*, she had no right to remain sentient on its green and happy Earth. It wrenched her, flayed her, crucified her, sought to pry the flesh off her bones, even where she crouched hiding from it. She screamed and screamed again, falling to the soft dirt floor and writhing in excruciating pain. She heard the Master, lying on his own pallet, give forth a dry rattling moan as well, as the fierceness of the attack hit upon him as well. Somehow she crawled onto the other bed, and then at last the pain grew so much that she lost awareness, and knew no more.

6.

There was a draft from some unidentifiable crack, wafting in a cool sharp breeze which revived her, bringing her the awareness that the crushing agony had once more faded into the usual dull ache of pain. Elizabeth lay on her pallet, drinking in the softness of the air, the blessed sweet darkness, and found within her spirit a certain contentment, perhaps even a state of bliss. Yes, perhaps this was the way for her, the stealthy hunt, the thirsty mouth waiting to be filled... She cast her senses forth from her body, to detect what lay around her shelter, threat or prey, but she was surprised to find her awareness was cut short at the edge of the building in which she was hidden. She could detect beyond it. "Master," she said, "what's wrong? I can't feel the world around us, the way I could last night."

"It's raining," he explained. "I told you last night, about how water is the only element we can't control. It's sort of a mixed blessing. The clouds hide the light of the Moon, and that gives us a little relief from its agony. But on the other hand, the falling rain is like a veil which is difficult for us to penetrate. Our senses are muted and confused by it. It drives our victims into their homes and shelters. It makes the hunt more difficult on a night like this, but the need is not so pressing."

"But will we go out on the hunt, even on a such a night?"

"We hunt always, every night. We'll hunt even in a blizzard, when the wind and the snow blow our forms to shreds, and we have to concentrate all our energy even to maintain existence. For the hunt *is* our existence."

At this he arose, and bade her dissolve herself. As they slipped into the night Elizabeth encountered the curious feeling of the rain passing right through her. There was no pain or discomfort, merely a peculiar cool slicing sensation, not even wet. They were forced to maintain human forms, for their mist-selves would be wholly washed away, and they were limited to the ordinary senses of mortal humans. Elizabeth could almost convince herself that her death and revival had been only a dream, that she was still nothing more than a mortal woman. But the dark presence of the Master, brooding in his human visage beside her, prevented the delusion from lasting for long.

As they walked in a fast wolf-like lope through the streets, Elizabeth gave thought to their condition. "Master," she said as they were passing under some awnings, "are the stories the mortals tell about us the truth?"

He paused, and there was a sharpness in his gaze. "Which stories exactly do you mean?"

She was somewhat embarrassed to think back on them, and hesitated a moment before going on: "Um, you know, the stakes, the cross, the garlic. I, I don't feel anything in me which tells me that these things have power over us, but is any of it true?"

He gave a short and curt laugh. "They're a pack of lies, but there's usually at least a hint of truth in every lie, and these are no exception. There's a great deal of history behind the symbols of religious belief. But think about it this way: the vampires are a fraternity spread all over the world, hidden in every city, in all cultures. Why should a vampire in Mecca be afraid of the crucifix, or the vampire back in Peru before the coming of the conquistadors?

"No, it is not the sign itself which has power. That is just two sticks glued together. It's the *faith* behind the symbol, the faith in something beyond the human's petty self-centeredness, which has power to drive us away. If a mortal has a strong belief in a force above his or her own life, then, and only then, can he or she defeat the vampire, to thrust us from him or her, even to destroy us, if we're not careful. And this belief can be focused on any of the holy symbols which humans conjure up for themselves: the Cross, the Star, the

Fivefold Path..." He smiled grimly. "I remember one time, many years ago, when I sought out a great man of science, for I desired to savor the taste of his life of materialism. But he had such strong faith in his own rationalist system, such terrible conviction that a vampire could not logically exist, that he drove me away with the most basic sign of his scientific reason: the right triangle.

"But, happily for us, even in the wildest and most zealous of times and places, when religious fever breaks open among the mortals like a sore, it is only the tiniest of minorities who can attain to this degree of selfless belief. I think you remember, from your mortal life, that humans believe out of habit, or as a social exercise, or thinking that they'll make some gain out of it. And those, by far the majority of human folk, are our fair prey. I've wondered at times that maybe we serve the purpose of whatever God that might really exist, to cull out the flock of his false worshippers..." He paused for a few moments, as if lost in some reverie. "Here, let me show you; this talk inspires me to give you a demonstration of what I've been talking about."

They hurried through the storm, and Elizabeth found that they were coming to a great cathedral, a tall and imposing monument to what the mortals claimed to believe. They entered, and found a late service drawing towards a conclusion. The patter of the raindrops added a staccato rhythm to the droning words of the priest at the altar. The Master made a gesture, and rendered them invisible, but able to perceive and communicate with those they might choose.

There were only three worshippers, coming to such a late service in the bad weather, and the Master guided them to the first one. It was a young-looking, ragged woman, who wrung her hands with terrible passion as she mouthed the prayers. Elizabeth was afraid that the young woman would have strength against them; the fear combatted the ravening increase of the hungry pain as the vampires drew near. The Master, casting a glamour, knelt down beside the woman and whispered in her ear, with a concerned tone (containing just a touch of mockery), "Dear child, what troubles your soul, making you pray with such ardor?"

The woman replied to him without looking at him: "I'm moved by the Spirit. I want to give myself wholly to our Lord." But in her words Elizabeth could hear another message, which was saying: "I'm hurt by the world and rejected. Why doesn't everyone love me for what I am? I've given up my fight. Let God come down from the heavens and rescue me, because I'm not going to try anymore."

Elizabeth hissed to the Master, "Is she ours? Shall we take her now?" But he replied, "Not her. She's common stuff. Let's look at the others before we decide."

The second worshipper was an aging man, balding, lines about the face, dressed well but possessing the look of intense suffering about him. He prayed quietly, but sweat ran down his brow. "And what of you," asked the Master, "what is the underlying root of your faith?"

"I am unworthy, a sinner beyond redemption. I cast my failures before my Lord and beg for His mercy," he murmured. But his eyes told a truer tale. "I'm a butcher among my fellow-men. I'll perform any craven act, I hesitate at no treachery in my quest for betterment, and I love every moment of it. But I'm afraid that I'll be condemned to suffering unless I pave my way with a little bit of superficial contrition." Once more Elizabeth slavered to attack him, and the Master again held her back. "He's an empty fruit. He'll fill up our belly but give us no pleasure in his destruction," said the Master as he turned toward the last supplicant.

It was an ancient woman, worn beyond even her advanced years, so that Elizabeth ached to think of the weight upon her fragile bones. She seemed to be paying only slight attention to the order of the service, and Elizabeth wondered if she was asleep. The Master strode boldly to her: "And what is your tale, old bag? What's your excuse for bothering your God with your tired old prayers? Wouldn't it be better for you be making your plans for meeting Him any day now?"

She didn't even appear to notice him for a minute, and then slowly looked up from her reverie, and croaked out with surprising vehemence: "I see that you aren't the great tempter coming to torment me again, not this time. You are just a cringing shadow, hiding from the light, and with a second shadow crouching behind you. I don't need to be afraid of you, or even pay you any attention. I know He keeps me safe!" And at that, she arose, and the very fire of the Sun shot out from her flesh at the Master, fierce and all-consuming. Elizabeth screamed and, although the sight and sound were invisible to their senses, both of the other worshippers were disturbed from their own concentration for just a moment. Perhaps they caught a fleeting glimpse of the power of her faith before they fell back and returned to their atrophy.

The Master had vanished into dust at the flash of the woman's faith. Elizabeth reeled in the dread of loneliness. Then the Master slowly gathered himself back into a human form, collecting himself in the shadows, and Elizabeth ran to kneel down to him. "I was so afraid, afraid that she'd destroyed you." He laughed shortly, giving no sign of having been fazed. "No, I'm old enough to have the wile to elude the enthusiasm of maniacal old women. But the demonstration has been good enough: you see now how physical appearance counts very little in consideration of the strength of human souls.

"But we still aren't finished with our survey," he continued, seeing her looking hungrily over the prospective victims once more. "There is still the priest."

Elizabeth felt a fearful doubt. If the old woman contained such a blasting power, what destructive might could the priest command, trained in the ways of sanctity? She hesitated before she followed him behind the sanctuary. The service was ended, and the priest was laying his vestments aside. He was a portly man, red-faced, satisfied-seeming in his livelihood and his God. But when they entered, he spoke angrily in his piping voice: "How did you get in here? Mass is ended, and these aren't open hours for confession."

"But we're lost souls, looking for a little guidance. Won't you help us?" said the Master in a honeyed voice.

He flushed even further, and his voice quaked in rage. "Get out of here! Go on, or I'll call the police! It's late, and I have to be going. Come back in the morning. There'll be someone here who'll listen to you then. I have to be on my way." And Elizabeth looked into the pool of his words, and descried there vanity, self-centeredness, gluttony and the most hateful of prides, the disdain of others whom he deemed lesser than his own demonstrated holiness. "Yes," said the Master hungrily, "you are the one for us tonight." The priest backed nervously away. "What do you mean? Get out of here, right now! I don't have any time for games..." But the Master only took a step nearer, and Elizabeth was close behind.

This time she succeeded in holding her hunger in check, allowing the Master to take his fill, as his due. For just a moment, as his spirit faded into nothingness, the priest abandoned his pretensions, casting himself onto the bosom of his God at the last possible moment, and there was a weakening in the Master as he supped. But even as the Master weakened, the priest strengthened in opposition, and as he did so, he again took up his pride; this cost him his victory. He slumped back again, and the Master made a quick end of it. Elizabeth finished up what remained after he stopped; only a few flashes of childhood memories were left, which the Master allowed her to swallow down. But even that was good.

Later, as they lay down to await the dawn, Elizabeth took thought. "Master," she said, "I pray you won't be offended at my words. You're now my only God and object of worship. But I can't help but think about what happened tonight. Was there something beyond the merely mortal taking place, when the old woman repulsed you? Isn't there anything true in their belief? Is there a God out there somewhere, who saves the humans? And does that mean we are cut off from Him if He does exist?"

The Master paused for a long time, so long that she was afraid he was angry. At last he replied, and she thought to detect the slightest of sadnesses in his words: "I've been walking the Earth for more years than you would believe, and I've seen a remarkable number of actions by the mortals which have caused me to suspect a supernatural cause... But nothing is certain, and I don't know of any of the undead who have ever obtained that kind of knowledge.

"Are we cut off entirely from the hope of salvation which the mortals preach to each other? Their myths about us tell us so, that we are damned by our nature. Maybe. But wouldn't divine mercy apply, even to creatures like us, if we repented at the moment of our destruction? That kind of question has been greatly troublesome to me at times. I knew a theologian once, whom the mortals eventually decided was a heretic, who taught that even the demons of Hell (should such beings, and such a place, exist) could still have the hope of mercy, at the end of all things..."

His voice trailed off. But as the pain of dawn smashed down upon them, she heard him give out a last murmur, before they were crushed into insentence: "But just think of it, the chance to sneak our way into Heaven, and there to drink of all those supposed saints who escaped me so long ago, and even perhaps to give a deadly little kiss to God Himself..."

7.

The nights flew by, and Elizabeth slowly learned the ways of the vampire. She discovered the abilities within herself, the molding of appearances, the control of the forces around her, and the never-satiating pleasure of the feeding. There came to be a pattern to their existence together, the Master and she: a ritual of the hunt, the meal and then the return to their cellar, where they would converse for the short while remaining before the dawn. It was a pattern, but it never became a drudgery to her. The pain of the hunger was too much a constant, and the thrill of the attack rescued her life from the routine. She thought that this must be akin to the life of the wild hunting beast, fulfilling the instinctual patterns but never straying from the cutting edge of destruction. She suspended as much of thought as was possible, and believed that she had attained a state of undead purity.

The Master spoke of many things. He drew down deep from the wells of history, from those whose memories he had taken, over the long centuries. He knew so much that at times she would have doubts, disbelieving that he could have been in three or four places simultaneously for the great moments of mortal history. But she came to understand that the vampires were not alone in their ability to drink of the souls of the humans around them; the mortals themselves regularly practiced the technique on each other, battening down on one another in their own endless quest to pour meaning into the insignificance of their beings. They read of others, they spoke to others, they dreamed and fantasized of some occult way to bring themselves effortlessly to the higher planes of existence; then they died, broken and disillusioned. The realization comforted her, on the occasions when she doubted the justice of their depredations.

One evening, as they awakened to the call of the night tide, she asked: "Master, you've told me so many things. You've given me knowledge which has spread my consciousness throughout the universe, and you've made me wise in the way of the undead. But there's one thing you've never spoken of directly: how many others are there like us? And where do all the other vampires dwell?"

No blood flowed through the Master's veins, and hence his countenance did not physically darken, but Elizabeth sensed the harshness of his reaction from the subtle narrowing of his eyes. "That's not a subject which I'd like to bring up at this time," was his only reply. "I'm sorry, Master," she persisted, "but how can I go on in this way, not knowing how to find others, or even to know if they exist?"

"A predator in the wild hunts alone, abandoning even her offspring if she has to. Do you want me leave you to yourself?"

This threat sank deeply in her, as she realized that the Master was her only foundation, her one security in undeath. To be alone, she knew, would be the deepest pit of despair. "No, no, please never do that to me, Master!" she exclaimed, and he detected the utter sincerity of her plea, and was moved to smile. "I won't bring the subject up, not ever again. But please don't even suggest the thought of leaving me. I beg you, Master."

Pleased in his vanity, he was moved to answer her, after all (but as ever, with just the hint of derision below the surface of his words): "I find myself warmed by the depth of your devotion. I'm pleased to such a degree that I will answer your request, just this one time. But don't let the subject of the others ever come up between us again, or you'll find out just how unpleasant my anger can be.

"I am the first and foremost of the vampire kind. My memories extend back, back, to the very beginning. I've always been undead, from the origin of all things. But I've grown so lonely, time and again, more times than you can possibly dream. I look around and see the strength the mortals can achieve, when they have the support of others beside them, bonded to them by birth and affection, and so I have tried, time after time, to bring others into undeath to accompany me. You're only the most recent of a long line of companions I have selected for myself, Elizabeth."

And a deep-rooted, inexpressible note of despair came into his voice. "But the joy of having another vampire with me almost never lasts long. You and I are alone, in the world of the vampire, Elizabeth. Do you understand now why I was trying to keep this from you?"

And Elizabeth felt trapped, trapped in the spell of his mood and his words, so that she had not choice but to complete the subject, like an incantation that can't be reversed, although her spirit was now recoiling from the question she needed to ask next: "And how did the others die?"

"I never said that they were *dead*, my dear. Oh yes, I suppose a few have ended their own existence, despairing of immortality and surrendering themselves to the Sun. And a very few, three or four, perhaps, in the last five hundred years, managed to allow themselves to be captured and destroyed by the mortals, despite the ease by which they might have escaped, had they used only a trifle of the intelligence I tried to give them. But a vampire doesn't have to die, save only by his or her own wish. No, they aren't dead. They survive. I know that there are some in this very city: mortals die here every day, and they would quake in fear at the realization of how few of their deaths truly result from what they describe as *natural* causes.

"You recall how once, back on the very first day of your new existence, I talked about savage, bestial vampires? The time when I chided you for your surrender to your passions."

"I remember," she said very quietly, embarrassed by the recollection.

"The others, all of them, have failed where you succeeded. Each one, soon or late, lost the will to battle against the inner savage. They gave up the fight, male and female, young in undeath or aged, and when I attempted to save them, they turned against me and fled, away to join their wild pack. I held out to them the promise of an eternity of splendor, and they stumbled, falling to a level below even that of the mortals. And this is the greatest of my many sorrows."

Elizabeth paused in silence, considering the impact of his words on her own situation. Was she too doomed to lose grip on her intelligence, to descend to a state of mindlessness, like the others? She was afraid to ask, but he detected her thought. "Yes, there's always going to be danger, so long as you're a vampire. I myself have to keep myself ever vigilant against my own inner nature. But you have already survived longer than many of the ones I've chosen, and I'll stand guard over you, correcting you when I see the worse instincts begin to come out in your actions. Finally, the night will come when I will decide that you have achieved the control I have over myself, when you shall no longer be my slave. That'll be a night of celebration for the both of us, for then you will walk with me as an equal, forever."

She was overwhelmed, thinking of the great love he possessed for her. Never again, she pledged to herself, would she seethe against his discipline, or rail against his chastisement. Truly the Master was a kind and just lord, and well-deserving of her heart-felt service.

8.

That very night, chill with the approach of winter, with ragged clouds swiftly traversing the sky, alternately hiding and unveiling the troublesome Moon, the Master led them on a new path, which Elizabeth failed to recognize as leading to their normal haunts. She made no comment or complaint, still basking in the glow of her devotion. Surely he would never lead her astray. Each night would bring the pounding thrill of the hunt brought to a successful completion, the happy resolution of the blood spilled for their drink.

She had by now learned that the pain inflicted by the Moon was not to be completely fought. That path led to the wasteful dissipation of her energies, waging a battle that could never be won. No, the gnawing was to be used as a *tool*, to sharpen her razor sensibilities, enabling her to hone in on any source of life which might alleviate the ache, if only for a moment. She was an automaton of destruction, and wholly dedicated to the Master's will.

Their new path led into city streets busy with late-night traffic, but they walked unheeded and unthreatened by the milling vehicles. At such times as this, Elizabeth reflected on the insignificance of the mortals' hurries and scurries, racing from jobs to homes, and never suspecting the predators walking in their very midst... But this time she further thought of how the wild, bestial vampires might be among them also, unknown even to her and the Master... How could they be discovered? Could they even pose a threat of destruction to her and the Master? She would have shivered, if human reflexes still had sway over her.

The Master pointed ahead, and said, "That's where we're going tonight." A hospital. She blanched a little then: the very idea of a building dedicated to suffering and death had held the greatest terror for her during her human existence. With her extended senses she felt the tendrils of mortal agony radiating out from the building to engulf her, the pulsing of screaming nerves, the feverish reproduction of bacteria in inflamed tissues, the slow ebbing of vitality. The Master laughed at her trepidation. "What, you're still afraid of the hospital? Their knives and needles can't hurt us now. Just think of the depth of the emotions of the mortals in this place! Trying to pour an entire life into the last agonized breaths. It makes me tremble to even think of it. There's no other place in the entire world, except maybe a battlefield, that can give us such a ripe harvest."

He boldly led her up to the very entrance, and there paused. "Stay still," he ordered. "Let your senses go forth, so you can feel the power of this place." Reluctantly she did as he commanded, and was stricken by the vastness of the suffering, the enormity of the human agonies enclosed by these walls. They were screaming, hundreds of them, not necessarily out loud, most of them, but on the inside, despairing of life and health, begging to any deity who might listen to them, to bring the gift of healing, or failing that, the bliss of oblivion. Elizabeth could feel the soul-pulse of every one. The Master strode into the doorway, fairly dragging her along after him, and immediately the clamoring dirge lessened. "They can feel us drawing near," he hissed. "Yes, the humans trapped in here are closest of all to being undead like us. At the borders of death, they can feel those like us, who stalk on the other side. They're waiting for us to come to them now."

For all the future ages of her existence, Elizabeth knew she would recall this night as the deepest of nightmares. They fearlessly walked among the mortals, taking their pleasure of them, openly, heedlessly. And the reactions which the humans had were those of *adoration*, blessing her as she stole their weak-flowing blood out of their veins, bringing the last satisfaction of the cessation of their pain. The Master laughed as he guided them among the victims. He chose only the sickest, only those for whom no hope remained, spurning those who would recover, however loud they plead for his mercy. Elizabeth felt profaned by their actions. They were no longer the bold hunters, stalking the fearful and reluctant prey; instead they were now scavengers, picking among the dead meat that had not yet fully cooled.

She could not comprehend the Master's pleasure at this uncouth business. He was giddy, as if drunk on the polluted and disease-ridden blood he was drinking. He laughed merrily, both at those he chose and those he spared. He rarely even showed the foresight to cast a glamour on the night nurses, sitting glassy-eyed and insensate. For the first time, she found herself wondering if his was the way to guide her, after all.

Their last stop was on the top floor, in the quarantine zone. The shadows were deep here, and the silence unquenchable. The hall was nearly empty; few plagues ran rampant in this modern hygienic age. And there was one room that was dimly lit, from which she heard a raspy uneven breathing. And here the Master led them.

A young man lay there, wan and very thin. She involuntarily cast her senses into him, and detected the virus running rampant in his system, the ebbing vitality, the speedy approach of his death. Seeing his beauty and innocence she suddenly felt herself thrown back into the thoughts and desires of her mortal self. She thought of his life, and hers, and of how things might have been different, had their paths crossed before their divergent fates had taken hold of the two of them. What might have been and could now never be. She might have wept, if her tears were water instead of blood. Then she raged at herself in embarrassment at this unseemly display, knowing the Master was watching every moment, detecting everything she thought.

He had an enigmatic smile on his face, and instead of reacting with anger, as she feared he would, he merely said: "Don't worry. I understand, you're still only a child in undeath. It's only natural to remember what used to be, now and again. But you have to set aside childish mortal desires again. He is yours to take now, yours alone, and you must take him now, in the way of the vampire."

To destroy him was the vilest thing she could imagine. Her body was filled with the blood of the dozens they had taken together, and she was revolted at the thought of taking more, even though the hungry pain cried out for it. She realized that the Master would become angry is she disobeyed, and that he himself would do the deed if she shirked. That would be even worse. She at least would take him kindly, and lovingly add his soul to the collection milling in her heart.

And she did so, barely breaking the skin. She allowed the blood to flow into her quietly, at its own pace, without sucking it forth in greed. She allowed the young man to softly flow into herself: brief, bittersweet memories, unfulfilled dreams. She learned his name. In some inexpressible way she felt as if a part of herself was flowing back into him, although she knew the thought was absurd. At last it was done, and the corpse was still, and the Master smiled down upon her.

And then they left.

9.

Elizabeth awoke in the unbroken darkness with the blackness that had invaded her spirit. The life of the undead had lost all its flavor for her, replaced by the endless ordeal of repetition, never to be relieved by the mercy of death. Never to experience change or newness, never to find hope. She began to understand those who gave up this non-life to the merciless purification of the Sun.

"Master," she said, "is this all? I feel so drained of vitality. What's the use of this existence, when there isn't anything to look forward to for the future?"

"Just wait a few minutes, child," he replied. "Despair never lasts as long as you expect it to. Only a little while, and the thrill will come back to you."

"No, Master, it can't ever be the same, never again. I feel like there was something hidden from me that got revealed last night, and can't be concealed again."

He sneered. "You can't hide your thought from me. There was this noble ideal you still had, wasn't there, of the glory and splendor of the vampire, but now it's been exploded. You haven't learned anything of what I've been trying to teach you. You still think that this existence is some sort of romance, a fantasy from which you'll wake up with the snap of a finger." He reached out to grasp her in his crushing grip. "It isn't. This is your reality. This is eternity.

"Do you think a lion out in the wild is going to turn away from easy prey? Of course not! The prey must be taken wherever it is available, at any time, whatever the circumstances. I would have thought you'd have been pleased with what we did last night. After all, weren't we showing *mercy*, bringing the easing of pain to humans who were suffering? We were like the angels of their salvation. But no, you won't allow us to serve such a role. No, we mustn't ever disturb your pretty picture, of noble hunting beasts, stalking the city like the savanna for our swiftly-fleeting prey...

"Take a look around you! Is this a vampire's castle, surrounded by the humble servitude of the trembling masses? No, we have to keep hiding from them, from their bright and seeking eyes, down here in the dirt and the vermin. You're a leech, not a lion, Elizabeth. The sooner you accept this truth, the sooner you'll be ready to graduate from my tutoring."

She struggled free of his hands, and sat sulking. At last she whispered: "I am a leech. I'm a leech and the slave of a leech. And we'll be leeches together forever."

And the Master laughed. "Very good, child, very good. But let me give you one tiny glimmer of hope. You're not really thinking anything new. Don't be afraid of that. Every one of us has had this kind of dark brooding. Me too. But this way of existence isn't going to last forever. No, the *night of reckoning* will be upon us soon, sooner than you might believe it to be, the night of the wrath of the undead."

She looked up. "Yes, Master. You mentioned that before. Tell me, tell me now, what is that night? How soon will it come?"

"It'll be here in its good time, its good time. Not tonight, and not tomorrow night, but soon, *soon*. The night of vengeance. The time of the final quenching of the pain. You think you've felt the fullest extent of my powers, but I'm saving myself. I'm hoarding strength within me, my might and the might of every mortal I ever drain; some night I'm going to reach out, and my arm will stretch up all the way to the highest heaven. Then I'll enclose the ball of the Moon in my hand and to crush it to ash. I'll blow on the Sun and snuff it out. Our night will last for a million years, and you and I and all the others I choose will have an eternity to kill and drink and torture, and our joy will never have an end. Be ready: you won't know the night and the hour, but it will be soon."

"Yes," murmured Elizabeth. The vision streamed through her soul, uplifting, renewing, just as the Master intended it. And together they ventured forth, she and the Master, to take that which would be theirs this night.

10.

The night was like crystal, piercing with a cold wind, yet clear of the city's usual evening haze. Elizabeth stared up at the uncaring stars, wondering if they would cause any pain to the vampire kind when the bright Sun was destroyed. She laughed to think of this, for the pain was nearly a friend to her this night, a close companion which was never gone, and she could scarcely remember any existence without it. Perhaps she had never been without it, even when she was alive. Maybe the mortals also held it within them, and deluded themselves into calling it love. The way of the undead was indeed the better way, she reflected; they at least suffered from no delusions of pleasure or merriment. To survive was to hunt.

And they hunted together, she and the Master, casting forth their keen senses into the howling wind, allowing it to carry them forth at its whim, high or low, so long as it led to the victims. The humans, however, fools that they were, were reluctant to venture forth on such a glorious night, and few were about who could entice them to the attack.

At last, they detected, at the same moment, a single pinpoint of flesh, far off in the older section of the town, walking alone in the night. Like hounds pursuing the hare, the vampires sped on the chase. There was a strange, distant sensation to the victim, which caused Elizabeth to hesitate just for a moment. It was as if he was behind a curtain or waterfall, blurring and confusing her fix on him, but this was of no matter. They would bring him forth, and empty him.

An open lot, overgrown and full of trash. The human was poking aimlessly in the underbrush. Probably the blurring of his spirit was due to alcohol or some other drug. Elizabeth grinned in savage hunger. They would soon grant him the escape from life he was seeking. "Wait a moment, Elizabeth," the Master began, "there's something wrong here." But she boldly strode forward, into the lot, and he followed after her.

And suddenly, the victim was gone. Elizabeth paused in puzzlement, for the mortals surely couldn't simply vanish beyond her detection... "Run, Elizabeth! It's the others! They're after us!" the Master cried out, but it was too late. The trap was sprung.

Bands of pressure descended upon them both, knocking them to the ground. Elizabeth was shocked to find herself pinned flat. She stretched forth with all of her power, bidding the Earth open to allow her escape and the wind rise to blow her free of her bondage. Some other force, a vast and terrible strength, brushed her will aside, and piled the entire weight of the atmosphere down upon her. She couldn't even muster the will to change form. She was trapped.

She screamed a piercing cry. "Master! What's wrong? What's happening to us?"

There was a sad resignation in his reply. "It's the others, child. I didn't think the time would be so soon."

The others! The term sent a chill through her. She pictured an image of the mindless walking corpses, the flesh falling off their restless bones, never still, never satiated, surrendered entirely to the way of the beast. She saw a motion behind the cluttered garbage and screamed again. She cried out, "Let us go! We don't have anything for you! Leave us alone, you filthy animals!"

A quiet and melodious voice, with a strong hint of amusement, replied. "Filthy animals? Now that's certainly not a nice way to describe your brothers and sisters on the occasion of our first meeting." Then the others stepped out into the open, where she could see them all, nine or ten in number.

And they were beautiful.

They were tall and clean in flesh, and the light of merriment was in their eyes. They were garbed in bright, festive colors, red and blue and white. Elizabeth detected a notable odor of freshness like perfume from them. She contemplated her tattered funeral shrift, sunken flesh, and the bones protruding from her fingertips. The vile smell of decomposition which clung to the Master and herself had gone unnoticed before this. It hadn't occurred to her that such things didn't need to be among the vampire kind.

The one who had spoken first, a portly male with thick, sensuous lips, laughed out loud. "I might venture from the looks of you that you are the savage beasts, myself. Of course, a great deal of your accouterment and, ah, *fragrance* stems from Master's sense of the dramatic, I'm sure," he continued, with a mock bow towards his nemesis. The Master made no reply, seeming to be little heeding what was happening.

The stranger vampire walked up to Elizabeth and stood over her. "So can we trust you not to do something drastic and idiotic if we set you free? At least long enough to hear what we have to say?" She nodded guardedly. The other made a gesture, and the pressure upon her frame was suddenly released so that she could arise. She did so, warily.

The vampire looked her over. "Master is a strict and thorough teacher, but there are one or two subjects in which he has perhaps been amiss. For instance, he has certainly taught you of the control of the elements of earth, fire and air. That is elementary, so to say. But he failed to mention to you, didn't he, that since your own physical form consists of nothing more than those very elements as well, you are free to alter your own appearance to anything you might desire. Let me show you," he said, and he reached out towards her. She shied away, but his touch was not violent, like the Master's, but gentle, caring, and possessing healing virtue. He touched her hands, and the ragged skin healed over the bones. Her face, and her sallow collapsed cheeks filled in. Her hair, and its matted filth gave way to silken tresses, long and smooth. "The way of the undead needn't be that of the charnel house," the vampire said, "and our touch need not be only that of anger. One only needs to make a *different* choice." And he nodded, down towards the Master.

"You, you aren't beasts?"

He laughed once more. "Well, that's certainly a matter of opinion. But I think the evidence, if you care to weigh it in an objective fashion, would tend to show that we are not so, at least not in the manner you mean. We are still the hunters, and the mortals would find a certain objection to our activities, let us say, if they were aware of us. But think about this proof: if we were savage creatures, unable to resist our lower impulses, as the Master says we are, could we have been able to imprison you, by the sole means of our collective will outweighing yours? And don't forget, we still are keeping dear Master under our power, even as I am speaking to you."

"What do you want with us?"

"With Master, nothing. He understands, although he might not admit it. We have, over the years, developed a certain arrangement with him, whereby we do this every now and again, when we decide the time is propitious. No, we are here for you."

"For me?"

"Yes. We are here to offer you a choice. Ever since Master brought you up from death, we have been observing, from our hidden vantage points. We waited until Master was finished showing you all the aspects of the undead of which he is capable. And now, you need to make an important decision. You may remain with Master, and he will keep you in this existence, to which you have maybe grown accustomed. Or you can come with us, and learn our ways. I have to remark, in my own humble opinion, that the latter choice would be the more intelligent of the two."

The Master stirred, enough to look at them, and say, with a vast world of despairing weariness in his voice, "Elizabeth, stay with me. Please."

Her defenses melted at his tone. She ran to him, crying out, "Master!" But as she came close to him, she saw that the emotion which was in his eyes was a glittering satisfaction, that she was still submissive, still a slave in spirit to his will, and she paused. "Master," she repeated and then her face became hard. *"You lied to me!"*

She struck down at him, and turned her back to him, and joined her mental force to that of the others standing about, so that the pressure crushed down upon him; he cried out and crumbled into dust.

11.

They were floating in the upper air, basking in the coldness of the wind, yet maintaining enough solidity of form so that they were able to hold conversation. "Is the Master dead now?" Elizabeth asked of the friendly vampire.

"No, we haven't the power to destroy our fellows, even when our full wills are joined. That is one ability the mortals have which the undead lack. No, your anger was such that it completely crushed his physical form, but it could not extinguish his vital essence. Our trap will pinion him for the entire course of the night, until the first rays of breaking dawn. Then, when our power dissipates, he will be freed, long enough to find some dank hole to hide from the day. And by then, he will be unable to track us down to take vengeance. As I said before, it's an old game which we have played many times before.

"And besides, who are we that we would dare to destroy the one who is the progenitor of all our race?"

"The Master? All of you?"

"Yes, every one who is in this group, and every one I know of in any other band of the undead, each of us was raised by Master, and served him, just as you did, until the others came to offer the same choice which we gave you. And each of us made the same decision as yours."

She paused. "But did I make the right decision? Has anyone ever chosen to stay with the Master?"

"A few, a very few. But let me assure you that every vampire who has allowed himself or herself to remain chained to Master has sooner or later gone out to meet the Sun, or surrendered to the inner beast. Every one. We're a proud race, and Master's dream of creating a group of slaves to his will destroys all who stay in submission to it."

"I feel like the whole world has been stretched out of its old shape, into some new and inexplicable form. I thought that I knew all about the way of the vampire, and suddenly I find myself a fledgling again, knowing nothing. I don't even know any of your names."

"Names aren't the most important thing for us. We change them from time to time, to suit whatever moods may be upon us. Most of those in our group call me Jonathan. You have my permission to call me that, as well. And what do you wish to be known as?

"Elizabeth."

"You wish to keep that name, even though it was the name of your servitude to Master?" She nodded. "Very well. Elizabeth it shall be, for now."

And all the group of vampires gathered around her in the midst of the air, and they spoke to her the same formula which the Master had said to her, so long before, but while the Master has spoken scathingly in mockery of its sentiments, these vampires spoke in full candor, a formal message of welcome and greeting:

"We welcome you, Elizabeth, once child of mortal flesh, now heir of the unending mastery, to the brethren of the night-tide, the keepers of the blood-quenched thirst. Spurn the agony of the day and abide with us, until the dark has conquered and ceases not."

And she accepted their invitation.

THE PEOPLE OF THE THIRST

1.

Elizabeth laughed at her fellow vampires when she first saw their lodging. She was still very young in undeath, and persevered in many of the romantic fantasies of the humans regarding the vampire state. It would of course have been foolish to imagine that they would reside in a haunted mansion, or mausoleums, or a desecrated chapel; a dozen children a year would stumble upon them, and that would be disastrous. Despite this, Elizabeth somehow imagined that there would be something unique, something somehow bone-chilling, at least something a little bit disquieting about the stronghold of the vampires....

Not a condominium.

"But of course," explained Jonathan, "what better arrangement could you imagine? This enables us to be in one place, but allows for a desirable privacy for those who wish it. We have a glamour on the lower stories, so that any mortals who happen to look in the windows won't see anything that might cause a disturbance."

"But aren't there any problems? I don't know: door-to-door salesman, tax collectors, building inspectors?"

"Don't underestimate the potency of the will we vampires can manifest. We carefully broadcast a message at all times, radiating out from the walls themselves. 'Ignore us,' we say. 'There is nothing here of any interest.' 'You aren't going to make any sales here.' 'There are no apartments available for rent.' It is highly effective. As for taxes and regulations, any which we can't discourage, we can satisfy by our command of the elements, creating any coin or paper which might be required."

"Is everyone free to come and go as they wish?"

He laughed. "You were too long under Master's tender care. Let me assure you, we are completely free here. Each and every one of us. We go out on the hunt either singly or in groups of our free choice. We are free to live here, or to go wherever we wish. Through trial and error, however, we have found that this communal arrangement presents the fewest problems. Any questions which affect us all are made by joint decision. Such as the resolution to gather tonight to rescue you from Master's clutches, for instance."

"I see..." she commented noncommittally. The excitement of her sudden liberation started to wear off her. She grew doubtful of her course. The Master had been a harsh and cruel lord, but he had at least provided a certainty in terms of which she could define herself and her role in the world.

After leaving the Master they had quickly fanned out, splitting up to accomplish the hunt. Elizabeth had been afraid they were about to abandon her, but Jonathan remained with her. He led her to a fraternal lodge, where the mortals were gathered together in a group. It was a swift and easy task to find two victims together, middle-aged men of empty lives who could be taken in the parking lot. Elizabeth found herself not wholly satisfied with the taste of her chosen prey. Not the taste of the blood, of course, which was as ever sweetly salty and savage to the tongue, but due to the loneliness of the attack. She hadn't realized that when the Master had shared in the feast, he had also shared something of himself as well. This solitary attack lacked that convivial atmosphere, like eating fast food alone when she was used to a festive gathering. Afterward, Jonathan conjured up the evidence of a hit-and-run driver to disguise their feeding, and then they swiftly flew to the meeting place, in front of the condo.

Elizabeth didn't know what to expect next. The night was old, but at least an hour remained before the morning twilight would drive them into hiding. She had anticipated at least some sort of camaraderie among the vampires, greetings or introductions to the others, who were still no more than barely familiar faces to her. But there was nothing of that nature. They waited in utter silence, as each of them reappeared. Finally, when all had been accounted for, they turned and entered the building, and each made for his or her individual rooms. Jonathan again took her in hand, leading her up to the top floor to an empty apartment. "I trust that this will be suitable for your needs. Feel free to make any alterations that come to your mind. We only request that you cause no changes to the lodgings of anyone else. We are very private in our habits here, and I hope that you will respect us in this." He turned to go.

"But wait!" she exclaimed. "Is that all?" She hesitated, not knowing quite how to frame the question.

"What more do you want?"

Irritation was beginning to fleck her words. "I mean, well, after you went to so much trouble to go and rescue me from the Master, it just seems to me that it would've been common courtesy for me to get a chance to meet everyone else here. I just want to get to know the people I'm going to be with from now on."

Jonathan smiled warmly, but there was a cold note in his reply: "I said that we are very private here. I wouldn't think of intruding upon the others without their invitation. If they don't wish to make your acquaintance, far be it from me to insist upon it! No, we have done our part. We have freed you, and now you can find your own best path in undeath. Now you must excuse me, I tend to ramble on and on, as you may have noticed, and I have already said too much. I wish you a good night."

And at that, he strode away, leaving her alone in the hallway.

2.

Still more than a little miffed, Elizabeth turned and tried the door. It was unlocked. She entered and automatically bolted it behind her. When she realized what she had done she smiled. There was no need to fear mortal trespassers, and the door would give little protection from her fellow vampires. Still, she kept it locked.

There she stood, in her new home. Spacious, but empty, devoid of any character or memory. It was just like any other unfurnished apartment. Empty rooms had always depressed her, filling her with thoughts of the transience of earthly life. Though she had escaped that transience now, she was still depressed by it.

What had happened to all her old possessions, she wondered, her old broken-down bed, her cluttered bookshelves, her ragged old clothes? While Elizabeth lived her mother had kept all her daughter's childhood belongings in her room at home just as she had left them, hoping vainly that she would have come back to live when she moved back to the city. She wondered, would her mother have finally thrown them all away when she died? An unsettling thought, that (and it was a shock to think about her mother at all: she hadn't given her a moment's thought, all the long weeks she had been with the Master).

There was no a chance to reflect further, for even as she first conjured the mental image of the belongings of her old bedroom, they appeared before her, occupying all the empty space of her room. It was merely another manifestation of her power over the worldly elements, operating unconsciously, bringing into existence duplicates of what she had once possessed.

Still, despite being aware that these were only copies, Elizabeth was somewhat comforted by the familiarity. She sat on the old bed, and relished the familiar creak. Once again, she could almost suspend the knowledge of her undeath, and pretend to be a simple mortal. This made her frown. It was childishness to hide from her present, she decided. She was a vampire, and no power on Earth could make her a human again. With a blink, she caused her old things to begone.

The question was, what should she create to furnish her rooms? The traditional vampire settings, coffins, cobwebs, bats and the like, had a certain romantic appeal, but she felt that to be a little too conventional. No to that idea.

She thought back, back to the dreams of her childhood, and from the depth of her imagination, she brought into being an Oriental fantasy. Rich brocades of tapestries adorned the walls, between elegantly arched doorways leading back to rooms of jeweled treasure. Pillowed divans were placed about the floor, surrounding an ornate table, laden with pomegranates and honeyed wine. In the corner, the form of a young eunuch softly played the lute. In another corner, she decided to put a small fountain. Water cascaded upward...

Then she remembered, and tried to uncreate the fountain, but too late! The water, the one element beyond the control of the vampire, poured out of the fountain, dissolving everything in its path. Nothing was left, but a vast sticky swamp. How appropriate, Elizabeth thought. Stuck in the mire again.

She felt a stab of fear that the water would soak all the way through the floor and fall down on top of whoever lived directly beneath. That certainly wouldn't be the best circumstances for introducing herself to the occupants of the building. But it was too late, dawn was about to pounce upon her. She hastily conjured up a simple hammock swinging freely over the muck, and climbed painfully in. One last thought came to her, before the oblivion overtook her: if the vampires were totally unable to control the element of water, how then was it that she had been able to create the water in the first place?

3.

Elizabeth awakened with a sense of defeat. She had tried to create beauty, and produced only a ruin. Her room remained barren and undecorated, and this was fitting with her own sense of inner emptiness. But the night's blood called to her, and her loneliness called out as well. So she got up.

She reflected that it might be a good idea to check on whether anybody lived in the room directly below her, to make sure she hadn't caused any damage. She descended, and, coming to the door, gave it a knock. Immediately there came a melodious male voice from within, "Come in!"

She tried to open the door, but there was resistance. She pushed harder, and slowly, with a grinding sound, the obstacle was cleared away. Books. Hundreds of books piled high weighed down the floor, which creaked as she stepped upon it. At least there was no sign of water damage. "Sorry about that," came the voice from deeper within, "I forget that visitors might not realize what things are like around here. I usually just float around, to keep from stepping on anything important."

With a reluctant frown, Elizabeth made herself weightless and wafted herself out of the alcove. As she came into the front room, she gasped, for the resident had warped it so that it was expanded into an infinite-looking space, receding as far as she could detect. All over the floors and walls and countless shelves she could see books, records, videos, prints, sculptures: all carefully ordered, although she couldn't figure out the system to it. She couldn't even detect the person who appeared to live in this chaos.

"Just make yourself at home," the voice said again. "Make a chair, get comfortable. What sort of subjects are you interested in? Whatever they are, I can guarantee that I have an excellent assortment pertaining to it, somewhere or other. I pride myself on that. I'll be with you as soon as I get there."

"I guess I'll just browse, thank you," Elizabeth replied guardedly. There was the solemn watchful air of a museum in this place which was making her very ill at ease. She floated over to a large bookcase containing quarto art books, and she picked one out at random, paying no attention to the name. But when she opened it up, the pages were blank. And so were all the others on the shelf. She frowned again.

The denizen of the vast library at last appeared. It was a short, somewhat pudgy male vampire with a preoccupied look about him. "Please, be welcome in my little domain. My name is Stephen. I'm perfectly delighted to have an opportunity to show off a little bit of what I have in my collections to a new enthusiast. Ask me about anything you want to know. Forgive me, I'm very bad with names. You said you were?"

"Elizabeth. I'm glad you're so willing to let me just barge in here. Jonathan gave me the impression that the vampires here weren't very sociable. But I'm really not sure I understand what all this is about."

"Hmpf. I wonder why Jonathan would say something like that. But what were you asking? What's this *about*? Why does it have to be *about* anything? I'm just a collector. I like to have a little bit of everything that interests me. And it so happens that, heh, I'm interested in just about everything you can imagine. I do admit that my wide range has left my living space a little cluttered, maybe, but you have to understand that the whole point of a collection is to have the most complete set possible."

Stephen was floating away as he spoke, gesturing with avidity at various of his collectibles as he passed, and Elizabeth had to float behind him to hear what he was saying. "Becoming a vampire was the best thing that ever happened to me," he was continuing. "There isn't anything I can't get now. When I take a victim, I can learn everything there is to know about him. There isn't very much I haven't found out by now. And there are no doors that are locked against me, no guard who can keep me from getting what I want.

"Just look at this!" he exclaimed, showing off a long gallery of artwork. "In here is the original canvas of every painting of every one of the great masters, both those known to modern scholars and also those they don't know about. As a vampire, I of course possess the ability to create duplicates precise down to the subatomic level. I have to laugh at all the museums, who talk and talk about their careful preparations against theft and forgery, when every one of the most precious pieces belongs to me." Elizabeth nodded vaguely at this as she stared at the pictures. Try as she might, she could not detect the slightest evidence of pigment or image on a single one of them. Acres and acres of blank canvass. She shook her head in puzzlement.

The next several hours were easily the dullest Elizabeth had spent since she had joined the ranks of the undead. Stephen was in his element: an opportunity to display his painstaking erudition about every conceivable subject to an apparently captivated audience. Elizabeth tolerated it as best she could. She eventually made a glamour of her own face with an expression of raptured interest, which she put over her own to hide her astonishing boredom and growing irritation. The night was getting on, and the pain was spurring her hunger. Didn't Stephen ever go out to seek satiation?

Apparently not. The night dragged on.

4.

The most exasperating aspect of Stephen's endless collections was the lack of anyone else there. If there only was some companion to share Elizabeth's misery, she could perhaps have found it faintly tolerable.

They were drifting past yet another shelf of blank ancient manuscripts (ancient Khmer scrolls unknown to any mortal scholar, or something equally inane), when she detected movement behind it. She cried out in surprise. "What? What?" exclaimed Stephen. Was there some interloper who dared to breech his domain? "Oh, it's only you," he said, as Jonathan stepped into their view.

"Sorry if I'm interrupting anything, Stephen," Jonathan said with a nervous tone, "I just thought that, with the night drawing on and such, you to might be wanting to go out. To look for victims, that is," he concluded sheepishly.

"Oh!" exclaimed Stephen. "Of course! I'd completely forgotten! Forgive me, please, for such a terrible breach of manners. I'm just so devoted to my collection, and so excited at a chance to show it off like this... And we need to go out, to get blood, for me to show you the best part! Come on!" he exclaimed as he rushed past Elizabeth towards the distant portal. "Oh, and thank you very much for reminding me this way, Jonathan." The other vampire replied to the compliment with a big beaming smile.

Elizabeth looked back at Jonathan with puzzlement. He looked much the same as the night before, perhaps a bit taller and thinner. But his bumbling manners and uncertainty of speech startled her. Not at all in character for him, she thought. But she hadn't the time to think about it, as they were already at the door.

Stephen was babbling on in his usual overwrought fashion as she hurried behind him. "I like Jonathan," he was saying, "but I wish the lad had a little more self-assurance."

"Jonathan?"

"Well, certainly. He's such a nice, quiet boy. I like that. Wouldn't want him rushing about disturbing me at my work all the time, would we? But he's always so shy, so, I don't know, withdrawn seeming, whenever I run into him. But a good head on his shoulders. Like the way he reminded me of how we hadn't gone out hunting tonight. Don't know what I'd do around here sometimes without him to remind me of the little things like that. I've tried to get him interested in collecting, of course. He seems the type who might jump into it with both feet, you know. On the other hand, I guess there really wouldn't be very much point for him to do it. Start collecting, I mean. After all, I've already got everything that anyone would ever want to collect. Still, Jonathan never seems to be that interested when I've shown him around. Oh, he's polite and all, of course, but I suppose the collecting bug just hasn't ever bit him. Not like you, of course, Elizabeth. You can't hide from old Stephen, girl. I could see that you were just dying with envy at all the goodies I've got. It's a gift I have. I can sense when a body has that collecting lust, no matter how hard they're trying to hide it. The Master was just like that, too. You couldn't hide anything from him. And he always said I was one of his favorites. Hurt me more than I can say when I had to leave him. But I had just grown beyond him. It's sad how both people and vampires can turn into different tracks and lose sight of each other. But I say you should never hold onto things too long. In relationships that is, ha. An unkind critic might remark that my whole collection consists of things I've been holding onto for too long. But that's just a matter of opinion."

There was much, much more, but Elizabeth (who hadn't the least interest in collecting anything) had by this time completely tuned out Stephen's monologue, and didn't hear a word more.

She suddenly realized that they had gotten themselves into another unfamiliar area of the city: a suburban zone, row upon row of identical houses, each nestled in its wooded lot, carefully designed to give an illusion of rustic ambiance with a stained wood exterior and traditional furnishings. Hedges painstakingly trimmed. Two cars in every garage, parked in front of the gas grill. The wind blew leaves from the gutters, into which they had been so diligently raked.

Continuing to ignore Stephen's unending prattle, Elizabeth reflected on where they should go. Lights burned in every home, and she could see the glowing of a hundred television sets. She shrugged, realizing it really didn't matter, since every place would be alike. Stephen pointed to his selection.

She felt a feral surge within her, eager for the destruction of this orderly place. There was a family in front of the screen, absorbing its essences in much the same way the vampires absorbed the humans. And when Elizabeth struck against the man, she found that there was nothing within him He was an empty shape, a reflection from the television screen, filling her belly but not easing any of the pain. Like Stephen's empty books and canvases. The children, however, were not the same. The rot was inside them, too, but hadn't consumed them entirely. Withering creams and stunted desires burned sweetly on her tongue. She supped on their hollow and irradiated spirits, and when Stephen tried to join her she snarled like an animal to keep him away.

As they glided back towards home, Stephen remarked, "I love going back to my old neighborhood."

5.

"Stephen," she said. "Listen to me." She was sated now, comfortable on a couch she had conjured to sit upon within his infinite library.

She found herself having difficulty expressing what was so obvious. "Stephen, about your collection."

"Yes. Isn't it something?"

"Yes, it is. But, well, no, it isn't. It's, not right."

"What? How can that be? What don't I have? Do you know about something I still need to get?"

"No, no. You don't have *anything*. There's nothing here. Everything is empty. The books, the pictures, they're all blank. You don't have a collection at all!"

Stephen looked at her blankly. Slowly, very slowly comprehension seemed to dawn on him. "Oh. I see what you mean. The pages are all blank to you, aren't they? I wasn't thinking again. I didn't realize that you wouldn't be able to see anything there."

"Exactly!"

"Ah, but they're *not* blank, not really. Or, not in the realest sense. Only to superficial appearances."

"I don't get it."

There was an unwholesome look of eagerness on Stephen's face as he brought it close to Elizabeth's to explain. She recoiled back from it, but still he spoke intimately, "You know, there's an awfully big difference in what you think you're seeing and what may actually be there. That's the way lots of things are in the world. And it's the same way with my collection. Everything I've been showing you is authentic. Everything. But it's all blank. That's because it's all inside. Inside me." He paused in satisfaction, patting his stomach.

"Inside you?"

"You're a vampire. And so am I. We're empty, and we fill ourselves from the world around us. We take blood every night, and we suck up souls and memories, too. But we can drink and drain everything (except water, of course). I've absorbed my collection. It's all inside me. I am the embodiment of the entire history of human creative endeavor." He bowed a little.

Seeing her dubious gaze, he continued, "Let me prove it to you."

He hurriedly led her down a corridor which he hadn't shown her before, twisting among the stacks like a labyrinth. "This is my private zone. I don't let just anyone in here. You're only the second, in fact. Just you and Jonathan. It's hidden in the very center of my whole collection. For safety. For protection. Both to protect it from the world, and to protect the world from it. It's safe here."

The light was increasingly poor as they passed deeper into the private area. Elizabeth felt claustrophobic, as if Stephen's vast collection was drawing in under the force of its own gravity, inward to smother her.

They rounded a corner, and a bright light, like daylight appeared. Elizabeth hesitated, until Stephen pulled her forward. "There's nothing to be afraid of. Everything's under my control."

One more corner, and they arrived at an open space, surrounded by a shadowy mass of books. Floating in the center of the space was a sphere, the source of the light. It was a small Sun, no more than twenty meters in diameter. Elizabeth gasped in pleasure, for the light caused no pain to her. Its radiance was gentle, easing to the eye and caressing to the flesh. A fantasy Sun, as if the cosmos was a joyful place for the vampires, rather than a world of suffering and strife.

Orbiting this miniature Sun was, naturally enough, a solar system, with each planet at its proper size and position relative to the Sun. Elizabeth searched for a moment until she found the Earth, compete with a duplicate Moon encircling it. Beyond the solar system, the light glistened off the lettering of the books' spines, very much like an array of stars.

"It's lovely, Stephen," she said, with unfeigned admiration.

"But this isn't all. Look closer," he commanded. And as she did so, she felt as if she was passing through veils, and each one she crossed added to the illusion of depth within the tiny globe of the world, until she began to wonder if somehow Stephen's handiwork was the real Earth, and the larger one outside was merely an illusion.

Behind her, Stephen spread his arms wide, and, with a joyful shout, he poured out of his body all the blood he had taken earlier this night, a dark red cloud that flowed forth from his fingers and his mouth, and the cloud of blood poured down and engulfed the solar system he had made and permeated his model Earth. The little world absorbed the blood, and was not stained by it.

And Elizabeth gasped, for the tiny Earth came to life.

The waters raged, the winds blew. The billions of tiny figures that were human beings scurried across the globe's face. They walked in their paths, worked their jobs, fought their wars. They lived, loved and died. It was reality. And it was more than reality, for the essence of this artificial world was the beauty of art, and the thematic elegance of literature. The people performed all their actions in an exquisite and graceful way, speaking their words in moving and lovely prose or verse. There was no boredom, never a fading of the romance of their passions, and their deaths always served to make some dramatic point. It was the world, but it was better than the world; it was the world the way humanity would have liked it to be. And it was good.

But slowly, imperceptibly at first, the world began to fade. The motions of the mortals upon it slowed, like manikins winding down, and the glow of their vitality turned to ash. Elizabeth cried out. Stephen, floating behind her, began to weep. She turned about and was shocked at his appearance: withered and aged, grey of hair and wrinkled of skin. "It's the blood," he explained in an infinitely weary voice. "The blood gives us life for a night, but the next night we must kill again. I try to turn the blood I steal to a positive use, to animate my world, my collection come to life, but it's not enough. Just a few precious moments, and then it runs down again... I give everything for my world. Everything, and all I get back is just one single moment of perfection.

"Don't you see, Elizabeth, that try as I might, I can never finish? So many billions of mortals are out there, and all of them alive and vital with their creative urges. Every day, a hundred thousand new works of art or writing, and I just can't get them all! It's almost enough to make me give up hope."

But then he smiled through his red tears, "But that's where you can help me."

Elizabeth wakened from her daze, which had been cast upon her by the tiny and perfect panorama of Stephen's world. "What? How can I do anything to help you?" For she had been overwhelmed by his vision, and felt, at that moment, that she would perform any service Stephen might need, to help his endless quest.

He laughed briefly. "Not much, not much by yourself, I fear. But just think! Look at how much I've been able to accomplish by my solitary efforts. The others make fun of me, absorbed in my own little world, and they won't even come to look at my collection, except for Jonathan now and again. But just think, if you only joined me. If you would come with me every night, to share in the taking of blood with me, and then sacrificed it with me for this great cause. We could double my world, my collection, or maybe even more! So much greater depth to my world, our world, you could bring. And then, maybe, just maybe, the others might come to see what beauty we're making. Maybe they would come join us too, all of them, even the Master! And he could make even more vampires to join us, our fellowship, our cause! And someday, someday, all the humans could be with us, and this world would no longer be just a poor little copy of what's real, but it would become the true reality, and the bad old Earth outside will be the copy, which would slowly fade away to nothing.

"And I, the one they all mocked, I'll be the one who started it all. Wouldn't that be a just reward for all my long and hard labor." By now his voice, which had been fading slowly as he revealed his dreams to Elizabeth, was a tiny whisper, and then it ceased, as he fell into private reveries.

But Elizabeth was listening to each word, and she understood now that Stephen's collection and world and dream were all nothing more than another trap, just as had been the dreams of the Master. And she shuddered.

"No."

With that one word she brought his vision to a crashing end. He looked up at her, and his face held the hurt of a kicked dog in it, so that her heart was torn, but she was resolute. "No, Stephen," she repeated.

Just one word he said, "Why?"

Elizabeth was crying a little herself now, but she smiled as she replied, becoming more certain of her decision as she explained: "Stephen, I am sorry. I really am. All night long, I've been holding in all these unkind thoughts against you, and only now, when I see that I can't help you, I see that you really are a beautiful person, and I hope that I can still be your friend, just like Jonathan. But don't try to make me join you.

"It's just like you said. The world, the universe, is infinite, and so is the creativity of the mortals. And you are just one person, with finite, limited abilities. You can't ever hope to succeed. Art, literature, they are infinities, as infinite as everything that is possible. You can never encompass it all. Your collection, in the end, is useless.

"And I wouldn't help you, even if I thought you could achieve your dream. Because it's your vision, and I won't sacrifice myself on the altar of another person's dream, not anymore. You intend well, but if I or any of the others ever tried to help you, it would all go sour, and turn into a nightmare of control and restriction. You would become another Master, and you wouldn't be yourself anymore. You would lose your dream even as you were in the process of accomplishing it. And I don't want to be the ruin of such a beautiful dream."

Dawn was approaching, so Elizabeth left him in his desolation.

6.

Night came abruptly, with the swift onslaught of a late autumn storm system, heavy and foreboding. Elizabeth regained awareness to the sound of the rainfall, pounding at the defenses of the vampires' abode. But the fortification of their magic was strong, stronger than could be overcome by the mere strength of natural forces. Elizabeth huddled down in the feather bedding she had made for herself, revelling in luxury and ease, but the hunger was awake within her, and she was stirred by its insistence. Never to find rest.

She realized that she was struck with the need for normalcy. Habit. All the undead she'd met seemed caught up in exotic other worlds of their fantasies, without any relation to what she in her earlier life would have considered to be reality. This was beginning to disturb her. Her human instinct contained an urge for romance, for thrill, for excitement, but it also had a compulsion toward security, quietude. Home. Perhaps, being no longer human, she would have to excise such feelings. This was not a pleasant prospect. She frowned.

With this in mind, she got up and dressed herself in the most casual garb she could picture: jeans and a comfortable blouse, with good walking shoes. It was as if she was back in school again, and the years with their many changes (not the least of which being her death) dropped away from her spirit.

She ventured out. A quick check had revealed that the top two floors of the building held no other occupants than herself and Stephen, so she headed for the next floor down, knocking on doors until she heard a lyrical female voice cry out, "Come in!"

And, as if her mind had been read, Elizabeth found herself home.

She reeled back and shut the door. She shook her head. "Can't be," she said, and tried the door again. But it was so. The room she entered was an exact image of the living room of her old house, where she had lived and grown up with her parents for eighteen full years: the old fashioned, overstuffed chairs and sofa, the worn plush carpet, the withered-looking plants along the windows (her mother had been repeatedly unsuccessful in her attempts at cultivation). Elizabeth heard the occupant come out from the kitchen, and hesitated for a moment before she looked at her; she sighed in relief, as the female figure which stood before her, short and highly matronly, bore only a slight resemblance to her mother.

"How do you do?" asked the other vampire. "My name is Deborah. I've been meaning to pay you a visit, but I'm sure you understand how things are. First there's this which needs to be done, and then that. Time certainly flies when you're immortal. It might have taken me years before I finally got around to paying a call."

Elizabeth felt herself taken aback. There was something about Deborah which she couldn't put her finger on, that was softly and gently insinuating. She felt a compulsion to trust her, to spill out every secret which she had ever kept, and allow her kindliness and goodheartedness to flow over her and wash her clean.

They sat for a few minutes on the sofa, and Elizabeth could never afterwards recall precisely what was said between them. She only could remember the warm glow of the fellowship of two women, different in rearing and background, but united in the unlife in which they found themselves. At one point, Elizabeth managed in casting off the spell sufficiently as to say, "It's all so very strange, the way we seem to have grown so close, when we've only just met. I don't understand. I even see it reflected in the way you've arranged your rooms. Everything is exactly like what I remember from my childhood home."

Deborah smiled back warmly. "Well, I have a little confession to make," she replied. "I've played a bit of a trick on you. This room doesn't really look like your memories. Or rather, it looks like the most comforting memory of anybody who comes to visit here. I've made the perfect mirror-spell, very similar to the one that makes the building unobtrusive to the mortal passers-by. When you enter the door, you are greeted by a vision of the place where you felt most content and relaxed in your life. I've found that it helps put my guests more at their ease than they might be, otherwise. And it works, doesn't it?" She gave a polite little laugh. "Although it can cause a certain amount of confusion when I have more than one visitor. Each person perceives being in a different room. People tend to get a little disconcerted when they see someone else walking through the place where they see a certain favorite chair, or something. I hope you aren't too upset by things like that."

"No, not at all..." Elizabeth replied hazily. Inside somewhere, she had an idea that she really ought to be bothered by this, but she couldn't crystallize the thought, and it slipped away again.

Deborah offered to give Elizabeth a tour, to show her the perfection of the illusion. And perfect it was: winding their way through the kitchen, the den, down to the basement and up the stairs, Elizabeth marveled at a thousand details of her childhood which she had consciously forgotten: a certain throw rug which had been thrown out when she was eight; the cuckoo clock which had always chimed one less than the hour; the soft texture of the upholstery in her father's big chair. Deborah's glamour had delved into the deepest recesses of Elizabeth's mind, to conjure forth a flawless reproduction.

They came to the upstairs hall, and Elizabeth began to rush forward, for she saw the door which would lead to her room. She was eager to see what cherished memories were to be invoked there, but Deborah halted her. "I'm sorry, my dear," she explained, "but that's my own personal room. It isn't a part of the larger spell over the whole place. You wouldn't begrudge me a little bit of privacy, would you?"

Elizabeth's feelings were hurt, but she understood, and so they left that room unvisited.

Not long after this, Deborah and Elizabeth went out for the evening. It was a cool and wet night; although the rain had stopped, Deborah insisted that Elizabeth make an umbrella to carry with her. She was experiencing that certain catharsis or regeneration which was only known to occur when a woman goes shopping, especially with another trusted female companion. The holiday season was drawing upon them, with the stores staying open late for their convenience, and the crowds were heavy. But Elizabeth was far from oppressed by the rushing mobs, because they always seemed to part as she and Deborah walked along, leaving them a sure path. She wondered if this was another form of Deborah's glamour, or merely the native discomfort the mortals felt in the presence of the undead.

They didn't purchase anything, although it certainly would have been easy to create any cash or credit which they might have required. It was sufficient just to be there, absorbing the thrill of the crowd, like being there for a race. All the blood pumping and gushing around them warmed and excited her, and she listened to a thousand heartbeats, measuring each one, as they moved through the crowds soft like satin against satin.

It was getting late, but the throng was only beginning to thin, when they finally decided to end their browsing and make their selections. There was a small shop in one of the more isolated corridors of the mall (although there was no such thing as real emptiness in the choreography of the building), and inside it were sold small knick-knacks for the household. Nothing of any great utility, or even of any particular grace or loveliness: just small items which the average homemaker might find useful to have handy, extra towelettes, refrigerator magnets, trivets, napkin rings, assorted pieces of wicker furniture. The proprietors were two ladies of early middle-age, slightly frumpy perhaps, but not unattractive in their conservative work dresses, and suited perfectly for their line of business. Elizabeth followed Deborah's lead into the store, and joined her in browsing idly for several minutes. She was amused to sense the slowly kindling irritation in the shopkeepers as they poked about, showing no inclination to buy. Finally, one of the ladies (the assertive one, who always dealt with unpleasant customers and salesmen, as opposed to the quiet brainy one who did the majority of the paperwork) mustered her courage enough to say, "Excuse me, but we're about to close up shop. I'm sorry if I'm rushing you, but if you ladies were going to be making a purchase, there isn't very much time."

Deborah smiled keenly. "Oh, I suppose we'll be doing our business in just a little while. But go on and take care of anything you have to, and don't worry about us."

The other woman frowned but turned back to whatever she had been doing before. Elizabeth impishly put a glamour upon her, so that she forgot their presence altogether for many minutes. She giggled lightly to see the women hustling about the processes of closing down their pretty little store: running the vacuum, straightening the shelves, setting out stock for the next day.

Finally, as they shut out the lights, letting in the soft sweet darkness, the vampires relented and allowed the women to perceive them again. "What? How did you get in here?" the second woman screeched in aggrieved tones.

"But we've been here all along," Deborah replied in a purr.

"We're not looking for any trouble! Get on out of here! Come back tomorrow!"

"But won't you let us make our purchase?"

The second woman began to make a biting reply, but the first one cut her off: "Of course we'd love to let you buy everything you want, but we've already closed up the cash register. It's against rules to open it back up again, and it'd make a frightful mess of our records to have to go and write you up by hand... I'm sure you understand our situation. Couldn't you come back first thing in the morning?"

"I'm afraid we won't be able to do that."

"But we open right at nine o'clock sharp for the season."

"No, I don't think you'll do that tomorrow, at that."

The women felt the spread of the darkness then, deep and echoing, and the shadows were gathering around them deeper with each passing moment. Elizabeth made a tiny step forward, and the women made an involuntary jump back. The second woman, who was behind the counter, jabbed out a finger to activate an alarm, but naturally Deborah had taken care to silence it. And Elizabeth took a second step forward.

"You know," said Deborah to Elizabeth in a light, airy voice, totally out of keeping with the gloom, "I am always amazed with the way the humans react when they're faced with certain destruction. Some scream and thrash about. Some faint dead away. And others are just paralyzed, frightened out of their wits, but so fascinated by the sight of their death that they stay conscious and aware for every second... It's like they're savoring it in almost the same fashion as we do ourselves." And she took a step forward herself.

"Oh, I know, I know," Elizabeth replied, moving closer still. "I wonder if we would react in the same way. Of course, I don't imagine a similar situation would ever arise for us of the undead."

These words broke the first woman. She shrieked and leapt away, pushing the second woman, her closest friend and bosom companion of many years, in front of Elizabeth, sacrificing her for a moment's escape, but Deborah moved like thought itself, reaching out to grasp her and bring her in to herself. Her mouth opened like a chasm. The second woman, however, remained rigid, with perspiration causing her make-up to run down in rivulets down her face, as Elizabeth finished her quiet approach. Elizabeth bit into her throat, feeling the rushing sensation of what was nearly relief stream out of the woman into her. Elizabeth moaned in pleasant surprise. The woman, so small and mousy, had been holding inside a seething volcano of frustrations all her life, in all her schemes and dreams, and secretly she had always harbored a vivid hatred for her partner; she gloried that the other woman was now finding death, even though she herself was also to be sacrificed. Elizabeth tasted the sweetness of the woman's suicidal triumph, and found it akin to her own inner promptings. She spoke to the woman's fading consciousness, comforting her with the words: "Be still and happy, sister. I am absorbing you into myself now, and you will always be a part of me now."

Afterwards, as she and Deborah cleaned away the debris of their attack and tidied up the little shop (inspired by the second woman's hatred, it amused them to set up the appearance of the proprietors having murdered each other in an argument), Elizabeth thought further of these things. Every human she devoured lived still within her memories. Even as she thought of them all, she felt them inside her brain, like worms squirming. Perhaps, as the years waxed into decades and centuries, the sheer number of victims within her would grow until they utterly overwhelmed her own dominant personality... Was she even the same person that she had been the night the Master brought her out of the grave? Would she be capable of telling if there was a difference? She frowned as they left the shopping center, without Deborah noticing.

7.

They went back to Deborah's apartment. Flushed with new blood and excitement, Elizabeth babbled like a schoolgirl. Elizabeth was still distraught by her uncertain thoughts and remained quiet for the most part. There was a subtle feeling of malaise growing in her mind, a suspicion she couldn't bring out into her open consciousness. She ignored the feeling, but it slowly came to dominate her, and their conversation slowly dwindled into silence. Elizabeth stared at Deborah, and Deborah stared back at her, with her beaming smile gradually fading. "So," Deborah said at last, "you've been a vampire now for, what, three or four months?"

"Um, I'm not really sure," Elizabeth replied. "I had a lot of trouble keeping track of time, at least when I was with the Master. I think I died back before the beginning of autumn; it feels like it's been three or four years since then, so many strange things have happened! And I don't know exactly how long I was in the ground before he came for me. I was thinking that it was only a couple of days, but with the weather getting so cold all of a sudden, I'm starting to wonder if I was down there for a couple of weeks. Or even a month."

"Well, the cold weather is coming early this year, as early as I can ever remember it. And I remember quite a few, you know."

"I don't want to be rude, but have you been undead for many years?"

Deborah chuckled, but with an odd expression. "Oh, it's all right to ask about that. I at least don't hold stock with much of these modern manners. But my years go back, back, for a long, long time." She arose to open a window with her hand. The late westering moonlight shining on her face gave her a chalky but translucent appearance that was almost like the beginning of decay. She said, "How old were you when you died? No more than twenty-three or twenty-four, at the most?"

"Twenty-six."

"Ah." She looked down with a twinge of pain. "How cruel the Master was, to have taken you so young. I, I had lived a good life, as full as could be had for a woman back then. Forty-seven years old. That's how old I was, when the Master came for me. And since then, I've seen three hundred and sixty-seven more years come and go." She turned toward Elizabeth. "Doesn't that frighten you a little bit?

For you to sit here and talk with a woman who's more than ten times your own age?"

"Well, I hadn't thought about it that way before. But haven't we had a good night together? Aren't we alike in a lot of ways? Maybe we should feel happy instead of frightened, to see how the years go past and yet we remain vital and joyful in our undeath."

"Yes, you may be right, you may be right. But don't forget, there's one thing more. I have lived four centuries as a vampire. And every single night, I have gone out into those streets, and I have taken a victim. Each night of my long existence has meant at least one less human being on the Earth."

Elizabeth shifted with a growing sense of unease. "That's true, I guess. But that's not something we can really control. We are compelled. We have to go out. That's what our nature's all about."

Deborah seemed not to be paying attention to Elizabeth's words. "So much blood spilt. So many lives cut short. It becomes difficult to continue to justify such a thing, as the years creep onward....

"I told you, didn't I, that I lived a rich and fulfilled life when I was mortal? I remember it well. I grew up in a happy household, fair and healthy. And I married well, to a good man, a holy man. He taught me the word of God by drilling it into my poor head, day in and day out, with a cuff for any mistake I made. But he almost never beat me on any other occasion, and that was a pretty rare thing in those days.

"Our crops and our herds took a full day's work, but they yielded well enough to feed us and give us a little extra for barter, so that we were fairly well-off for that region and time, although you'd have thought us dirt-poor peasants, judging from the modern standards of this land. I worked hard and prayed hard, and, if I didn't have very much time for laughter and gaiety, I didn't miss them.

"And our final and greatest blessing was our daughter. She was so lovely, pretty as the first flowers of fresh springtime and slender as the reed. Her father was not well-pleased, as sons were more valuable to have at that time, but I never bore again, and so he made room in his heart for her, our little Rebecca. My life was complete then. I had fulfilled every expectation which I woman was supposed to have: marriage, land and childbirth. What else was there?

"Alas, that those happy years were so brief. War came by, not close enough to destroy our own holdings, but close enough to wreak havoc in the country about. We were forced to give up our crops and cattle to the soldiers, more than once, and then they compelled us to house their wounded and to nurse them with our own hands. They were filthy, ridden with lice and fleas and other vermin. For weeks we slaved for them, without food or sleep. And then they left, without a word of thanks or apology, much less even a penny of recompense.

"All they left behind for us was the plague. We all got it, along with every one else in the village. A nightmare. I still cannot bear to think about it for more than an instant. So many died. But I was strong and I recovered, and so did my Rebecca. But not my husband.

"Things were very hard after that. I was a widow with a child, in a war-torn and ruined land. I could expect little help from my neighbors, for everyone was in the same condition. But I fought against adversity, and I worked harder than I would have thought possible, and we lived.

"But then the Master came among us. He trailed after the armies in those days, battening himself like a leech on the despair and hardship which accompanied the fighting. The strongest of those who survived the plague he took, leaving nothing but the dregs to carry on. But I alone he brought back from death, to serve him.

"We walked together for long vile years. Time after time I tried to overpower him or trick him into destruction, and instead he forced me to minister to his wants, to the consuming fire of his eyes. And deeply in the glamours of evil did he immerse me, until I was stained beyond redemption.

"And then, after the long war, he cast me aside without a moment's remorse. I was to him no more than one of his mortal victims, a thing to give him sustenance until I was used up, and then tossed aside like an empty bottle.

"After I was abandoned in such a way, I had nothing, no purpose in existing and no place where I could go. So what else could I do, but wend my way back, back to my home?"

Deborah paused. There seemed to be a struggle going on inside herself, whether to go on. Elizabeth was frozen in horror and pity at her tale. But she knew that she had to hear it out to its conclusion.

"My darling Rebecca had grown up in those years, to become a lovely young woman," Deborah finally continued. "She was enough to make any mother proud. But I was afraid, afraid to reveal myself to her. She had thought me dead for fifteen years. I knew that I would be a thing of revulsion to her. But I watched, from the deepest shadows, as she performed her profession in the evenings."

Suddenly she stood up like a shot. "It's time," she said to Elizabeth, "it's time for me to finally show you my own private room." Elizabeth started to decline politely, but Deborah was firm. "Oh, you must now. I insist. You won't really understand until you come with me."

8.

And so they walked up the narrow staircase, down the hall which held a life of memories for Elizabeth. She was beginning to tremble in fearful uncertainty, at what she suspected might lay within Deborah's (which still in Elizabeth's mind should be her own) room. There was a large lock on the door, not at all like her memories said there ought to be, and Deborah fished out a rough-hewn wooden key from her pocket. The door creaked open, and she gestured for Elizabeth to enter.

The room was dark and windowless, nearly barren with unpainted wood walls. Primitive oil lamps were burning in the corners. The back of the room was covered with a thick curtain which trapped the light, casting twisted and phantasmagoric shadows. And on a bier in the center of the room was the body of a young woman. "This is Rebecca?" asked Elizabeth in a flash of intuition.

"Yes." The vampire woman stepped forward to gently caress the waxy dead face. "The days that passed were agony, huddled in the corner of the ruined old mill, with discovery possible at any moment. The light of day seeped in through cracks and seared like brands. There was no rest. But much worse were the nights, for I feared to assuage the mounting hunger, which grew into a torment that never ceased. I was decaying, losing my intelligence and my will, as I slowly lost strength. Soon, I was unable to leave my hiding place even had I dared.

"It was in that condition that they found me. They had bright flickering torches and steely evil eyes. They were ready with stakes and holy water, and I had no will to resist them. But sweet Rebecca strode out in front of the crowd, and stayed them with a gesture. She said, *'Inside that rotting thing was once my mother, and perhaps she is still trapped in there.'* She sent them away. Then she picked me up with her own hands, and brought me back to my house which was now her house.

"She nursed me, all through that dismal night. She tried to feed me with thin broth, but I couldn't help but spew it back in her face. And when the dawn came, I screamed for the pain of it, and she screamed too, to see me in that state. And she let me crawl under her bed.

"At last the night came again. I was reduced to a mass of comatose flesh. No one who hadn't known me before would even have thought me a human creature. But she spoke to me. For hours and hours she talked and she told me of the hardships of her life. How she had been forced to lower herself to being a charwoman, and finally a whore, she who had grown up the free daughter of a landowner. Dimly, I could sense that she wished to accuse me, to berate me for abandoning her, but such was her sweet love for me that the words never passed her lips. And she struggled to comprehend, to understand what I had been put through, what I had become and how. I couldn't speak, but I managed to bring her to an understanding, with brutal and ugly gestures. She was repelled, but she didn't turn away.

"No, she stayed, and she talked further. And slowly it seemed to me that she was growing to realize that there was little really different between the two of us: both forced into dark and evil deeds, but while I had no choice in what I had become, she came to think that her own course had resulted from her own decision... I shook my head violently, denying this again and again. But she wouldn't listen to me. I lay there, and listened as my precious young child cast herself into a pit of degradation and despair."

Deborah fell silent again, and Elizabeth was shocked to see that the other woman had begun to tremble, the vampire who was in control of all realities, but no longer able to control her own emotions. When Deborah spoke again, it was in a savage whisper that cut across the room: "She saw herself as lost, evil. Not deserving to live. And so, she offered herself to me, her flowing blood and swift heartbeat. The pain, the pain of the hunger was thrashing within me....

"And I killed her."

She looked up and her voice rose into a screeching wail. "I killed her, and I drank her blood to the last delicious drop. Do you know how it tasted, the blood which had arisen out of my own living flesh, quenching that thirst from the depth of hell? I tore her apart, lapping at the red flood like a dog, not even tasting of her being, so that her soul was wholly lost, unpreserved. I rent her flesh and cracked her bones to suck out the marrow. She was dead." She looked significantly at Elizabeth. "And she died in her twenty-sixth year."

After another pause Deborah spoke again, pacing the floor, tracing lines around the bier which Elizabeth felt must be ingrained by long habit. "That was all. I fled away, and I never returned to that place, to that country. And the nights have passed in their long and lonely spiral. And so many more have I added to my toll of destruction. In every land, in every city, I sought out the women, to taste of their hearts.

"But Rebecca won't ever return to me. Never to her mother. See how I have fashioned flesh for her to dwell in? If she would only forgive me, and come back to me in one of the ones I kill, I could keep her, and put her in this body, and we would never be apart again. Why can't she forgive me of my one transgression? Ungrateful wretch!

"No, what am I saying? She was my pure one, she was the one who was dragged unwillingly down her path. I am the sinner. I am the beast." Deborah suddenly halted directly in front of Elizabeth, who quailed and drew back. Deborah reached out to grab her arm in a grip to break mortal bones. "We are the beasts. We're unnatural, vile things, against the will of God and of man. We've rebelled against the grave which is our rightful place, and we slay them to slake our dire thirst. We're sin, we're the darkness incarnate!" And after a pause which seemed to last hours, she added, *"And we must be punished."*

With a gesture she pushed aside the woolen curtain which dangled behind the bier, revealing to Elizabeth a long chamber filled with the devices of torture. There was the rack, and the bone-crusher and the fingernail-piercer, and other less identifiable items. But what frightened Elizabeth the most was the presence of Jonathan, standing solemnly in the corner, with wild eyes and solemnly dressed in a hairshirt. He made no comment, but nodded to them in greeting. Elizabeth thrashed and squirmed and tried to will herself into vapor, but Deborah, holding her by arm and by will, dragged her forward into the room. They didn't pause at the rack or the wheel or the electroshock apparatus. Deborah took her to the very end of the room, where the exposed wall was broken by a number of circular openings covered by shutters like portholes. "We have made a careful study of the endless ways the mortals use to break and crush each other, Jonathan and I," Deborah hissed, "but of what use are these means to such as we? Our bodies re-mold, our flesh flows to cover up any harm. No, there is only one torture cruel enough to expiate our evil." She threw open a small hole. Through it there came the faint light which precedes the coming of dawn.

Elizabeth recoiled from the light in fear, and Deborah laughed in a bitter fashion. "Don't try to run away. You mustn't. You can't. You will stay here with me. All day." She thrust Elizabeth's hand in the opening up to the wrist, and clamped a heavy bolt around it, to hold her in place. "You're young and still soft in your sin. You can bear the pain only in proportion to what you have earned. Later, maybe, you will require a more stringent punishment, like mine." Deborah left Elizabeth chained there, and went over to a square of larger holes; she opened them, emitting a blinding rush of near-dawn light. And she put both her legs and both her arms within the opening, all the way up to her torso, and she brought down the bonds to hold her fast, yet dangling freely over the floor. Beside her Jonathan stepped forward, still without making any sound, and inserted the top of his skull as far as the eyebrows into an oblong hole, binding leather bands tightly about his neck to hold him in place.

There was no escape. There was no escape. She felt the Sun rushing upon her like a juggernaut of fire. With each instant the sizzling agony of her hand was increasing, exponentially. She prayed to any god of the living or the undead for freedom, and cursed them all when there was no answer. The chain withstood the fullest force she could exert, with either her limbs or her will. She called down the very walls of the building to surround her, to hide her and leave her inviolate, but every effort was evaporated by the thrusting heat.

And then came the dawn.

The Sun's anger fell upon her. Blisters bubbled forth on her hand the size of balloons and exploded, expelling the ichors of grey humours. There was a suction, a pulling out of every corpuscle she had ever stolen, rushing from her soul and down her writhing arm, gushing forth into the open unholy air. Her scream was so high that it lay beyond the pitch audible to her ears, and so loud that the linings of her mouth pulled loosed, flapping around her shattering teeth. A galaxy away Deborah trembled as her limbs dissolved, her body thrusting against the wall as if with sexual heat, and beyond that Jonathan gave forth a low moan as his brain steamed within his captive skull. But Elizabeth knew nothing of their travail, as all thought and memory and dream and desire ceased. She was the last creature of an extinct species with her entrails torn out and dripping. She was a nerve ending exposed for a thousand years to the gnawing of beetles.

And then the second moment commenced.

There was still a flicker of mind in the darkest recesses of her being, and the Sun was a burrowing thing ripping through sweet brain meat to root out the last vestige. Like a pinned insect she squirmed, dashing her skull against the wall to find the glorious silence of oblivion, but the Sun had no mercy. Awake and aware she remained fixed as it uncovered her final sanctums, and it touched her with the breath of the dragon. She withered like a flower in drought, like ice brought forth before the flames.

And then came the third second.

Below the human lies the bestial. Below the bestial lies the vegetable. Below the vegetable lies the mineral. And below the mineral lies the fundament of waves and particles and motions which cannot be detected without causing their alteration. Yet being persists even unto the deepest wells of the creation. She sank down the layers of essence like a diver, seeking the bottommost place of hiding. She was returned to the point where her existence had begun, a thing which knew itself only as the subject of agony, but try as she might, she could not flee that last and elemental knowledge. And in the dark aloneness she was found by the Sun and the light, exposed and resourceless. And she was extinguished.

9.

Oblivion is dagger-fast, but recovery is slow, slow like wading through the quagmire of returning being. So it was for Elizabeth as she struggled to return herself to awareness in the evening. The sensation was like diving deep into the sea, and losing the direction back to the surface. Her mind turned about, searching in a state of near-awareness for the proper direction which would bring her to consciousness. At last, when she was nearly out of the breath of her spirit, she found the way.

She slowly opened her eyes with trepidation. There was an ache seated in her bones, like the feeling of impending influenza among the mortals, and she moaned as she moved. The hunger, the hunger for blood to replace that which was lost to the Sun, was like wheels grinding together without lubricant.

She looked about the shadowy room of torture. Deborah was slumped loosely in her bonds, mouth in an open rictus, through which her breathing hissed unevenly. Jonathan was gone. Elizabeth forced herself to stand, and found that the strap holding her arm was no longer taut. Slowly she pulled her arm out.

Her hand was gone.

Dissolved. By the Sun. She lost command of her limbs then, falling against the wall with a thud. Her head was level with the empty opening, and a faint tingling of light, the last echoes of the Sun's daytime fury, lit upon her eyes. She recoiled. Once again, she caused herself to stand, and, shaking her remaining hand, she cursed the Sun, by the most terrible thing she knew. She cursed it in the name of the Master.

She staggered to where Deborah dangled. She seemed much older to Elizabeth, sagging, weary, flaccid. She reminded her of a frog, ready to be dissected. Elizabeth felt an urge to strike her as she was helpless, but she mastered herself. Deborah gave forth a faint moan, and Elizabeth knew she had to escape while she was able. As she passed the bier on which lay Rebecca's body, she brushed against it, and it toppled, dumping the body to the floor. A stench of decay arose, and the body broke open. Without Deborah's will upon it, the flesh had swiftly corrupted in the course of the day. Elizabeth fled with a gag, not caring what she knocked over as she ran.

At last she was free of that room, and she stumbled down the stairs. She fought to ignore the spell which caused it to recollect her home; she wanted no reminder of anything of her past. She made it out the door, and fell flat in the hallway outside, so sterile, giving no clue of the horrors that went on inside the innocent-appearing doors. The thought was unbearable, and she stumbled onward, and made it outside, where she collapsed again. She lay there senseless for a minute, and then she felt a light touch. There was an old man, weathered in face but kindly in appearance. Somehow fetched despite the glamours of protection around the building, brought by the radiating hunger to her. "Are you all right, dear?" he asked softly. She managed a smile. "Oh, yes, I'm going to be all right now," she replied, and her smile grew wider to show her sharp, sharp teeth.

10.

For several days, Elizabeth remained secluded, avoiding all contact with the other vampires. She opened a doorway in the back of her apartment which connected with the fire escape, and she skulked in and out secretly. She later remembered little of her activities at that time. She crept around the edges of the mortal populace, striking suddenly at a human without a moment's planning, but then sparing the next after a painstaking stalk of an hour's duration. The time she spent in her room she concentrated on growing a new hand. She felt compelled to make it perfect, tracing the path of each individual muscle and nerve, and destroying it again if she detected the tiniest hint of flaw. She used her hand as a focus for her old Zen disciplines, suppressing all her conscious thought processes, trying to lose her identity in the instinctive motions of the cells. But, just as had always happened while she was still alive, *satori* eluded her, her concentration flagged, and she found herself once more pondering her life and the diverse ways of the vampires.

So once more she set out to meet the others. That night, she met Charles, who, after freeing himself from the power of the Master some two centuries in the past, had sworn an oath never to taste of human blood again. He transported Elizabeth far away from the city into the surrounding countryside, and together they hunted in the wild. The blood of animals tasted raw to her: strong in flavor but lacking in the spiritual element, which was what it needed to be fully nourishing. Each furry soul gave only a quick taste of fear, of hunger, of sexual need, containing only the briefest tang of self-awareness. And so, to obtain satisfaction, they had to kill and kill again. And as the night wore on, her soul and Charles's took on a feral nature, gradually forgetting the city and civilization.

Late in the night, their animal sensibilities became aware of another inhuman presence. A presence that was seeking them. They crossed the line from pursuers to pursued. All their undead wiles they utilized, attempting to elude the hunter. Their own forms they altered, taking the shape of a hundred different animals, or trees, or inanimate rocks or clouds of mist. But the hunter was not deluded. They constructed barriers, thick walls of stone and earth and metal, but the stranger penetrated them all. They fled in panic, but the follower calmly closed in.

The inevitable happened. First Elizabeth, who was inexperienced in bestial flight, was captured, and then Charles also, by the shadowy unknown hunter. Bound and trussed they were, helpless, exposed, and the figure stepped silently up to them, to administer the death-blow. But there was no blow, only a firm grip taken on their heads, and thought and memory came flooding back into their minds. The hunter, Jonathan, said only, *"Dawn is soon,"* and then he vanished.

As they were returning to the city, Charles tried to put the best face he could on their misadventure. "It happens every night," he explained with a sheepish expression. "It's so easy to lose yourself among the animal souls. And so, every night, Jonathan has to come out and save me." But Elizabeth was sullen. The fear had cut her deeply.

The night after Charles, Elizabeth met Claire. Claire was of the generation of the first World War, that first class of mortals who were confronted with the widespread rupture of cultural values, and whose response was the era of the flappers, the bootleggers, hot jazz and blues sung with no thought for tomorrow. The first generation that grew up without innocence. She withdrew from the world at the Depression, knowing that her time was passed and the excitement could never be recaptured. But she had been in error, because it was then that the Master came to her, with his cruel kiss, and took her into a new world where she could regain that innocence.

Softly she enveloped Elizabeth in her spell, a spell that cast away the travail of the decades that had passed them by, and brought them out into a world that knew how to dance. In their tasseled dresses they glided down the dark streets, lit by gas lights and the occasional passing Model-T, until they reached their destination. It was a perfectly decent and clean-looking club from the outside, but on the inside, on the other side of a hidden portal, there was a raw and rowdy speakeasy, where a fat black woman belted out the blues in the smoky air, and the bottles and reefers were passed around freely, with no intimation of guilt. There they danced with swarthy and attractive men of uncertain background, who whispered colorful suggestions in their ears. But when Elizabeth chose a partner and accompanied him into the private chambers in the back, the man found that her kisses were not of the nature he had intended.

Afterwards, as they returned to their flat, Elizabeth felt sullied. She demanded that Claire unleash her from the glamour, and Claire did so with a frown. The gas lights flickered a little, and turned into glaring arc-lamps. The soft friendly buildings that surrounded them became a row of crumbling warehouses. Their gay dresses were transformed into dull and flat modern clothing. The past was over and unreachable. "And where did we go?" Elizabeth demanded. "What present day monstrosity did you take us to, what kind of disco or fern bar or crack house?" she spat out in disgust. Claire shook her head sadly and replied: "No, I promise you, that part of the vision was truth. I'm not the only being in this city who longs for that old time of laughter and innocence. My spell slips through the alleyways and the hovels, and seeks out those old and broken-down mortals who remember those good times, the time before the world turned old and respectable. They're happy to shed their stooped bodies and grey heads for a taste of reality the way they remember it ought to be, in a kindlier universe... And they don't begrudge me the blood which they know is the price they have to pay for it."

11.

The next evening, while she was still in the process of gaining consciousness, there was a hard pounding on the door. Before she could answer or cause it to open, it opened wide and in stalked a tall, gaunt and ugly figure, who spoke in a grating voice: "I'm Gregory, and you're Elizabeth. So much for the amenities. I've heard that you are progressing all around the moronic crew who occupy this building, so I decided to skip the wait until you deemed it necessary to come looking for me. Don't think that I'm showing any degree of affection and favoritism for you. I figured just to save a little time for both of us. Now hurry along, we could've already taken a dozen or more victims by now!"

The sky brooded under a deepening overcast. A mighty storm was brewing. The light of the Moon was diffuse and dim, but all-pervasive. Elizabeth felt it surrounding her like a thin fluid though which she had to swim to progress. With each step it resisted her, with a little bite of pain and mockery. She couldn't forget that the ultimate source of this light was the Sun. The streets were filled with mortals, hustling about their petty unthinking errands. She felt their small thoughts as they brushed by. The weather was troublesome to them as well, and each was hurrying to find their own safe refuge before the storm came upon them.

But Gregory was not impeded. He was like the embodiment of the mortals' poor conception of the vampire, swooping down upon near and far like a vast black bat with his long tails flapping behind him. There was no planning, no thought behind his attacks. No wit, no elegance. Elizabeth thought him crass and unimaginative. But seeing his greed inflamed her own pressing need, and so she shortly found herself joining him in his reckless abandon. They leapt from mortal to mortal, and Elizabeth barely had the chance to taste of their essence, before Gregory hurried her on to the next one. It soon became almost pleasurable to her, to cast aside what she felt to be the better nature of her vampirism; Gregory, sensing this, grinned evilly back to her as he raced forward to claim yet another victim.

They were gross and inelegant. Gregory's mouth was blood stained, and he didn't bother to clean himself off before grabbing at the next human. For just a moment he would wait, to renew his spell of invisibility, and then fall upon the next one. Each corpse in turn he re-animated into the appearance of life, to walk down the streets for another day or two before collapsing in what would appear to be a death by natural causes. The sheep were unaware of the wolf loose among them; they hadn't even the sense to flee. Elizabeth had never felt more distant from her human heritage, as she joined Gregory in the reckless slaughter.

After a while she noticed two things. First, the streets steadily emptied of potential victims. Had they depopulated the entire city already? She decided that more likely the night was growing too late for them. She frowned, for this meant greater effort to keep on killing.

More slowly, she noticed that Gregory's appearance altered as their toll of kills increased. He seemed to be swelling, expanding from his earlier slenderness. It shortly became obvious that he wasn't even taking the time to properly digest the blood he was sucking into himself; he stored it under his skin, as a cow might store its cud. As his skin stretched out he began to take on a reddish pallor, the hue of the thickening gore which pressed within it. Elizabeth wondered, amused, what would happen if he should burst.

Vast and bloated, Gregory less resembled a bat by now than a huge pulsing toad hopping from human to human, round like a wrecking ball, casting about for more destruction. A red juicy grape. Despite his appearance, he remained nimble. Elizabeth was suddenly surprised to discover that she had been doing likewise in imitation of him, and abashedly paused from the havoc for several minutes to take the blood into her system, and bring herself back to her desired slenderness.

At last, the clouds, bloated with moisture almost as much as Gregory, began to disgorge their contents, in the form of a chilling sleet. This sent the few remaining mortals away from them, away to safety. Gregory looked as if he desired to run off to pursue them further, but after a minute he cursed and slowed to a halt. "Bah!" he spat in a deep gurgling voice, "always something. The world conspires against me, Elizabeth. Every night something happens to keep me from getting quite enough, enough to fill up all the nooks and crannies. Still, it hasn't been a bad night. Might as well go back to the building now. No more use standing out here in the wet."

They made their way back to the condominium. Frozen precipitation was a new experience for Elizabeth as a vampire, and it inspired and delighted her as much as it had when she was mortal. She ran and danced and slid on the freezing pavement, laughing at Gregory's scowls as he trudged grimly behind her. It burned her, as all moisture must, but she was strong, filled with the essence of more victims than she could count. She was free from the tyranny of the Moon, at least for the moment.

Only Gregory called out to her: "Stop acting like a cretin! Every moment you're wasting enough blood to last you for a week. Keep every drop like a miser! Tomorrow you may not even be able to leave the building, if the weather keeps up like this. You'll be sorry then. Do you think blood grows on trees?" She only laughed at his metaphor, poking his bloated belly to see if he'd pop.

As they returned to their home Gregory lumbered down a broad first floor hallway, at the end of which was a massive carved wooden double door. Elizabeth followed eagerly, until he held up his hand to stop her. "You aren't going to follow me into my private chambers," he said. "Didn't I refrain from looking into your rooms when I could've if I wanted to? I demand the right to a certain privacy." And with that, he opened the doors with a snap of his fingers and sprang though them with surprising agility for one of his bulk. With a slam the doors shut in Elizabeth's face, like a great trap.

Considerably irritated, she returned to her own room, at this time spartan and utilitarian, still reflecting her harsh mood of several days before. She settled herself down on her simple bed and tried not to think too much, but it was inevitable that she began to reflect on Gregory's boorishness again. Her irritation kindled to a flame. Then she realized that there was no moral barrier to her voyeuristic impulses since she felt that Gregory's inexcusable behavior justified any counteraction she felt appropriate.

She encountered more difficulty than she had expected. He was serious in his determination to maintain his privacy and had set a number of barriers and traps to ensnare the prying eyes of his undead compatriots. Elizabeth was determined and patient, and she slowly unraveled the complicated thread of glamour with which he had surrounded himself, until she descried a distant picture which revealed his actions after he closed the double doors behind him.

Elizabeth felt a thrill unlike anything she could recall, the thrill of the forbidden, like the violation of a trust. She almost conjured up a bag of popcorn for herself. Slowly and serenely, the image of Gregory cast off his black garments until his rippling flesh was grotesquely bare. Then he stepped through another wide portal into an inner room. The room was enormous, a vast atrium, lit by a diffuse glow like clouds. It was elegant, pristine. Tall Corinthian columns towered between fluted arches softly cast into shadow by gauzy veils. Refined statues of nymphs and fauns tastefully cavorted in the corners. Gregory's face visibly relaxed from its prior mirthless visage, and Elizabeth smiled too to see him reveal his true expression.

In the center of the atrium was a gigantic pool, which Elizabeth was puzzled to notice was empty. Gregory didn't pause as he slowly waddled up to its edge and knelt down before it. He leaned forward, and he heaved, casting forth all the great volume of blood and gore which he had taken in the course of the evening, a vast steaming torrent pouring forth from his throat. On and on he vomited it up, while Elizabeth reeled back in disgust from the picture. More and more and more, sticky, red, hot yet congealing. Soon he once again had his painfully thin figure. He had spewed forth every drop.

And then he stood up, and, gracefully assuming the posture of a diver, he plunged into it.

For a moment, Elizabeth continued to watch with disgusted fascination his swimming and splashing and cavorting about like a schoolboy on vacation. He was quickly covered by the gore from head to feet, unrecognizable if she hadn't known who he was and what he was doing. He swam laps and did handstands and playfully splashed it about to make waves which overran the edges and stained the flagstones. She wasn't able to hear any sounds, but it appeared that he was singing merrily. Finally, she was unable to bear it anymore, and she ended the vision. Fortunately, she thought, vampires don't have to vomit. Unless they want to.

12.

The next night, Elizabeth put Gregory out of her mind, and met Una. Una was an anarchist, brimming over with grandiose schemes for actions to achieve the perfect state among the vampires. Elizabeth (whose political views had never been more than muddy) was somewhat puzzled by her insistent denunciations of their current state of being. "But how am I being exploited, the way you say I am?" she asked. "I'm perfectly free to do absolutely any activity that enters my mind. I can create any item I want, so it's absurd to claim I'm enslaved by poverty. And none of the vampires do anything I'd describe as work... So I don't understand why you think a revolution is needed, much less how you plan on going about it."

Una, sitting opposite to Elizabeth in the smoky dark confines of the coffeehouse, leaned forward to speak more softly. "Keep your voice down," she said, looking suspiciously at the other political types sitting in the surrounding booths. "No one here knows what we really are. They think I'm just another mortal who's committed to the cause, who happens to sleep or work all day. Half the humans in this room haven't seen the Sun themselves in six months, I'd bet. But be careful of what you say when anyone else is around."

She sipped at her coffee, and Elizabeth did the same, frowning at the bitter taste. Not like the hot and pleasant saltiness of blood. Drinking another, lesser liquid only made the craving stronger, and it was bad enough already with all these humans so near but unattainable. Una continued: "I respect your opinions. Really I do. Most of the others won't put up with any criticism of their pet theories for more than a second. They'd decide you were a fool or a tool. Or a spy. But listen to a few points I have to make."

She assumed a schoolteacher's expression and voice. She had obviously given the same lecture many times before. "You say that there is no person or force which exploits the vampires. But have you already forgotten the so-called Master? It's an *undisputed* fact that for some time he has been planning some form of revolutionary action of his own, which he claims will put the mortals at our mercy. That may be so. But I say that, from what we know of his personality and techniques, what he's *really* aiming at is a state of dictatorship, in which the undead rule the living, and he will be the ruler of all the undead.

"As evidence, I give the fact of his unjust monopoly of the means of production: the method for creating new vampires. He is the one person who has caused all of the vampires known, at least in this city, to revivify, and, as far as is known, he is the only one who is even capable of doing so. Why? *Obviously*, he needs to keep this method as a secret in order to keep us in line. It is quite likely that he is just as capable of returning us to the grave as he took us out of it. This disturbs you, doesn't it?" she asked, seeing Elizabeth blanch at her words. "It ought to. *Ultimately*, we haven't the slightest guarantee that our current state of apparent freedom will last. At any moment, he could pop up and take over again, threatening to destroy any vampire who resists him. *Therefore*, my first expressed goal is to bring the group to a decision to take the so-called Master prisoner and keep him until he releases the information we require, or destroy him if he refuses."

"But wouldn't he just kill us if we try to strike at him?"

"Our only safety is in numbers. That's why I'm content to allow the current situation to go on as it is, *for now*. The more vampires we free from his clutches, the better our chances will be when the time comes, to *take action*.

"But on to my second point. You say that we are free, and that we don't do any work which is being exploited. But do you know that this is the case? Isn't it very *suspicious* that we have all been convinced that it is vitally important that we all dwell in that one building? 'For *safety*,' we're told. Might there not be some other motive? Could it be that the presence of so many vampires together gives some benefit for someone?"

"But who?"

"Who else but the *one vampire* who continues to argue persuasively for this arrangement, the one who always seems to pop around the corner when you least expect it, the one who..."

"I appreciate being the subject of conversation, even if that conversation is going on behind my back," said Jonathan, who had appeared beside their table without their noticing. He was dressed all in black, like the majority of the people in the club, but there was a casual impeccability about his bearing, almost a regal quality, that stood out from the mangy look of the humans. Elizabeth jumped nervously at his sudden appearance, but Una just leaned back, closing her eyes in visible irritation. "Why don't you just *admit* it?" she accused. "You're the only one who insists that we stay penned up in that building, that *condo*," she said, spitting out the term with acid.

"There is no reason other than what I've said a hundred times before," he replied, sitting himself expansively beside Una. "What if we suddenly leapt out in front of this crowd and bared huge fangs and started ripping into them indiscriminately without taking any precautions? They'd fall back in a panic at first, but we wouldn't last three minutes, before they'd tear us apart. Individually, they're helpless, but collectively there's no stopping them. *'The people united will never be defeated.'* Isn't that one of your revolutionary aphorisms? Nothing for me, thank you," he added aside to the waitress who appeared at his elbow.

"The bourgeois always finds a good excuse for their abuses," Una replied sullenly, looking down into the bottom of her cup. Jonathan laughed. "Ah, at last the argument decays, as ever, into the case of the haves against the have-nots," he commented.

"And why not? Isn't that what *history* has been teaching us time and again for five thousand years? Has dear Jonathan ever given you any hints about his own origins, Elizabeth?" She shook her head. "Of course not. He won't *admit* it unless you corner him. Well, I'm not so reticent. Our dear friend and companion Jonathan is a *scion* of ancient French nobility. The blue blood of a dozen *comtes* and *ducs* runs through his veins, or at least they did before the so-called Master emptied them for him. His personality was *irrevocably* shaped by his mortal experience, twisted until he is unable to perceive the truth of the proletarian struggle. This is the mind-set of the *sheep* whom we'll lead to the guillotine, when the first blow of the revolution is struck!"

Jonathan's air of amusement had slowly faded during this speech, and he replied to Elizabeth as if Una was no longer present: "What we see here, my dear, is an excellent illustration of one of the greatest dangers to which the undead is subject: the loss of the realization of our true identity in relation to that of our victims.

"Una has accused me in her most scathing terms of being bourgeois, as if that were a capital offense. Well, I'm afraid that I don't see that as such a terrible thing. Yes, I am a member of the nobility. And so are you, and so is Una, little though she wants to admit it. We as vampires are a natural aristocratic class, a separate breed above the level of the mere humans. We may imitate them for the purpose of disguise or amusement, but in the end, they can be nothing to us more than sustenance or entertainment. Nothing.

"Now, there can be no objection to Una playing her game of revolution as a pose, in order to insinuate herself in this gathering of mortals. But when she remains among them for an extended period, as she has unfortunately done, there is an enormous peril for her losing the awareness of what she is. You have already seen this same effect to a degree when you hunted in the wild with Charles. That was a minor danger compared to this, and it was easy then for me to save you.

"But when Una remains among them for many months like this, the humans tend to become, well, too human for her. She must recall that they are not to be anything more than food for her."

"Or else?" Una hissed.

"Or else, you will inevitably forget your undead nature. I've seen it happen a dozen times before, my dears, a dozen time. I'll admit that it's not usually done due to political fervor. More often it happens when one of us has the misfortune of developing an infatuation for one of them. As if the wolf could fall in love with the sheep. Or an even better metaphor, as if the sheep could fall in love with a clump of grass. Vampires can be just as ridiculous as the mortals. Without consciously realizing it, they can conjure up the hormones in their own bodies and let themselves be led on. At any rate, it's all too soon that the human will demand too much of the vampire. Probably it'll make the vampire agree to meet it during the day. And with all those chemicals stirring in his (or her) brain, the vampire is foolish enough to do it, and poof! he is no more. A tragedy. Especially when it is so important that we keep up our numbers, as Una insists we must."

"We have, *of course*, no independent way of finding out if what you are saying has any truth to it," Una noted.

"That is true. If I am the manipulative devil you believe me to be, I certainly wouldn't fail to stoop to any low means imaginable to keep you in my evil clutches. I wouldn't trust me either, in the same circumstances."

Elizabeth had followed their exchange in silent consternation. She had been attracted to Una's sense of committal, her dedication to a cause worthy of her fullest abilities. A welcome change from the egoistic obsessions of the other vampires. But Jonathan's arguments were calm and reasonable. Appealing to the head rather than the heart. This dichotomy was the precise reason Elizabeth had always striven to avoid politics whenever possible.

As she was thinking this, Jonathan was in the process of summarizing his case. "In short," he said, once more referring to Una in the third person, "she is a victim of her own radical mind-set. Her heart beats for those she perceives as down-trodden, and so she is willing to act to the detriment of herself and her own kind for the victims' sake. Even though she understands that she would be the first to be executed if her revolution ever does come to pass.

"Although of course, the revolution will never happen. Our power over the humans is absolute. They would never dream that vampires such as us exist, possessing such astonishing power over them. It is an affront to their pride. Taken in this light, Una can in fact be seen as being no more than condescending to them. As long as she plays the game of anarchy with them, they will never learn the truth about her and about us, and therefore never achieve their illusory freedom."

Without further comment, he arose and left them, with Una bristling silently behind. After he was gone she suddenly broke into a peal of laughter. "It's no use," she said after her chuckles died down, "trying to be reasonable with him when he gets on his soapbox. What a pompous *windbag*. He can't stand to ever lose a single point of debate. So the only way to shut him up when he gets on a roll is to just be quiet and let him say his piece. That way he'll leave satisfied, thinking that his superior *nobleman's* brain has refuted all opposition. But while he rants on with his chatter, others are taking *action*."

She led Elizabeth out of the cafe. The night was bitterly cold. Clear and icy enough for the stars to reflect off the snowbanks, glittering and blinding. Una flew to the wealthiest section of the city, stopping before a dark brooding mansion. "This is where the blow must *strike*." And lightning-like, with no forewarning, she crashed through a bay window. She was a vortex of destruction, tearing apart all the trappings of luxury. Draperies flew, furniture shattered, ornaments were flung about. The human dwellers, both owners and servants, were herded into a corner, shuddering and defenseless. Una grinned evilly. "Be proud, for you are about to die for the Cause!" she exclaimed, bearing great shining fangs, and she battened herself upon them.

And Elizabeth joined her, solely for the sake of satisfying the hunger. Jonathan had in fact largely convinced her with his arguments, no matter how long-winded they might have been. Una's act, she realized, was useless for her revolution. One ruler slain tonight

68

would only produce another one tomorrow. But the taste of the terror she had generated by her attack was excellent, a superb vintage.

13.

Elizabeth continued on her course of investigation into the ways of the vampires.

The evening after her night with Una she knocked on another door and entered at a booming and good-hearted invitation. At the door she was stunned by the appearance of a huge stuffed hippopotamus in the foyer. Negotiating her way around it, she saw that there was a long narrow hallway extending back for some distance, with any number of creatures standing at each of its frequent turns. On the walls, between the taxidermy specimens, there hung an immense collection of rifles, swords, knives, harpoon, blowguns, nets, *nunchakus*, bolos, and dozens of other categories of weapons and implements of destruction. After she passed all the weapons she reached a corridor lined with every imaginable variety of sports equipment, and every other possible instrument appropriate to recreation. The next hall consisted of an endless-seeming selection of wines, beers and spirits, from all over the world and many differing periods of history.

When she finally got through all the twisted length of the corridor, she arrived at a masculine but comfortable room with the appearance of the interior of an A-frame house. Reclining expansively in front of a roaring fire was the denizen of this place. "Hi," he said in a deep voice and with a warm smile. "I'm Phil." He stood up, and, had Elizabeth been a mortal, she would have had to fight to urge to drool, at the appearance of his broad shoulders, trim yet muscular frame and cleft chin. As a vampire she new how artificial such an appearance could very well be, so she kept her hormones in check. He gave her hand a firm squeeze as he shook it and led her to the sofa.

"Let me tell you something that's concerned me for a long time," he remarked, "about the nature of the majority of the vampires who seem to join our group. Especially the male ones. Now don't get me wrong: I'm a live-and-let-live man myself, and I'd never try to force my beliefs down anyone else's stomach, you know, but it seems to me that there's an unusual number of, er, non-manly types that have been getting raised from the dead. Not trying to cast any sort of suspicion on any of the others here, or on the Master, who's always seemed a really solid guy to me, but I have to wonder, what'd be wrong with having a few more normal, masculine, everyday sort of men around?"

Elizabeth shrugged. "Maybe the sort of man you're talking about isn't the sort the Master wants to revive?"

He gave a laugh. "Well, that'd make me feel kind of awkward then, wouldn't it? I mean, that sounds like there's something wrong with me, that makes me like one of those other types: the ones that all seem to be, well, *missing* something, if you follow what I'm saying."

She hastened to deny this. "Oh no, I'm certain that can't be it. I don't know, there could be a dozen other reasons. Maybe the others who are more like you might be, um, more independent. They might have left the Master and not come to stay in the condo."

He nodded. "You know, that could be it. Sounds reasonable. But me, I have a few theories of my own. You know, I look around, and I think to myself that they all act like they're all independent and original in their thinking, but none of them is what I would describe as a strong personality. They'd be very easy to dominate, I think. They are being easy to dominate. Just look at the way they're all huddling here in the condo, when they could so easily be out in the world, doing anything they want."

She couldn't resist the next question, "But what makes you any different from them?"

But Phil was ready with an answer to that: "I may look like I'm like all the others, staying safe behind Mama Jonathan's apron-strings. But I'm just playing things by ear. I do a lot of thinking about the sort of things that people like Una say. She's a kook, but she does have a head on her shoulders. One of these days, the Master is liable to be coming back looking for us. The way I have it figured, all of those others are all going to go running back to him like little babies. But don't count on old Philip doing that. I'm just going to sit back, and watch how the breaks fall. The Master's a big man, but I'm not too little myself. Don't be too surprised to see, when push comes to shove, the Master turns out to be easier to take down than the others think."

He invited her to join him on his rounds, to observe his techniques. She made herself invisible, and followed after him as he wandered around from nightspot to nightspot. His technique, she soon noted, consisted of doing virtually nothing. He allowed his god-like good looks to do all the work, alluring the finest of the women at each bar, while his glamours caused them to hear whatever it was they most wanted to hear from him. He remarked to her, "I feel that I'm performing a community service to the human males in this city. I'm removing some of the most dangerous ones, so they'll have an easier time of it. Sometimes I'm tempted to go and tell them what I'm doing, so that maybe they'll put up a statue of me or something."

Later, after she left Phil before dawn, Elizabeth shook her head in mock despair. There was no escape for the women of the world, not even in the wonders of undeath. She crept out of the building and found herself the biggest, stupidest, most gloriously masculine male she could locate on short notice. She made him grovel for mercy before she destroyed him. She felt she owed it to her sex.

14.

The next evening there was another storm. But this one affected Elizabeth differently than the last one had done. She felt as if the atmosphere was heavy, brooding, surrendering its precipitation with reluctance: big, formless clots of snow which dropped swiftly without being blown about by the rising wind. She felt that on a night such as this it would be ridiculous to have to go out in search of blood. This was the sort of night to lie around cozy in bed, warm and safe. But even as she had the thought, the hunger struck at her stomach insistently. She toyed with the idea of trying to cast a glamour to cause a human to come to her. She could call to get a pizza delivered, but the delivery boy would be the real meal... She giggled. But the dense and complex glamour which surrounded the building was too powerful for Elizabeth to budge. She sighed. She's have to leave, whether she wanted it or not.

And so, that night she met Alicia. Alicia was very small in size, frightfully energetic. Vivacious, if such a term could be applied to one who was not, strictly speaking, alive. She agreed with Elizabeth that this was no night for hunting, especially for the type of hunt which she preferred. But she shrugged, saying, "I guess we both know that the hunger isn't going to let us be, so we might as well get started. You know, I think I'm looking forward to having a new face along with me. I usually have to go find Jonathan, when I'm looking for company."

They ventured out in vaporous form, Elizabeth following Alicia's lead. The snow, falling in heavy clumps felt like burning coals shooting through her form, and the wind tattered her like a rag. She fought to maintain her being as Alicia glided silently beside her, with her senses spread before them like radar to detect the victims she sought. She showed her success with a joyful cry, and pulled herself into a compact shape which darted forward. Elizabeth followed with growing eagerness.

They were hovering outside the window of a condo not unlike the one where the vampires lived. Inside, Elizabeth's keen hearing detected the sounds of a human couple having an argument over the brassy blare of television commercials. A child was crying in the back room. Alicia quickly explained her plan, and Elizabeth recoiled distastefully. "Come on," the other vampire urged. "It won't work with only the one of us doing it. Don't judge this sort of thing before you try it: it's great, not like any other kill. And you'll have a hard time finding other game easily tonight." Finally, reluctantly, Elizabeth agreed.

Following Alicia's lead, Elizabeth compacted herself into a smaller size than she had ever tried before. Smaller and smaller. It was a curious feeling. Every sensation became stronger, more focused. With a smaller surface area, fewer of the snowflakes struck her body, but those which did were gigantic, in a relative sense, ripping through the entirety of her midsection when they struck there. But soon enough they were so small that they had to flit about to avoid the flakes, or they would have gotten crushed. Elizabeth reduced herself to a quintessence, a bright spark of thought and pain, in a body smaller than a flea.

They penetrated between the panes of the storm window, and floated swiftly into the room. The humans were giants, booming their angry and incomprehensible words, stirring whirlpools of air from their waving gestures which tossed them about like a tempest. And the sound of their blood rushing in those massive veins like rivers in flood stormed through Elizabeth's tiny mind, nearly overwhelming her thought processes.

Alicia, having suggested the game, chose the man. He would be more difficult, as the opposite sex. And so Elizabeth flitted to the woman. Simultaneously, they bit, but not to draw out that torrent of blood. Instead, they entered into the bodies of the humans.

Elizabeth slid softly and without detection through the skin and outer tissues, and penetrated into a capillary. Suddenly, shockingly, the hungry pain which was the definition of her existence vanished.

She swam and leapt about for joy, within the confines of the blood vessel. After a minute of unadulterated pleasure, she calmed down to think about it. Evidently, she concluded, the blood fluid must shield one from the radiations reflected by the Moon, which was the source of the pain. She began to have a better understanding of several of the mysteries of undeath: the brief cessation of pain which came from the sucking of the blood, which must give a partial shielding effect from the Moon; necessity for having to feed on a nightly basis, since as the living blood was digested and taken into the vampiric system it lost this protective aspect; and the peculiar pleasures of Gregory and his swimming pool.

Elizabeth was buffeted by corpuscles almost as large as her shrunken body. Although she didn't feel the pressing need of the hunger, she playfully nibbled at one, which ruptured, releasing all sorts of delightful-feeling molecules which surrounded her. She wondered if this might be the solution of the dilemma of the vampires, to turn themselves into microbes, hiding in the safety of their victim's bodies. (Or was this in fact what the true essence of all infectious diseases: hidden vampires within the very bodies of the mortals?)

Very shortly she learned the shortcoming of this solution, when a huge phagocyte, activated by the release of the red blood cell's inner fluid, ambled ominously in her direction. It reached a stubby pseudopod towards her, and she stabbed it with her sharp fingernails. And that only made the situation worse, releasing more chemical signals into the bloodstream, which summoned more cells to combat the invader. Antibodies, molecular structures so small that she could only barely see them even in her reduced size, swarmed over her, searching for a chemical grip to weaken her. She felt a slash of panic, but then she collected her thoughts, and carefully cast a glamour, which altered her own chemical nature to that of the host, so that its cells would no longer perceive her as foreign body, and so cease to attack her.

She sighed with relief, emitting a tiny bubble into the fluid. No, mortals' bodies were not the perfect environment for vampires. Although it was an excellent place during the night, the blood might not prevent her from losing consciousness under the light of the Sun, and if that happened, she would be helpless to resist the destructive ministrations of the white corpuscles.

This brought her finally to recall the plan which Alicia had told her. She tried to swim in the blood, but the strength of the flow was too great to move without a great struggle; then she remembered a little more of her physiology, and stopped resisting. The blood would carry her the way she wanted to by itself, eventually.

It was a bumpy ride, not unlike a rafting trip she had taken once when she was alive. As she penetrated more deeply into the mortal's body, the diffuse light lessened, and she had to radiate her own light to see where she was going. The capillaries fed into the smaller veins, and the small veins into larger ones. She recalled a description from school likening the blood system to the network of city streets. She was downtown in rush-hour traffic now, by that analogy.

The heart was an impressive sight. Loud. Tremendously strong. She could easily imagine it crushing her in its huge pulsing valves. Even in the microscopic state she could halt it with a single thought. She grinned to think of her power.

There was a quick trip through the lungs (she saw the damage the woman had done to herself by years of smoking: vile and ugly, withered structures where the blood had to struggle to pull the oxygen into its hemoglobin), and then back to the heart again. This visit was more difficult, as she was trying to maneuver herself to go into the correct artery to take her to her destination. She pushed through the throng of cells, which inevitably reminded her of an impolite crowd in a store. It was growing harder and harder to keep from anthropomorphizing the entire situation. She had to keep reminding herself that all these corpuscles and platelets were totally mindless, obeying only their instinctive patterns, following the molecular stimuli.

Finally, Elizabeth reached the brain.

She eased herself out of a capillary, and wandered aimlessly for a few minutes. She was in a forest of neurons. She was unable to detect their impulses. All appeared still and silent. She wondered how to go about doing what Alicia wanted her to do. Finally, she picked out a cell at random, figuring it was as good as any. She grasped it in her arms, hugging it tightly to herself, and bit into it. She injected herself inside its membrane, like a virus.

Once inside the cell, she dissolved, allowing herself to diffuse and occupy the neuron's volume. She was surprised now to be able to feel the tickle of the impulses which constantly passed through its, her, body. With a bit of concentration, she learned how to comprehend the messages. It was easy enough, once you tried it.

Then she asserted herself, and the messages began to change.

There was resistance, of course. As she sent forth her impulses, bringing an increasing number of neurons under her control, the native impulses re-routed themselves around her, attempting to surround her enclave and isolate it. But their opposing action resulted only from instinct, random, while her tactics were planned, sophisticated, subtle, subversive. She was a tumor, a mass of brain tissue rebelling against the human body's governance, and she was growing rapidly.

This growth required energy. Without a conscious effort, Elizabeth began to consume the energy of the host body. As she gained control of more systems, she altered blood-flow patterns, increasing the flow to her domain, and cutting off the blood to the enemy.

Slowly, she took over the victim's personality. As she conquered more neurons, she absorbed more thoughts, more memories. It was an ultimate act of sedition. Rapine of the mind. The enemy was shrinking now. Blurring. Losing her definition. In a series of rapid strikes Elizabeth took control of sight, sound, feeling. The other was walled in, blind and silent.

Elizabeth took possession of the personality. She put on its name, its likes and dislikes, like a new shirt. She made herself comfortable with it. Theresa Ryan. Age 36. School, work, marriage, childbirth. It was highly interesting for Elizabeth to discover the basic similarities but unique variations which came out of differing experiences. She could learn to like this, she realized.

As she took over Theresa's senses, she gradually noticed that the argument (the same old money fight which never really got resolved) had fallen into silence. Elizabeth began to look out her new eyes and saw the other human, Gary, the husband to the female body, had paused in its bellowing. She recognized the impish glint in the eyes, as the presence of Alicia. "I've been waiting for you a good ten minutes," she said with his voice. "What took so long?"

It took Elizabeth another minute of consolidation of her victory to learn how to use the new mouth and vocal chords to make coherent sounds. "This is, it's so much different from what I expect. I thought it'd be mostly like our usual way... But this is so much more. So complete. So, so..."

"So intimate. I know. We vampires think we know so much about the humans, from the way we absorb them as we drink their blood. But by doing that, we only get a taste of the surface of their beings. With this way, we drink of *everything*. You are Theresa now, down to the atomic level. And I'm Gary, completely. And this wonderful feeling, of becoming totally free of the pain, even if it can only be for a little while... It's almost a religious experience. For me, at least."

"Yes. Yes."

Gary's mouth frowned. "Oh, excuse me," said his lips. They had been talking very loudly, almost shouting, in order to hear themselves over the continuing squall of the infant in the back room. Brandon. Their son. No, the humans' son. But the product of their two bodies they wore, just the same. Elizabeth was having trouble keeping straight just where she stopped and Theresa started in this brain.

She'd have to be careful not to allow herself to forget her undead nature. She remembered Charles and his nightly hunt among the beasts.

Alicia caused Gary to pick up a cushion from the sofa and took it into the baby's room. Presently, the crying stopped. There was an instinctive pang in the female's body at that, which Elizabeth naturally suppressed, but she was surprised to detect, deeper but more pervasive than the anguish, a secret inner delight. The unspoken wish of every mother to destroy that to which she had given birth.

"What'll we do with this?" asked Gary's voice, holding the still red body up by a leg. It was more Theresa's will than Elizabeth's that moved her body to the kitchen for the big butcher's knife. They slit the little throat and drank. Not from need, not from the undead thirst, but just for the lust of doing what the mortals knew to be utterly evil.

And so it began for that evening. The vampires held fast their hold on the mind and will of the two mortals, but the mortals' suppressed desires rode the vampires like beasts of burden, urging them onward toward acts of greater malice and destruction. After a brief and bloody visit to the condo's superintendent, they ventured outside. The storm was continuing to rage. The streets were covered in drifts. No vehicles could get through. But the human bodies boldly strode through the snowfall, heedless of physical harm. Alicia and Elizabeth, fighting hard to maintain even a modicum of control, allowed the bodies free reign. But the energy costs of maintaining the torrid pace were dreadful. Under the vampires' command, the bodies commenced to cannibalize themselves, metabolizing tissues to provide energy for the pumping muscles and gasping lungs.

While Gary's flesh broke into a gun shop, Theresa's body made its way to the insurance office where it was employed. The fire was warm and cheery, and would be unquenchable by the time the fire department could get through. Then, heavily armed with weaponry, they jointly paid visits to friends, neighbors, relatives. The no-longer necessary day care center. The plumber. The tax auditor. The minister. Surprise provided the advantage. No one escaped them. No one had time to call for help.

But at last, as the night was growing old, the authorities tracked them down. Pursuit through the blowing wind. The bodies were little more than shells by now, emptied of everything except the vampires and the vile pushing will of the mortals. Flashing lights surrounding them to all sides. Loudspeakers calling on them to surrender. Theresa couldn't hear the words for the wind. Alicia in Gary's body took refuge behind a car, and shot at the policemen. Fire was returned. Bullets struck. Theresa gasped, unused to the mortal varieties of pain. She tried to keep the legs running, keep the blood flowing. But the will was finally ebbing. Surrendering at last to oncoming death. She fell.

At the last moment, she remembered. Not Theresa. Elizabeth. *Elizabeth!* She pulled herself out of the shell, returned to her microscopic form, breaking through the skin once more. And as she passed from the body, the human pain surrendered to the undead pain, viler, less clean. Elizabeth wept, but she saw the police running towards her, and dawn was approaching. No time for sentiment. The hunger was all, so Elizabeth quickly supped on the thin weak blood of Theresa, and it was rich, sweet, creamy to her throat, for it tasted of the experience they had shared. Together, forever.

Taking the form of mist, she arose with renewed strength, and she extended, re-acquainting herself with her keen vampire senses. How sharp and all-detecting they were, compared to the poor blurred sight and hearing of the humans. For instance, she immediately detected that Alicia had also escaped her mortal shell, and was quickly speeding back to their home. Elizabeth followed.

15.

"What happened?" she asked Alicia when they had returned to safety. Alicia was ecstatic, prancing about her room (which was a grandiose and bizarre spectacle of obelisks, madly-whirring machinery and banners blown by random geysers), babbling insanely about anything that came to her mind. She halted for a moment, contemplating Elizabeth's query, and set off again, "I don't know. It happens every time, and I've never really figured it out. I go and absorb the human's body, and then it seems as if it's the human that's absorbed me! What did you think of it?"

Elizabeth frowned, as her own excitement faded, to be replaced by an increasing upwelling of distaste. "Well, I don't know. I thought that you'd know it a little better. I'm the one that's new to all this."

"Exactly. Exactly. And isn't it funny? The vampire, the one who's supposed to be in charge of everything in the world (except for water, of course), can't even control a single little mortal! Sort of puts you in your place, doesn't it."

She stopped for a second, and heaved a big sigh. "I'm really sorry I get like this," she continued with just a slight lessening of her excitement. "I just can't help it. Taking a human in that way does it to me. Or maybe it's just my personality. I was always all bubbly like this when I was alive. I wonder why the Master would choose someone like me. I'm so unlike any of the others. But that's another story....

"But like I said, I don't know what happened, not really. But I have a few guesses. It's all the human's fault. I remember what the Master told me. Didn't he tell you the same thing? He used to say that if the humans have something to believe in, something which is totally important to them, then they can be more powerful than us."

"Yes, I remember him saying that. Usually religion is the thing they can use against us."

"Well, when we attack in the usual way, I think that, even as we rip their throats out, they still really don't believe in vampires. They've done such a good job of convincing themselves that we aren't real. So many stupid books and silly movies. They can't allow themselves to believe in such a ridiculous thing as vampires.

"But my way is so different. We go completely into their minds, and take them over. They have to believe it. It's undeniable. Even though we're in control of everything in their bodies, they're still stronger than we are. They make us move their bodies to do what they want.

"And what they want... Back when we were alive, I remember, we always thought that, in the deepest part of our hearts, we were basically good people. All humans do that. But you felt what happened to them, when they realized that death was upon them. They knew that they were free, for a few hours, to do anything in the world they could imagine, anything they could compel us to do for them... But what always happens, with me, with you, with Jonathan and every other vampire who's ever tried this with me: what they make us do, is kill and maim and annihilate, everything that was closest to them. It's like that deepest part, the innermost heart, which is in both the living and in the undead, is a will to evil. A will to smash, and kill, and destroy."

The whirring of the machinery died away to silence. As she spoke, it seemed to Elizabeth that Alicia was growing older, grey and weary from this unholy knowledge, but Elizabeth's anger had simmered as she listened to Alicia's words, until she couldn't hold it in any longer, "That's the most ridiculous thing I've ever heard!"

Alicia started back in shock, causing a raucous discord of sounds to emanate from the equipment behind her. "What, what do you mean?"

"I mean nothing but exactly what I said. How can you make such a statement about all of humanity, and all the vampires as well? I resent it, that you think that you can try to say such a thing. What do you know about what I have inside my heart, that it's good or evil?"

Alicia stammered a reply, "Y-you can't deny that the undead are practicing evil, by, by destroying so many lives, every day..."

"Yes, I'll admit that I've done wrong, both when I was alive, and, yes, maybe since I've come back into undeath as well. But you're not telling me anything other than what Deborah said, and I'm not going to accept her choice. I don't believe it. There has to be something more than evil to the world, to what we do... I won't let you cast everything into the darkness. Maybe we're really doing a favor to the mortals, giving them a taste of immortality they wouldn't get otherwise."

"But the Master's words: he told us beyond any doubt that ours was a path of evil..."

"But we've already rebelled against the Master. At least that's what everybody keeps on telling me, although it seems that he's the one we spend all of our time talking about and worrying about. I rebelled against him, once and for all. We already know that he told us lies. That leads me to assume, for anything he might have told us, the opposite may very well be the truth."

Alicia started to collect her thoughts, as her own anger began to emerge. "But what about our experience tonight, when we drank the deepest essence of the human soul, and found it total darkness?"

"I'm not willing to concede that we experienced anything of a human nature tonight. Nothing at all. We vampires are a very complicated and subtle group. Too subtle. Every night, it seems like I'm taken into a different world: each of the undead lives in his or her own personal reality, where everything is shaped and colored by his or her perceptions and desires. I can't be sure of anything I see or feel, because I can't know whether it's truth, or a trap. Anything may be nothing but a reflection, from the spirit of one of you other vampires....

"So, I think that what we went through tonight, what you say was an exploration of the depths of the souls of the morals, was really only an exploration of the twisted depths of your own heart. It was a snare, set and sprung by you, trying to lure me in and entangle me in your own ways."

The geysers sputtered and stopped. The machinery froze, and collapsed into rust. And Alicia knelt down in the dust of her works. "You've ruined everything. All I was trying to do was to have some fun, a few innocent delights, turning the humans to work all the darkest deeds that were suppressed inside us. To forget my own shadow by letting their evil loom larger than mine... But you couldn't let it be. You had to destroy it all, you had to be so damn curious about everything. It's all your fault, making me explain everything in so many details." She bowed her head.

Elizabeth replied, "I'm just trying to learn all the ways of the vampires. And to do that, I have to understand everything. I don't want to get caught in the throes of error. I was stuck in so much falsehood, so many twisted meanings, back when I was alive. I just didn't want it to happen again. I'm sorry if I hurt your feelings." Dawn was getting very near, and she turned to go.

But as she reached the door, Alicia picked up her head to call after her, "I was only trying to be friendly with you, Elizabeth. But you've succeeded in revealing everything I have inside me to be all tangled and evil. So I can't let you be my friend. We're enemies now. And I'll show you just how much evil there is inside me, someday. I'll show you in a way you aren't ever going to forget. And a vampire has all eternity to wait for revenge."

Elizabeth felt a shiver of dread. Feeling less certain of herself with every passing moment, she fled back to the safety of her own room.

16.

Elizabeth woke at the moment of dusk with a deep-seated anticipation, and fairly sprang up from her bed (which was an elaborate covered affair this particular evening). It was a feeling, she thought, very similar to the one she used to get on the day when an important school project was finally finished. You're weary from the long struggle, with the goal so far off as to seem unattainable. Then the climactic day arrives, and you feel a rush of relief and pride in accomplishment, but also a slight wistful sorrow. Another goal striven for and then reached which can no longer tantalize you with its fleeting reward.

This was the night, she knew, that she would at long last finish her survey of the other vampires in the building. She had trekked down every hallway, opened every door, except for the last one. Either it was another empty room, which meant that she was finished already, or it had one final occupant for one final night of discovery (and probably, the way things had been going, horror and disgust), and then freedom.

But freedom for what? She had allowed herself to define her existence in terms of this project of exploration, discovering the many ways of the undead, to see how each of them had chosen to spend his or her particular slice of eternity, but what would she do after this? She would have passed through every door of possibility, and (unless this night revealed something especially excellent), each door would have proven to be unacceptable. She would have to go out and make a decision. To join one of the other vampires in his or her own world. Or to find some new way, one of her own. The idea of making that choice haunted her. It was the one decision she had never succeeded in making when she was still alive, and she hadn't seen anything since her death to make the decision any easier.

(Of course, as she told herself to keep from getting over-excited, this was certainly not going to be the last night of her explorations, since she hadn't yet gone to visit Jonathan's own domain as yet. She had decided to wait and go to him last of all. There were so many questions she had which only he could answer for her.)

She went down the hallway to that last door. She knocked. No answer. Again, and still no reply. She concluded that this was one more empty room, and, smiling, turned to go, but then she had a hunch and turned back again to give the door one more try. She touched the knob and found it unlocked, opening inward with no effort. And she looked inside.

Inside she saw the desert.

Vast and uncompromising, an unending vista of sand, ranging in low dunes as far as she could see. Crystalline night above, shattered by the glistening of thirty thousand stars. At the lifeless distant horizon the stars were shaded by the forms of jagged mountains. A cold but gentle breeze blew in from the open spaces, rustling softly at Elizabeth's hair and shirt. It had no odor, but it conveyed a sense of freshness, of well-being, of contemplation and communion with the vastness of existence.

Elizabeth knew that she had to find the source of that wind.

In a dreamlike state, she stepped forth from the hallway and into the desert. It was real. Sand crunched beneath her shoes. No, not her shoes, she decided. She caused them to dissolve. Her bare feet tingled with the feeling of the grains against them.

It was colder than she would have expected. Not a winter cold, but a dry, renewing cold. The low humidity caused it to be a not unpleasant sensation.

The wind picked up a little, and suddenly the door flew shut, leaving no trace of its presence. Elizabeth now felt some stirrings of fear and suspicion, as she passed the place where the doorway ought to have been and could detect nothing. And the wind was blowing away her footprints. If she left this point, she would be very unlikely to locate it again.

She was intrigued by the mystery of it all. Where exactly was she? Was she still physically located inside one particular room in the condominium of the vampires, or had the doorway transported her to some other location? Was she still in America? Or even on Earth? The stars were so bright, so overwhelming in their splendor, that she was unable to recognize any of the few constellations she might have been able to identify. It should be possible, she reflected, to experiment, to see if she had the ability to alter this place to return her to the building. But she wanted to learn more. More about that wind. If it was a trap, it was a very cunning and enticing one.

There were a few larger rocks scattered about, and Elizabeth assembled them into a cairn which could be visible from some distance. Then she began to walk, facing into the wind. Unless it suddenly shifted in direction, she figured that she could probably find her way back to the cairn, and if necessary force the door to reopen for her.

She walked. One of the more desirable aspects of undeath was that one possessed infinite stamina. The dunes were higher than they looked from a distance, more difficult to traverse; her feet sank deeply into the sand with each step. She could have, of course, taken on vaporous form and travelled with no effort, but somehow she felt that it was appropriate to journey in human form, by foot.

The walking did expend energy. As the strength flowed out of her, Elizabeth began to feel an increase in her hunger. She didn't see anything alive in the desert, not even a lizard, not even a plant. The night was passing slowly, but she knew that soon she would have a great craving for blood. The desert floor was too smooth, too uniform. There ought to have been sharp rocks to cut her feet upon, she thought, or larger stones to stub her toes against. Each step was always too easy and painless. This fact, added to the lack of wildlife, caused her to suspect that this place was wholly artificial, and she was still inside the building.

She had spent most of the trip looking down at her footing; so it came as a surprise when she happened to look up and see a light already close by, flickering and wavering. A fire, apparently. She found herself eager for the idea of company. Another soul to share in the hugeness of the desert night. Or one to assuage her hunger.

Elizabeth rapidly neared, and soon could make out a figure sitting at the fire opposite to her approach. It was completely garbed in a robe and hood, unidentifiable, but its small lithe size suggested a female. She came directly up to the fire, and stood silently, feeling vaguely foolish for not having anything to say. The figure cast back its hood, and revealed that it was indeed a woman, matronly but handsome, and with solid black eyes that could swallow all the big night.

"You are hungry, and in pain from it," the other said in a quiet, flute-like voice. "But this is the place where you can learn to put that hunger aside. I welcome you, in the name of the one whom we all serve, whether we know it or not. I am Diana."

"Thank you. I'm Elizabeth. Is this, all this great expanse, real? All inside the one room in the vampires' building?"

Diana smiled enigmatically. "If I understand the sense in which you are speaking, the answer you are looking for is, Yes. I made this place long ago, and its boundary which intersects with the outer world is no more than the wall of one cubicle. But in the sense I prefer, the answer would be, No. I have surrendered all claims to possession on the physical plane, and thus this territory is an independent place having its own existence and being, and cannot be considered to be mine. Yet in a third sense, the answer turns to Yes, once again. That which I consider to be myself radiates outward from my body, and encompasses all this domain, and all the building wherein we dwell as vampires, and indeed all the city and the world. I am one with it, and therefore it is one with me, and is contained inside me."

Oh, Lord, thought Elizabeth to herself, *one of those mystic types.* In college she had more than her fill of them and probably could have considered herself one. She had long forgotten the lines of thought and arguments which one needed to communicate with them. Already anger was building up inside her mind, the same anger which had made her lash out at Alicia. She determined to try to get away as soon as possible.

"Please, sit and share the fire," continued Diana. "We don't have the bodily need for the heat, but its hypnotic beauty is one better shared with a companion."

With a sigh, Elizabeth complied. There was a pause for several minutes. Diana seemed lost in contemplation of the flames. Elizabeth fidgeted. Just when she was starting to think of excuses to depart, Diana began abruptly to speak again, "Tell me, Elizabeth, when the day comes and your mind darkens, do you dream?"

Startled, she jumped a little. She almost made a quick and flippant reply. But then she reconsidered and thought for a few seconds more. "You know, that's something I hadn't realized before now. No, I don't dream in the day... At least, I don't remember ever doing so. How strange, that I never thought about it."

"No vampire dreams. Ever. Daylight causes agony, and oblivion. Every dawn, we die again, and every dusk, we are resurrected. Yet one of the definitions of the human creature is that it is the being which dreams."

"So we're no longer human. That's something every vampire agrees on."

"We are not human, but we possess all the mental elements of the humans. We use speech and logic. Our thought processes are not foreign to the human condition. As far as we know, the sole difference, regarding the intellect and spirit, is that the humans dream, and we do not."

Elizabeth pondered this for several minutes. Willing or not, she realized that she was getting hooked on Diana and her mystic perceptions. "I suppose you're right, as far as you go. But are we sure that there aren't any other differences we aren't aware of? I mean, we have the power to change every physical aspect of our selves we desire. Don't we have the same power to change our mental or energy portions also, if we wanted to? To become truly non-human in the way we think and feel. In fact, I'm sure we can," she added, calling her adventure with Charles to mind.

"Would you have the courage to take such a course?"

"What do you mean by that?"

"It is your mind and spirit that is what you think of as your true being. If you dare to alter that, you may find that you are no longer Elizabeth."

She sighed. "I'm sorry, Diana. I know you mean well, but all this refined philosophical hair-splitting is just too much for me anymore. Do you know Deborah and Una? The three of you could have a very interesting discussion on the essence of our beings and the proper ethical course of action we should take. Add Jonathan if you need a fourth, I'm sure he'd be willing. But I'm hungry. Hungry for blood. I don't see what good philosophy or high thinking is when there is that need which we can never fill."

"But if we change ourselves, body and soul," replied Diana insistently in a quiet yet crystalline voice, "why can't we change to make the pain cease?"

That caught Elizabeth aback. "Well, I never thought to try. The Master said we couldn't change that."

Diana did not reply directly to her. "Behold," she said, pointing out and beyond the fire. Elizabeth turned, and she quailed at what she saw. It was the Moon. A waning crescent several days from being new, but in the vast openness of the desert, it was gigantic, threatening, terrible. There was nothing for Elizabeth to use to distract the Moon from her, or herself from it. It was a huge Eye, glaring down three-quarters closed at her. And it hammered down at her, demanding blood, blood to flow, blood to quench, blood to spread over all the Earth, to rise and cover it. She moaned. "Stop it," she cried to Diana. "Make a mountain. Make a city. Something to hide it away from me! Isn't there something here, anything I can drink, to let me sink my teeth into?"

"Nothing. There is no living thing in all this place, nothing to distract us from our concentration."

"How do you stand it? How can you stand to have it looking down on you? How do you stand the pain?"

"I feel no pain."

Disbelief. "How? Why? Why don't you hurt?"

Diana smiled at her. "Why, it is due to philosophy, of course."

Elizabeth was no longer capable of making a coherent reply. She bit into her own arm, and the thin trickle of her own blood gave no relief. She was rolling on the sand, no longer in a wholly conscious state, instinctively struggling to find a shelter from the Moon. It was very similar to Deborah's torture chamber: not as overwhelming in the severity of the agony, but like to it in the pervasiveness, the totality. Worse in a way, since she was already empty of blood. There was nothing in her but the hunger. The universe was reduced to nothing other than pain. Pain and further pain.

Then a familiar voice called out, "This is too much for her! She can't handle it when she's so empty." And there was a comforting flow into her, something from outside. The pain was still bad, bad, but she now had a little strength to fight it off, a little bit. She opened her eyes. She was not surprised to see the figure of Jonathan, standing over her and dripping blood from a container into her open mouth. He was dressed in sackcloth again, and managed to look very elegant in that garb.

During the following conversation Elizabeth was in no condition to participate. She lay weakly on the ground, soaking up the cool soothing sensation of the sand digging into her flesh. She wished she could burrow into it and hide, but she lacked the strength, and she feared Jonathan might no longer protect her if she tried to hide. But she listened.

"We were doing very nicely on our own," she heard Diana say crossly, "before you butted in."

"I don't know if that's the way I would have described it," replied Jonathan with a hint of humor in his voice.

"She was suffering, true, but an initial process of purification is desirable."

"I've noticed that what mystics call purification is generally indistinguishable from what laymen call torture. I know you always get angry at the comparison, but I for one don't see much difference between your methods and those of Deborah."

"Deborah considers herself already damned, and is trying to get an early start on the tortures of hell. I am trying to bring about a condition where damnation is itself averted. And it works."

"For some. For others, this way has caused only madness and self-destruction. As you certainly remember."

"I'll take that chance. I'll sacrifice a thousand in order to save just one. The chaff must be separated from the grain, the dross from the gold."

"And another thousand vampires must be discarded. Is there never to be an end? Must every vampire you get a hold of be melted down in your crucible? Won't you allow some other, gentler way? You know how I feel. I have striven to make this community a testament to diversity of thought and practice."

"And the results only argue the more strongly for my view. We are the most blessed of all beings. We alone of reasoning creatures on this world have been given proof that death is an illusion. And it is obvious that God and God alone can bring this about."

"That is debatable. It is Master who did this for us. There is no necessity to invoke any higher power. Do you propose to worship him as your God?"

"Master is above and beyond our petty squabbles. He is unique. He is the instrument by which this miracle has been wrought. He walks close to God, in His very shadow, even if he doesn't realizes it."

"I am certain he would be highly amused to hear you granting him such distinguished company."

"Mockery doesn't veil the clarity of revelation. No, it is conclusive that we have been chosen, through the actions of Master, to receive this precious gift. Immortality. Total power. We are the very angels come to Earth, but we use this gift for nothing more than glutting ourselves. Our chosen food is the blood and life of the humans, the ones whom we should be holding on our knees like little children, imparting to them the jewels of our divinely-gotten wisdom. Instead, we hunt them down to tear their throats out!"

"And so you say that merely by refraining from this natural impulse we magically ascend into the clouds of holiness. All our evil will be shed from us like a dead outer skin, and we'll spend all eternity singing hosannas."

"You're putting words into my mouth, again. I wouldn't presume to claim to understand the entirety of the wonderful plan, of which we are the key and cornerstone. But it is inarguable that we cannot bring about anything desirable by wallowing in the depths of depravity. Which is the way you teach."

"Now you're the one putting words in my mouth, old friend. I don't teach anything. I know you find it hard to believe, but it's the truth. I only attempt to encourage those around me to have an open mind, and to think for themselves. I don't presume to know anything at all more than what I can determine by my own existence. And that is where I am correct and you are in error."

"Bah! You come to me reeking of bloodshed and dare to lecture me on what's right and correct! You and your bottle of blood are a pollution of the desert!"

"Are you absolutely positive that you have not a single trace of the old hunger left in you? I notice that your eyes keep on turning toward this little container, which still has a few drops left in it... Does this reek I have about me which you're complaining about not stir up the tiniest yearning in your sacred and purified breast? Are you sure that what you're feeling is really contempt of me, or of yourself?"

He coughed. "But you've allowed me to fall too much in love with my own voice again. Not that it's an all-that-unusual thing to happen. I'm not here to quarrel with you. We aren't saying anything we haven't said to each other a hundred times before."

"That's true. But eternal hope is a virtue."

"So you say. But talk all we want, the question hasn't yet been addressed. Which is, what do you want with Elizabeth?"

"The answer is easy enough. I want to keep her here, and wean her away from the blood-thirst, and help her to purge away her innate evil."

"But have you done her the courtesy of asking her if this program is something she desires?"

A pause. Diana's reply was curt. "She would come to accept it. And as the darkness falls off her soul, she would wonder at the glories that would be revealed, and curse the nights she spent under the shadow, before she came to me."

"In other words, no, you didn't think to ask her."

"That's a most crass way of putting it. She has openly indicated that she wants to experience all the varieties of existence which have been brought about in the vampires' building. She has sampled what she would consider to be the good and the bad, joyfulness and suffering. I think that she would have said yes if I'd have asked her, if only to learn."

"But, of course, she has been listening most carefully to everything we've been saying. I think that, knowing now what the gist of your beliefs are and what she would be expected to go through if she remained with you, she would decline your invitation."

"It would be interesting to learn which of us is correct."

"So why don't we ask her? With your permission, of course."

Diana must have agreed, as Jonathan stirred up his power, and sent forth a great cloud, which blanketed the face of the desert, and obscured the hard light of the Moon. Elizabeth immediately recovered enough to come fully to her senses, although the pain was still strongly set in her bones. She stood up, and found herself with the urge to fawn almost like a cur, craven and bowed, before Jonathan, who had brought that blessed relief.

She steeled herself, and turned to look at Diana. The female vampire didn't seem to have moved a millimeter; rather the expression on her face was stern, uncompromising, enraged at Jonathan's interference but strictly in control. Her voice, however, gave no indication of strain or displeasure: "Well, we needn't beat around the bush, do we? You've heard everything. I could say more to try to attract you, and I'm sure Jonathan could do the same. Will you remain here, and accept my lessons? I am not offering an easy or pleasurable way. You will suffer here. We will feel agony together. Every night we will sit before the Moon, and we will allow it to beat down on us. And comes the dawn, we will huddle in a cavern without the meanest comforts.

"And though you think you felt pain now, and pain while you were exposed to the Sun by Deborah, you will plumb deeper depths of agony than you can possibly now conceive. You will bite the hard dryness of rock. You will burrow into the sand like a worm. You will tear your body limb from limb in your desperation for a single moment's respite.

"But, if you will persevere, if you fight your demon up to and beyond the threshold of insanity, you will come to find that the long years of austerity have worn away the limitations of undead flesh. You will become a light. A tiny flickering candle when compared to the cruel splendor of the Sun and Moon, but you will not die out. You will glow in the darkness and the darkness will lose its power over you. And you and I will be joined, two lights to shine out for the others to behold and take hope.

"Will you join me?"

And Elizabeth's heart started to melt, and pour out on the barren ground, for, despite the repulsion she had determined to feel for anything Diana told her, she was tempted to join Diana on her path, a holy and sanctified communion. Truly the path of blood and lives spilled away for her fill was a pale and tattered thing when compared to the glory which was now appearing before her feet, with but one step necessary to set her on its course.

She looked back and saw Jonathan. He said nothing at all, but only smiled a little. He was very sleek, she realized, very much like a well-fed and groomed rodent, with his perfect coiffure and refined mannerisms. He was sin. But he was comfortable.

Elizabeth suddenly realized that Diana's path was irrevocable. To join her would require her to cast aside everything she had thought and said and done since her return from the grave. That was too much for her. Too much for now.

At last she made her reply. "Diana, Jonathan, I thank you from the bottom of my soul that you've allowed me to witness your debate. I feel like an infant here, crying in my egotistical hunger, while you great and solemn beings argue the fate of the world. I'm not worthy to be subject of so much of your concern.

"I can't tell you how much I am attracted to the mystic path you've put in front of me, Diana. But I can't do it. Not yet. Maybe not ever. Or maybe someday. You'll always be here, won't you, if I ever find myself ready for it?"

"Of course, my child."

"Good. Good." And with that, Elizabeth's energy wholly failed her, and she fell into a swoon. Jonathan stepped up and lightly picked her up in his arms. With a nod to Diana, he opened up a doorway right beside the fire and took them through, back to the hallway where she had begun. With a great struggle, Elizabeth brought herself back to coherence once more to say: "Jonathan, don't go. There are so many things I need to know. I need you to tell me what's been going on. It's all so complicated, so confusing. I need..."

"Not now, not now, my dear. The night is late, very late. You must go out at once and find yourself a victim, to preserve your very existence. Come back to me tomorrow. I'll be waiting for you."

18.

And thus, early the next evening, Elizabeth found herself before the last door, the door to Jonathan's room, the superintendent's room on the ground floor. She had carefully made certain to go out at the very moment of dusk, and quickly found herself a victim. Probably too quickly, she realized. It was messy and gave her little pleasure. But she felt herself prepared for anything now. She hoped.

"Come in, come in!" Jonathan exclaimed with apparently unfeigned delight as he answered her knock. She stepped inside, and was bowled over with the sight of his chosen surroundings. The sole theme which tied together his furnishings was the lack of theme. Jumbled furniture from a dozen styles and periods, juxtaposed indiscriminately.

"Well," he said, "I am most pleased that your survived your survey of our community with body and mind intact. They are not an altogether easy group to learn to live with."

Statues and shelves and artwork and stuffed animals and whirring machinery. It was disjointed and disturbing, yet somehow there was something which appeared very familiar to it all.

He continued: "It's up to you now to make a decision. Or rather, several decisions. First off, you have to decide whether you want to continue to accept our hospitality and remain with us. If you do so, and I must say that I strongly urge you to do so, for reasons I think I have made clear to you by now, you must then decide which of the varied living styles you wish to adopt. Or, of course, you may adapt any other manner of existence you can imagine. Total freedom is available. Infinite possibilities."

On one side of the room, there was a window looking out upon a verdant forest scene, and on the opposite side, another with a view of a desert. In a small alcove, some very familiar-appearing torture devices. Slowly, Elizabeth felt she was beginning to understand.

"But Jonathan," she said very slowly, "you say I've seen all the different choices this group has to offer. But that isn't true. You haven't shown me anything of the way *you* exist."

Jonathan stopped. He looked aggrieved for a minute, and then his smile gradually returned. "Heh, heh. I perceive that I may be a tiny bit more transparent than I would have thought myself to be. Is it so obvious?"

"I don't know unless you tell me."

"Very well." He sat down in a plump armchair like the one her mother had. "I suppose that it's my lack of interior decorating that has given me away. It's true. I am not an imaginative person, I'm afraid. I've tried and tried, but I can't ever seem to think of a truly original idea, in how to act or what to think or do. So, I've gotten in the habit of utilizing the ideas of those who are around me.

"But don't think that I'm a simple imitator or fake. I do have a certain amount of pride. I am most helpful to them. I interact with them. I provide what they really need. You've seen. You understand, don't you?"

"I think so. For instance, for Charles, you..."

"I am the hunter who pursues him and saves him from himself every night."

"And Claire?"

"I am a footman, or driver, or any other servile figure she might be in need of, to facilitate her dreams and pleasures."

"For Stephen?"

"A companion even shyer and more withdrawn to listen to him and let him explain things to me."

"What about Alicia?"

"A companion to join her in her infectious adventures inside the humans."

"For Una?"

"For Una, and similarly for Diana, I'm a foil for their debates. Intellectuals are always in great need for someone who's their equal, but whom they can convince themselves they've overcome."

"Deborah?"

"A fellow penitent."

"What about Gregory?"

"I serve him by my absence, by allowing him the privacy he desires. But don't be mistaken, by doing that, I am still participating in his world, if in a rather paradoxical manner. I take part in the personal perceptual world of every one of the vampires who dwell here, in some manner, visible and invisible."

"But there are so many of them. How is there time...."

"I myself am many. Even as I am speaking with you here, I am simultaneously engaged in arguing with Una, and listening with rapture to Stephen's lecturing, and driving Claire in a hansom cab to her club. Soon, I must begin to pursue Charles, and then don my hairshirt for my dawn engagement with Deborah. As I keep mentioning, there is *nothing*, or almost nothing, which is impossible for us vampires to do."

Elizabeth began pacing the floor nervously back and forth in front of him. "This is all so very strange. I feel like a rug's been pulled out from underneath me. I don't know: are you even real? Real in the same sense I am and the others are?"

"Of course. Real, but multiple. I suppose you could consider this to be my particular manner of existence."

"But why? Why do you do this?"

He shrugged. "I have my reasons. It fills the centuries."

"Do the others know?"

"Yes, they know it, if they choose to recall it. But I have taken certain steps, in the casting of the spell which protects the building, which discourages them from remembering it on a regular basis. It tends to make them uncomfortable, to recall it."

Elizabeth halted her paces. "And, and you want me to join you. You want me to become just like them, creating a self-centered little fantasy world to live in, which you'll use for your own voyeuristic desires, spying on every move I make, using me to fill up the emptiness which you can't fill on your own."

"I would hesitate to put it in such a negative light."

"Like some huge grotesque leech, like a, like a..."

"Like a vampire?"

She stopped instantly, and stared down at him. Slowly, her anger evaporated, until she laughed out loud. "I suppose we should be the last ones who're justified in criticizing you, aren't we? We're all parasites on the mortals, and you're not doing any more than turning the tables on us, and doing the same to us as we do to them."

"Harrumph. Speaking of it in those terms tends to emphasize the least desirable aspects of this arrangement. Please look at some of the more pleasant considerations. I am infinitely adaptable. I can provide any sort of companionship you might desire. You've just scraped the surface of the possibilities by looking at the vampires who currently reside here. Why, I could tell you the most remarkable stories of centuries past...."

"Still, I don't know about it. There's something that feels wrong. And I don't like what you mentioned about the vampires forgetting the truth about you after they've been here for awhile."

"Well, I can give you the most solemn assurance, as having been an honorable man while I was among the living, that I will exempt you from the action of that particular glamour if that is the only factor which would cause you to decline the offer of staying here."

He stood up. He appeared to be wholly recovered from his episode of embarrassment. "And there is still one more thing you need to see to understand fully what we are and what I am. You have in fact not yet met every one of the undead who reside in this structure." He gestured her before him. Curious, she obeyed.

19.

Jonathan led Elizabeth out of his room, and turned toward the stairwell. To her surprise, they descended, down to the basement. It looked like the basement of any other apartment building or condominium in the city: washing machines, a furnace, a water heater, plumbing pipes. She supposed that the items were there to satisfy any human government inspection which could not be put off by glamour. Jonathan pointed to a small door in a shadowy corner. With great flourish he fetched out a key from within his pocket. "I am doing you an honor by allowing you to intrude to this, my innermost sanctum. Of the other vampires, only Master and Diana know that this room is occupied." With that, he unlocked the door and threw it open.

Inside it was dark, but there was an elusive glimmer present, the source of which she couldn't identify, and which illumined nothing. Jonathan caused the slight radiance to grow. The room was revealed to be featureless, but in the middle of it there floated the appearance of a nude male-child, wrapped in the faint shining.

Involuntarily, Elizabeth stepped forward, for the child was unspeakably lovely: no more than three years old in physical appearance, curled in a fetal position; flawless, and having an expression of total bliss on its features. She stopped after a step, fearful of disturbing that perfection.

"His name is Guillaume," said Jonathan quietly. "And long years ago, he was my dearest friend and companion. Together Master took us. We're the first vampires who came to this city. Together, the three of us, we ventured the long and perilous voyage over the ocean, where we were helplessly imprisoned. In coffins, just as the myths tell of us.

"But when we came to America, Master cast us aside. The wide land tempted him to exploration and conquest, and he thought us no more than useless baggage. There was a very harsh period which lasted for a long time. That was the experience which broke me, consumed my imagination, and made me what I am now.

"Guillaume, however, was such a gentle soul. He could not imagine that Master could have treated us with such cruel indifference. And so, rejecting that reality, he withdrew from the world. This was his escape.

"And thus has he been, ever since, for more than a hundred and fifty years. At first, he had the aspect of adulthood, but he has very slowly regressed in the appearance of his age. I wonder what will happen when he moves back before the point of his conception.

"But see! Even though he is still and withdrawn, he continues his existence, and thirsts with the lust of the undead. And see how it is that I give him satisfaction." Jonathan strode up to the floating still form, and he bared his arm. Gently, he offered it to the child, who didn't appear to notice for a moment. But then slowly, languidly, the small mouth opened exceedingly wide, showing just two long narrow teeth like a viper's fangs, and he bit down hard.

Elizabeth saw Jonathan wince at the bite, but after that, he showed no sign of discomfort. Instead, there spread over his face and form an expression of relaxation, of bliss even, like the reflection of the trance-state of Guillaume. They swayed together, merged into a single perfected being. Here, Elizabeth sensed, here was the reality which was hinted at in the fantasies of the others: the totality of Stephen's collection; the liberty of Una's revolution; the pleasure of Gregory's bloody pool; the forgiveness which Deborah could never attain; and most especially the mystic unity and vision of Diana's desert. She struggled with the impulse to shed tears of joy.

After a few moments that stretched out to eternity, it was finished, and Jonathan pulled back his arm. He was pale and shaky, but fulfilled. Guillaume continued to levitate in blissful contemplation as if nothing had happened. When Jonathan spoke, there was a nearly religious tone of awe in his voice: "Now you know everything. You see that I am not wholly egoistic. Every night, I come and share all with him. I give him my hard-won blood, and also I give him all I have experienced. And thus, since I partake of the experience of all the vampires who live here, I additionally give him everything which all the vampires experience. In return, I wish for nothing, except only for the joy of this selfless gift.

"And this is what is offered to you, Elizabeth. I beg you, join us. Eternity beckons to you. Seek out your role in my building. Create yourself a paradise, or plunge into your own inferno. Sanctity and sin, ecstacy and despair, infinite possibility lies before your feet. What better purpose could anyone ask for in this existence? Stay, and help me feed Guillaume, this child of perfection, silent and selfless and uncaring."

And like nothing else in all the days of her life and the nights of her undeath, Elizabeth desired to answer in the affirmative. She stepped forward and stroked Guillaume's silvery head. It was cool and faintly metallic-feeling. How similar to the harsh Moon in its shape and color! But how kindly and satisfying it would be to serve this head rather than the bloated satellite and its unappeasable hunger!

And in a sudden rush, she knew that it could not be. What Jonathan offered was yet another trap. Soft and appetizing, where the Master's had been cruel and uncompromising. But she could not surrender. She knew that she could take on no role which was not of her own will, her own doing.

With tears of blood flowing down her cheeks, she turned and fled.

LOVING THE UNDEAD

1.

Elizabeth was homeless. She had rejected the rule of the Master, and she had rejected Jonathan's communal building of the undead. By the requirements of her nature she was of course denied the public amenities which were provided for vagrant humans. And so, while she was joyful at the prospect of at last finding her true freedom, she was at a loss regarding how she was to survive so as to enjoy this liberty.

The first priority, she thought, was to locate some dwelling which would provide a degree of safety during the day, both from the deadly light of the Sun, and from the no-less deadly investigations of curious mortals. Yet she needed to remain within easy access of those same mortals in order to obtain sustenance from them. A dilemma. One more time she looked backwards at the vampires' condominium. Nothing at all to distinguish it from any of the other identical buildings amidst which it nestled. She felt a pang of homesickness already, but her mind was made up. She turned her back on it once more and for good, as she thought, and strode purposefully away.

Another cold night. Few wayfarers, which well suited Elizabeth's frame of mind. Mounds of hardened snow lay to either side of the sidewalk. Icy patches contained phantasmagorical twisted reflections of the world around them. In each reflection, she feared to see one of the other vampires stalking up behind her, about to wreak some unspeakable vengeance upon her for her betrayal. Or even worse, she dreaded seeing the shape of the Master. She dared not even think of what punishment he might have in store for her, if he came upon her while she was unprotected. Thankfully, the Moon was new, and caused only a slight gnawing of pain in her gut. One less problem to have to deal with.

She found her feet taking her to the cemetery. Back to the beginning. The grass had covered her empty grave now lay yellowed, grey in the darkness. She felt little emotion as she stared down at the stone. *"Elizabeth,"* she whispered, reading the name off the stone. Only a label, along with two dates. All that would identify her to the mortal world, through the passing of the decades, until the stone itself wore away to nothingness. Then, total anonymity.

The old rage boiled up inside her, the anger she had felt when the Master had first yanked her out of the warm comfortable coffin. Months had passed, and she had accomplished nothing.

Now it was time to return. Raising her arms, she commanded the wind to rise and the turf to roll back like a blanket. Down, down, she delved, and finally she exposed the casket. It looked smaller than she remembered. Nonetheless, she caused it to open, clambered down into it, and pulled it shut upon herself.

Dark. Quiet. Warm. The pain was died down to an ebb. It was good.

But sleep would not come.

It wasn't dark enough. She could still see, not with her eyes, but with her radar-like sense of position. She was innately aware of her surroundings at every moment: her depth underground (which she could calculate to the millimeter if she desired), the weather conditions above, the pattern of buildings in the vicinity. She was even aware of the astronomical positions of the Sun and Moon and brighter stars, in their locations relative to her resting place. In her mind's eye she could visualize all these things, and was unable to prevent herself from doing so.

It wasn't quiet enough. Her preternaturally sensitive hearing could detect the minute shuffling of insects and rodents burrowing for many meters around her. The wind softly whispering in the grass was loud as a shout to her. She could even detect very faintly the groaning stresses of the geological faults far below. She couldn't shut the racket out.

It wasn't warm enough. Now that the container was closed in around her, she was feeling a clamminess, seeping in from the chill of the ground. With each passing moment it increased. Claustrophobia was setting in. She needed to get to warmth. And only one warmth would do: the warmth of blood, flowing out of the humans, and into her.

With a cry she rent the coffin asunder, and thrust the dirt upward with a heave. Back up she climbed. Dirt on her face, in her hair, down her throat. She coughed and wheezed. And she lay down on the cold ground in misery.

Elizabeth thought of the dead. Hundreds, still and decaying, on every side. Maybe, she thought, maybe they're all conscious, down in their graves. Maybe they lay in the silence and were content, allowing the slow process of degeneration to dissolve them into nothingness. She and she only was denied. She stood up. She and she only must walk in the mortal city. She did so. She and only she must seek sustenance. And she did so.

2.

Elizabeth slowly adapted herself to solitude. She found an empty shell of a building in the decayed industrial heart of the city. Once it had echoed with the bustling of the mortals in the pursuit of economic well-being; now it was silent. There was something in the high ceilings draped with catwalks and mechanical belts, the heaps of slowly rusting machinery, the ghostlike quietude of the still loading docks, which appealed to her. The vanity of the builders, maybe, in thinking their proud construction would defy the ruination of time. Like her, they found their beliefs and plans outwitted by history. Like her, there was nothing left but the shell.

She recalled that both Jonathan and the Master before him had made mention of wild vampires roaming in the city and elsewhere, who had devolved so far as to lose their conscious identity, becoming no more than savage animals. Recalling her experience with Charles, she felt there was a good likelihood that these stories at least were true, and she felt considerable anxiety lest she succumb to such a fate. To prevent this, she got in the habit of spending time in the early evening at the main branch of the library. She was capable of absorbing all the contents of the books there within moments if she desired it; instead, she disguised herself as a mortal student, and read at a mortal pace. Any subject. Religion and the afterlife was especially appealing, from a professional standpoint. *Ecclesiastes* and *Job* were particular favorites.

She chose many of her victims from among the other library patrons, just for lack of the will to go to any further effort many nights. For others she chose those hapless vagrants and wanderers who happened to venture into her chosen building. These were few. She cast as much of a glamour of dread and avoidance on the premises as she was able to do single-handedly. Thus, the only persons who entered it were either those humans who were uncommonly strong of will, or those who were so immersed in their despair of life they just didn't care. Each variety made for a very satisfying repast.

Not every night, but regularly, Elizabeth found her inerrant feet taking her back, back to that empty grave. She didn't know what she was expecting to find there. She would approach it, and stand in front of the stone for just a few minutes, and then be off again. It came to be interesting to her to notice the subtle changes of light and shadow which played over the uneven ground as the Moon waxed and then waned again. Then, on other nights, after there had been snow, it was a mild diversion to hunt for the correct grave, among the hundred identical stones hidden under the drifts. At times she worried that she was sickly fixating on this place. At other times she comforted herself that here was a single point of continuity in her continuing undeath, never constant but fundamentally changeless.

3.

One night, Elizabeth awakened with a feeling of unease which she couldn't identify. It nagged at her, causing a discomfort not unlike the pain of the hunger, although much less, of course, in degree. Troublesome. Thoughtfully, she climbed out of the storage tank she had adapted as her bedroom, carefully dissolving all her personal effects afterward.

She looked out a broken window. Another vile night of the endless winter. Cold rain, occasional sleet. She turned away with a frown, only to experience a tugging sensation resisting that motion. The strange uneasy feeling was urging her in the direction of the window and against any other direction.

Intrigued, she gave in to the urging, for the moment. Taking a vaporous form, she allowed herself to be pulled by the feeling as if towards a magnet. She rose over the city, and slowly floated away from the industrial park, towards the residential areas. As she drew closer to the source of the pulling, the sensation strengthened, causing her to accelerate. But when Elizabeth finally saw the source, she pulled up and resisted. The source was the vampires' condominium.

It had been nothing but a lie, she cried out in her mind (having no existent mouth parts at the moment). They told her that she was free to live as she wanted, free from any interference, but she saw how easily they could bring her back. A fish on a reel. She fought the pull now with all the power she had, but the will of the others was united against her. She could not resist for long. Finally, she gave up the effort, figuring that it might be intelligent to conserve what energy she had left for the upcoming struggle.

She congealed in front of the door, and strode authoritatively up to it, projecting a confidence she lacked. But when she entered, she once more halted in her tracks. There in the lobby were gathered every member of the vampire community. The sociable ones like Jonathan, Deborah, Claire and Charles didn't surprise her much, but in addition there were also present the figures of Stephen, the withdrawn and passive collector, Diana the ascetic hermit and even miserly Gregory, who never made any secret of his contempt for the others. All there standing in silent solemnity (excepting only Guillaume of course, Jonathan's secret and hidden companion, who could not be strictly considered part of the group). After a pause, Elizabeth summoned her fortitude and took her place in the midst of them.

"So she's here at last," noted Alicia to Jonathan in a distinctly caustic tone.

Gregory added, "She's so late that we're going to have to rush now."

But Jonathan replied soothingly, "Now don't you forget that Elizabeth had to travel a long distance to get here, my friends, and there's no doubt that she has to feel a certain degree of suspicion regarding our motives." He cleared his throat, and came up to take her hands. "Welcome back, my dear, even if only for a few hours. I'm sure that I speak for all of those present when I say how delightful it is to have your lovely form grace our gathering once again." Elizabeth noted that only Charles, Phil and Stephen appeared to agree with this statement with any amount of enthusiasm.

"Except for Elizabeth, all of you know the rarity of such occasions as this, for all our community to be gathered. Privacy is the one creed we all support. There is only one cause for which we will sacrifice that belief, and draw together, to act in accord.

"And thus it is with great excitement and trepidation, that I report to you that Master has once more increased the number of the undead. He has brought into being a new vampire, and the time is now arrived for us to bring him liberation."

Jonathan's speech was interrupted by a flurry of comment.

"What? So soon?" asked Gregory in a shocked tone.

Deborah ruminated thoughtfully, "I don't recall the Master reviving more than one mortal within a single year since at least the period of the Napoleonic wars."

Una's tone was aggressive, "I'm very *suspicious*. Does this mean that for some reason he has a sudden need for more vampires? Or that his long-range plans are entering a new and more *uncertain* phase?"

Philip was laughing. "You said the word 'he', didn't you? That's music to my ears. I'm glad to see the Master's finally working to restore the dangerous imbalance of the sexes here in this group."

Claire sneered and was about to reply to that, when Jonathan raised his hand for silence. "Ahem!" he said loudly. "While it is grievous to me to interfere in any way with the free discussion of our ideas and notions regarding Master's deeds and motives, I must urge restraint for the moment. Although this is certainly a most unusual happening, it might be more desirable to save the talk for a later period. As Gregory would undoubtedly remind us, time is short, and there is a lot which must be done tonight." And with that, they quickly dispersed.

Elizabeth was left standing in the lobby, feeling little better informed than she was before. "No, I haven't forgotten you," Jonathan said in friendly voice. "I can't help but blame myself for the abruptness of your departure a few weeks ago. Perhaps I allowed my eagerness to have you join us to cause me to overly pressure you at a sensitive moment. Please accept my most sincere apologies." He bowed.

"All right, I suppose... But what do you want with me now?"

"Well, simply put, I hope you could help us. You know at first hand the terrible strength of Master's mind. He warps the very flow of the reality of the world around himself. All ten of us acting in concert can barely suffice to pin him down even for a little while. Another will to add to ours would be most welcome. Besides, I remember the night when we liberated you. Your rage was such that you actually crushed his bodily form to powder. I suspect that you have the ability to become the strongest of any of us, when you learn how to fully exert yourself. But that's something to think about another time. Will you listen to my entreaty, and add your power to ours, for just a short time, in the name of a purpose which you know to be good?"

She smiled at the glib and pleasant flow of his words, and realized that she had missed that swirling current since she had left. "Well, I guess it won't hurt. But I don't know what to do."

"Stupendous! Don't worry, it's not difficult or overly dangerous. Just consciously push your will to act together with the rest of us, when you feel the time to be right. But come along now, we have to rejoin the others before they start without us."

Jonathan led her forth, back into the night, and they took flight to rejoin their companions. Collectively they flowed over the city, like a storm-cloud or a flock of carrion birds, spreading their senses out across the sky like a net across the waves. They quickly located their catch.

On a frigid and ugly night, few attractions were sufficient to draw the mortals out of their secure homes. The most enticing of these attractions were sports events. Twenty thousand otherwise perfectly normal humans ventured out into the sleet to pack themselves into the coliseum, willfully pouring their energies into the handful of performers below. Hearts accelerating with each turn of the action, emotions on a trigger, rollercoastering from elation to despair in an instant. They formed a single organism, team below and spectators above. The vampires, needing a great pool of energy for the conflict to come, were drawn like a lightning bolt to a rod.

The news reports later that evening would be aghast at the accounts of the horrendous accident, the spontaneous collapse of supports over the roof of the arena. Probably due to vibrations caused by the cheering crowd, accentuating the stress caused by the weight of tons of ice and snow. Dozens killed, hundreds injured. The humans would be shocked and mournful, but reassured by the scientific analysis of the disaster. No reason to even dream of supernatural causes.

4.

Elizabeth rose from the carnage along with the others. Filled, elated, satisfied.

Following Jonathan's quickly-communicated instructions, at the moment of the attack Elizabeth focused her will simultaneously with the others, concentrating her energy to a central point in the center of the group. This focus was the source from which they could draw strength, to accomplish that which needed to be done. As she increased her concentration, she began to experience a pleasurable feedback, masking her hunger, and encouraging a further increasing of her willpower. The cycle spiralled upward in intensity, until her consciousness was overwhelmed. She ceased to be a separate being. And the same experience was happening to the others at the same time, so that they merged together into a new being, a super-vampire, containing all the might and the volition of each of the individuals, magnified. A being fit to attack and consume the vast thrashing being formed by the mortals in the coliseum below. With barely an effort, it reached down and peeled open the roof. It absorbed forty lives in four seconds, and swiftly slipped away, undetectable in the maelstrom of human suffering.

And now, with the vampires split back up into their individual bodies, they stood at the chosen site, a small paved park in the inner financial district, with many deep shadowy recesses where they could hide, and they began to weave the delicate strands of glamour and illusion, to trap the Master and his new slave. It was a similar operation to their previous merging: again Elizabeth turned over her personal energy to the group. This phase was different from the prior integration in that each vampire retained a degree of independent consciousness and will, so as to utilize his or her particular abilities to best effect. It was Deborah, for instance, who provided the talent to hide the vampires from any possible detection. Gregory, who stored vast amounts of blood for his personal use, contained the excess blood which they had obtained at the arena, and he poured it out now into the decoy body they had manufactured, to make it an irresistible lure. Alicia, taking her microscopic form, entered into the brain of the decoy and gave it the simulation of living thought and motion. Yet no matter what care was taken by the vampires in their spell-casting, there was a trace of undeath which clung to all they did, like an odor of decay; it was Diana (who alone had, through a supreme effort, not taken in any of the blood which the group had collectively consumed), who now used her power to eliminate all detectable taint of death and make the trap perfect.

Elizabeth, along with the others whose talents were not specifically required for the trap, used her strength to provide amplification, and a damping effect which would hide their presence and lull their victims. This required little conscious effort, and so she found herself with time to think and observe, as they waited.

She realized that she was feeling more than a little hurt. Remembering how long since she had left the Master, she could calculate that he must have spent almost no time at all after her leaving before he had gone out and resurrected this new vampire. A couple of days at most. She recalled his harsh treatment of her and brass assurances that she had meant nothing to him, but it was still a blow to her pride to see how unimportant she must have really been. No period of anger, no time of mourning. He just picked himself up, went out and raised himself up a new servant. She determined that, no matter who he had been and what he was like, she wasn't going to go out of her way to welcome this newcomer, this interloper.

This line of thought spread out to encompass consideration of her own relationship with the other vampires. Was she as unimportant to them as she evidently had been to the Master? Was she perhaps no more than an interloper among their community, a brief ripple in their eternal calm pool of existence? Did Jonathan's smile hide an inner sneer of disdain? She argued with herself about this notion. It seemed unlikely that they would have gone to such lengths, exposing themselves to real danger, to liberate her (and this new vampire as well) from the Master, if they had felt any degree of resentment... If anything, they seemed to be looking upon the whole event as a big party, an entertainment granting a respite from their normal repetitive rounds. The more often the Master resurrected a new victim, the merrier was the time to be had. She was immature to allow such unworthy thoughts to pollute the nobility and excellence of their motives.

Next, Elizabeth's thoughts took flight to light upon the vampires' merger of mind and being. It had been a very seductive experience. While their number had been added arithmetically, their power and pleasure had seemed to increase geometrically or even logarithmically. The pain had completely vanished during the amalgamation, snuffed out in the delicious enormity of their strength, of their glorious ability to destroy and consume. There had been more than a passing temptation to forego the separation after they were finished. To remain a vast, omnipotent being, stretched out against the night sky, a thing of unending doom and terror to the humans... Elizabeth began to feel a little afraid. What if the Master, with his titanic will and lust for dominion, could somehow take over the merging and compel them to form this higher being for his own dark purposes...?

Further speculations were interrupted. They were coming at last. She thrilled as she detected the familiar aura of the Master's being, distant but unmistakable. Less strong but still noticeable was that of the stranger. Like that of all of the undead, but intriguing in its unique quality... There was a nagging familiarity to it, which Elizabeth felt she should be able to identify, but she couldn't. She didn't bother to give it much thought, as she drank in the sweet knowledge that she could feel them, but they couldn't feel her.

Elizabeth was so lost in the observation that she didn't even notice the actual springing of the trap. There was a scream of shock, the sudden warning shout of the Master, that brought her out of her reverie. Yet there was a distance, a layer of seeming unreality, which continued to grip her, as she stepped away from her hiding place, creating shimmering clothes of festive colors. Just like the others. Just like her memory of when she was liberated. How very like her recollections were the words she heard exchanged:

"Keep away! The Master warned me about you animals!" cried the new one, whom Elizabeth still couldn't see clearly, as he lay pinned on the ground under their spell.

"Oh, did he now?" replied Jonathan in his most amused-sounding voice. "And what, pray tell, could dear Master have said that would cause such a distressed reaction, my young friend?"

"That you'll fall on us like a pack of wolves and tear us apart in both body and spirit, to satisfy your foul cannibal thirst!"

Jonathan gave forth a loud and short laugh like a snort. "Well, I'll have to admit that it's a tempting idea. But maybe not tonight. Is there any proof we could give, any grave and terrible oath we could swear, that might indicate to you that our intentions are most eminently honorable?"

The other vampire had a confused tone in his voice. "You're talking and reasoning like an intelligent person, and not like a ravening brute. But..." He paused in perplexity.

"But we all know that the clever hunter is the one who camouflages himself until the prey is won, no?" Jonathan ventured. "Being able to mimic logical reasoning is not proof that intelligence is really present here. We seem to have caught ourselves in a dilemma. There seems to be no way you can be assured that I and my companions are the friendly and reasonable beings we appear to be. Can you think of any way to solve our difficulty?" he asked rhetorically. When the imprisoned vampire remained silent, he continued: "Well, allow me to suggest an idea. If we are savage and unreasonable creatures, we would certainly keep you pinned down and helpless until we are ready for the feast. If we were to allow you the freedom to arise, it would indicate that we are capable of the feeling of trust, trust that you will stay calm and remain and listen to our explanations and our offer without attempting anything violent. And the capacity to trust is one criterion which would demonstrate that we are intelligent. Don't you agree?" The other assented, and Jonathan, with a wave of the hand, released him. He stood.

And Elizabeth reeled back, suppressing a cry.

Flashes of memory.

With the Master.

The night of horror in the hospital.

The taut and wasted body laid flat on the hard hospital bed. The weakening pulse failing under the relentless battery of disease. And her sharp teeth, granting remission. Absolution. Extinction.

And now the same body stood before the gathered vampires as if alive. Whole. Healed.

Waves of betrayal swept over her. He was hers. Hers alone to hold within herself, to cherish for eternity. The Master had taken him away from her. Thief, skulking in the night. There was a hollow empty hole now where he was supposed to be, and it would never be filled again.

In her anger and self-absorption, Elizabeth didn't see what transpired between Jonathan and the Master and this new vampire.

Suddenly it was over. They were leaving, leaving the Master trapped behind and taking to the air. Elizabeth was torn between two conflicting urges: to stay behind and confront the Master, to hurt him, to punish him while he was helpless and the compulsion to trail after the others, to listen, to learn. To get him back again. To consume him again.

She floated on the periphery of the group, which was surrounding their new recruit as if to protect him from harm. Feeling very much the voyeur, she eavesdropped, hearing Jonathan asking: "Is there any particular name you wish to have among us?"

Oddly, the stranger hesitated for several moments, before he answered. "You can call me Daniel. I think."

No. That wasn't right. Elizabeth screamed at him from inside her brain, but made no sound. She knew his name. And it was not *Daniel*.

"You paused before you answered me," Jonathan noted. "Does that name feel uncomfortable to you now? Are you wholly satisfied with the name Daniel?"

"It's what the Master called me."

And it's a lie, she thought.

"Ah, but that's not what I was asking you, my friend. There are many of us who have memories of Master which we would rather not call up, if we can help it. We are very relaxed about names and identities. Feel free to take any name you might desire, at any time."

"I don't know. This is all too unreal. Maybe I should just stay Daniel for now. It gives me some feeling of security, somehow."

"Daniel it shall be, then, until you decide otherwise."

But Daniel was an aberration, a falsehood. Elizabeth was tied in a knot. If she didn't speak out now, she would be sacrificing any right she would have to speak in the future. But she couldn't. That tiny piece of him which she still contained would be consumed, if she admitted her prior knowledge of this not-Daniel.

And now the vampires were gathering together, about to speak the hallowed words of the ritual of welcoming. Twice Elizabeth had heard it invoked before, once in jest and once in solemnity, but now, as she mouthed it along with the vampire chorus, the words were an empty mockery, a prayer to a non-existent deity, a rite which, rather than welcoming her, excluded her from joy and fellowship forever:

"We welcome you, once child of mortal flesh, now heir of the unending mastery, to the brethren of the night-tide, the keepers of the blood-quenched thirst. Spurn the agony of the day and abide with us, until the dark has conquered and ceases not."

5.

Elizabeth was alone and desolate.

She had drifted quietly away after the speaking of the ritual words, and no one had noticed her absence. Except possibly Jonathan, who perceived all matters relating to the undead, but even he gave no indication. He was wrapped up in his new acquisition. The new toy. The new tool.

She felt that a wall was now erected between her and the others. She could have gone back, up to now. Jonathan would have welcomed her. Diana or Stephen or Charles would have welcomed her. All it would have taken was a little sacrifice of her self-esteem. But now, with their act of accepting that new one, she was cut off. He was her replacement.

Despite all the events which had happened this night, it was still before midnight. Elizabeth walked the street paying little mind to where her footsteps were taking her. Her thoughts continued to churn.

Maybe everything was a lie. Maybe the not-Daniel was a sham. A false being conjured by the Master as a snare for the vampires. A homunculus which would lead him to them, in order to take a terrible retribution. In that case, it was her duty to go back and warn them.

Or maybe he was a lure especially for her. Made by the Master. Or by Jonathan. Don't forget that it was Jonathan who had summoned her, Jonathan who was the only source of the information which had led them. Or maybe he had been made by one of the other vampires out of spite. Or by the humans. The mortals had learned of the existence at last, and had manufactured a deadly automaton which would explode at an unguarded moment and destroy them all... Or just destroy her. It would tempt her, taunt her, force her into the daylight and destroy her.

Her unconscious walking had brought her back once more to the graveyard. She smiled grimly. Her last sanctuary. She stood at the gate. It was open. She experienced a dull shock. Too overwhelmed by previous events to react with the level of surprise which this shock deserved.

Some one was in the cemetery. The false Daniel, come to envelop her in his glamour of doom? The Master, come to claim her once more for his own? That thought made her gasp, recalling that he certainly must know where her grave lay, where she had been coming so often of late... He had restored her consciousness when he brought her back to animation. Maybe he had planted this urge to return here into the depth of her soul, so that she'd always come back to this place where he could reclaim her with ease... Everything she had thought she had freely chosen for months had been preordained by his will. A puppet.

No. No. No. She hit her hand hard on the rock wall, willing herself to feel the pain. Stay rational. Stay in control. Think. Her only recourse now. A vampire wouldn't bother to open the gate like this. He or she would simply fly over the wall, or at most pass through it in vaporous form. The way she did when she came here.

So, it was not a vampire. A human, or a group of humans. Children playing pranks. Violating her domain. Elizabeth snarled. She'd give them a game, all right. A lesson they wouldn't forget.

She passed through the gate, sending out feelers to sense the location of the intruder. It was just one. No matter. She sliced through the air.

And once more she froze.

Not a child. An older figure, female, shivering in the deepening cold despite her heavy bundled coat. Standing, head bowed down. Flowers in her hand, about to lay them down on the grave, Elizabeth's own grave.

Mother.

6.

Elizabeth stood wrapped in such silence and invisibility as only the undead could command. It was only an instant before her mother stood up, and, with barely any indication of surprise, turned to face her. Elizabeth saw how the muscles of her throat constricted as if about to utter a shriek; the sweet hot blood she could feel in the mortal woman's body draining from her face, as if she might faint. Instead, with such suddenness that it almost surprised even her vampire sensibilities, her mother fled, legs pumping, lungs gasping in desperation for air. Up to that moment, Elizabeth had felt little or no desire for the life of the old woman, but, catlike, the very sight of the human in flight before her plunged her into the hunting mode, and she felt herself compelled to pursue, with the hungry pain on the rise in her essence. It was of course only a matter of moments for her to swoop around her mother, trapping her between three gravestones which made a small alcove. For another moment the hunger came close to overpowering her. Then, suddenly, she looked down into the old woman's eyes, and recognized in them the eyes that had gazed lovingly down at hers through the years of her childhood... And the desire passed. Still her mother had not made a sound.

Then and only then it was that the woman shook a little, awash in the depth of torrid emotions which could not be named. Elizabeth wanted to flee, wanted to call up the ground of the cemetery to form a mountainous wall to separate them. But instead she took the tiniest of steps forward, and whispered, "Mother."

The woman slowly exhaled her pent-up breath, forming a mist around her lips, and replied, "Yes. I felt it every night in my dreams. In the morning, I awoke and laughed at myself, insisting that it couldn't be so. But then, the next night, back came the feeling again. At last, I couldn't hold it in any more, I had to get up out of bed, and come here. I had to come and look at your grave, I said to myself. It would prove to me beyond the shadow of a doubt that you were laid here. Now, now I can see that it was my dream that spoke the truth. The truth that you were alive."

She made a motion of beginning to step forward to embrace Elizabeth, but she held up her hand to stop her. "No. Not alive. Don't call me alive, Mother. And don't, I beg you by everything that's holy, don't touch me."

With a hurt look on her face, her mother stopped. "But can't I even get a close look at you?" Finally she relented. "All right. Look, there's a bench right over there. Can't you come over and sit with me there, for just a little while?"

The woman walked to it and sat down. Elizabeth hesitated. She was remembering the terrible story told by Deborah, who had met with her only child in a similar circumstance, and had consumed her. Elizabeth wondered why she wasn't feeling the same urge. There was a murmur of the hunger inside her, generated by the sound of a mortal heart beating, the blood softly flowing through the veins. But not the overwhelming gnawing she was expecting. She was actually feeling a touch disappointed by that.

She sat down on the opposite side of the bench. There was a lengthy period of silence. Finally her mother broke it. "You're looking very well. Your hair. Your skin."

"Maybe I should've died a long time ago. It seems to have brought out the best in me."

"Hmpf. Don't say that. So how are things going for you? You should have called when you came back from the dead. Are you eating well? Do you have a nice place to stay?"

"Well, if I'm a corpse, do I need anyplace other than a hole in the ground?"

"Now here I am trying to be as polite and civil as possible under the circumstances, and there's no need for you to speak in that tone of voice."

"Okay, I'm sorry. It just seems so silly to be making all this small talk. Yes, I have a place to stay. It's alone and quiet. I was staying with, with some others who are like me. But we had a falling out, and I left a couple of weeks back. So I'm on my own now. It's better this way. Don't worry about me."

Another pause. "You're happy, then? That's what's the most important thing."

"As happy as I guess I can expect to be."

"Any men in your life?"

"No!" she frowned. "Yes. I don't know. And don't call it 'my life', because it's not life. Everything's different on this side of the grave. But everything's still the same. It's still confusing. It's still difficult. And men are always the same. They dangle what you want in front of you, and then when you grab the bait they pile on the obligations. All they want is to change you into what they want you to be."

For the first time Elizabeth looked up and into her mother's eyes. "There was someone. Someone who I had and held close. But just tonight, he turned into something completely different. It was just another trick. Just another lie."

"I remember hearing those same words from you time and again when you were alive. And the way you say them again is finally proving to me that it's really you, really the Elizabeth I bore and raised." And she smiled.

"And you always took me into your arms and held me close. You spoke all those soothing words, but you never tried to deny what I said."

"But now you won't let me comfort you. Can't a ghost come into her mother's arms the way she did when she was a little girl?"

Elizabeth almost went ahead and did it, but she steeled herself again. "I'm not a ghost." She looked down, and for the very first time she felt a little shame at her existence. "I'm a vampire, mother."

Her mother kept looking at her without a change in her expression, still brimming over with that motherly adoration. Elizabeth couldn't stand it. She had to shake her out of that blandness, that complacency. "Didn't you hear me? I lay in a trance all day. I rise out of a tomb when the Sun goes down, and I go and drink the blood of living humans. Doesn't that bother you? Doesn't that move you in any way?"

"A mother has to learn to accept a lot of things about her children. Things which would tear her apart if she allowed herself to think too much about them."

"But don't you think this might be a little bit more extreme?"

"It's only a matter of degree." She paused. "*My daughter, the vampire*. It sounds like a movie they would've made back when I was a little girl." Another pause. Then, with less levity, "So, have you killed people?"

"Yes."

"How many?"

Pause. "I don't know."

"That many. I see. You know that I don't approve, but it isn't for me to keep you from the lifestyle you want."

"You think this is something I chose? That I want to be like this? Jesus Christ, Mother."

"No need to get profane, Elizabeth."

"Why not? What's it matter to me? My soul is pretty well damned for eternity as it is! That's what the priest would say, isn't it?"

Another pause, a long one. Elizabeth started wondering if she should just get up and get on her way. Finally, her mother spoke again. "I'm sorry, Elizabeth, for a lot of things. We had lots of chances to talk when you were alive. I know I did a lot of things that made it difficult or impossible, back then. And now, I'm getting the feeling I'm doing the same thing, now that you're not alive. It's my fault."

"Oh, Mother, that's not true. God knows that I was doing just as much to keep us apart. And I'm still doing that, too."

"There's just this pattern, the one we always seem to fall into. I'm trying my damnedest to avoid it. And I thought that we could do it, with things as different as they are now. But I'm human. I can't change."

"I'm not, but I still keep falling into that pattern, too. It's bigger than the two of us."

With a visible effort, her mother got up. "So is this the end? Shall I just go away and leave you to whatever it is that you're doing with yourself?"

"No." And Elizabeth stood up too, and faced her. She was tall, taller now than she had been in life: an unconscious alteration which she'd caused in her body in the course of her new existence? She had to look down to meet the older woman's eyes. "I've made a decision," she said. "I've been running around for months, looking for friendship, looking for direction. All I've gotten are kicks to the head. So I'm going back. I'd like to stay in contact with you. Close contact."

"Well, maybe you can come home and visit."

"All right, maybe I will. Tomorrow night, about an hour after sunset?"

"Good. I'll be waiting. You know the way."

7.

Elizabeth awoke with a pleasant feeling of excitement and anticipation which she hadn't felt for a long time. It was a very good sensation, and she stretched out her body luxuriously for a minute. This was a mistake, however, because the motion kindled the pain. She sighed and got herself up.

And then she remembered the new vampire, and her spirits sank down to the bottom again. She pictured him going through the same experiences she had gone through when she joined the vampire community. She grimaced to think of him having to meet the mental cases like Gregory and Charles. She was surprised to notice a definite stab of jealousy when she saw an image of him learning the ways of Diana and Stephen, and especially Alicia. And when she thought of him undergoing the ministrations of Deborah, she began to feel a strange fear.

What did she care, she told herself. He's nothing to her. Less than nothing. A stranger. Deborah could take him and stick him in the heat of the Sun until he shriveled up like a raisin.

And now, getting back to business. She had to go find herself some blood early. She couldn't picture herself lusting for her mother's life, but it was best to satiate the urge, and lessen the temptation. She didn't like it, the idea of having to go hunt as a chore. The hunt was supposed to be a joyful thing, an experience using all of her talents and raising herself to the height of mystic ecstacy. This was a lowering of her self-esteem. It was a fight to keep herself from blaming her mother for this sensation, and using it as an excuse not to show up.

The night was cold but clear. The city was still mostly frozen in from the previous night's ice storm, but there were a number of humans about, mostly work crews performing various emergency repairs. It didn't take too long to find a man from the electric company who had gotten a little separated from his fellows. She took a compact form like an insect, and with a rush and a stab to the back of the neck, she paralyzed him, and drained him quickly. She made it look like an accidental electrocution.

Thus, she was right on time when she arrived at that familiar street. The house was small. Smaller even then she remembered from her last visit last summer, just a few months back... Becoming a vampire must expand one's picture of one's self, she reflected. No longer strictly confined to the compact human form, she found it hard recalling that the mortals were stuck in such tiny bodies.

Her mother must have been looking out for her, as she opened the door just as Elizabeth stepped up to it. She had been careful in her preparations, making herself a heavy overcoat which hid her body until she saw what her mother would be wearing. As she saw the conservative dinner dress which her mother had on she conjured up a complementary outfit for herself under the coat. Flattering the figure but not revealing. Her best color. She was gratified to see the smile of satisfaction in her mother's face as she looked her over.

As she stepped inside, she was hit by a not-altogether pleasant cooking odor. Like every child's mother since the world began, hers had pictured herself a wonderful gourmet cook, better able to satisfy her child's hunger and need for nourishment than anyone else on Earth. For Elizabeth's mother, however, this had not been quite the truth. Her late father took them out to eat more than regularly. It had been a joke at his funeral that he had worked himself to a heart attack just to get away from his wife's dinners... Elizabeth berated herself for the fact that she hadn't realized that an invitation for the early evening would be naturally assumed to be for dinner. This could be a problem, from several different points of view.

"It's nice to see you again," her mother had been saying. "That's a good dress for you to wear. Better than that thing you had on last night. I'm glad to see that you have a chance to do some shopping with the way you are now."

"Well, it's really a little bit different than you're thinking, the way I get my clothes now...."

"Come in, come in, where are my manners. Let me take your coat. Would you like something to drink? Oh, never mind. I suppose we might as well go ahead and serve dinner. I'm afraid I'm really famished tonight, I've been running around so much today, trying to get everything just right. I haven't had anyone over here for months, since the funeral. Oh, I'm not doing very good at keeping the conversation heading in the right direction, am I?" She laughed nervously.

"It's all right, I don't mind. It's something that's very much on my mind all the time, you know. One of the main subjects of conversation around the gang, talking about how we died, and the way things have changed since then."

And now she was in the living room, She remembered Deborah's imitation, which she had made out of a reflection from Elizabeth's mind, and she smiled now to see how pale and false the copy had been. A cheap snapshot. This wasn't exactly as she remembered: a new chair, a slightly different arrangement of the pictures on the wall, but it was so much more. This was the real, this was the truth, this was her childhood and youth and the source of all her memory. She almost had to cry. Her mother said, "You've mentioned others a couple of times now. Do you have many friends? Are they living or people like you? Maybe you could bring some of them over sometime."

"Good God, no! Um, well, I mean, it might not work out very well. There are some odd people I hang around with at times. You probably wouldn't really get along with them. It's sort of hard to explain... And I guess it isn't right to even call them friends, not really. They're more like my business acquaintances. Or like the members of a social club. Or the members of a church. Yes, that's the closest way to describe it, I think. We all have things we happen to believe in common, because we must; there are some people in your church you really wouldn't want to have over to your house."

"I understand. It's perfectly all right. I just thought it might be a way to help break the ice, to bring us a little closer together."

There suddenly appeared two small heads, peering around the corner of the hall. After one moment of hesitation, they came forward, and rubbed themselves against Elizabeth's legs. Purrs arose. And this brought her even closer to her long-resisted tears, as she realized she hadn't given them a single thought in all the long months since she had risen from the grave: Felix and Dana, her two old cats. "They remember me," she said, reaching down for them. "Even after all the changes, I still must smell the same...."

They finally sat down at the table. Her mother, with a proud flourish, presented two thick steaks. "Look," she pointed out, "I tried to cook this one as rare as possible." Dark blood welled out of the meat as she poked a fork into it, mixing with the fatty juices on the plate. Elizabeth felt nauseous, but she smiled and nodded a little. She meant well.

Elizabeth cut a small piece and put it in her mouth. She chewed, and a puzzled look came over her face. "What's wrong? Is it too rare?"

"Oh, nothing, nothing. I guess I'm just not used to this kind of eating anymore." The steak was flavorless. Except for the cooked blood, which gave out a burnt, bitter flavor, there was no other discernable taste. Elizabeth added a liberal dose of salt, tried another piece. Nothing. Put on some steak sauce. Still nothing. She tried the vegetables. Nothing, nothing.

It was as if she was eating sand or mud. The food no longer had any nutritional value to her undead body, and therefore her mouth had lost the taste receptors for any flavor other than blood. In a way, she told herself, this might be a blessing in disguise, in that she was now forever free from her mother's unappetizing meals. But that failed to provide more than a momentary comfort.

Another problem, she found, was that naturally the food she was ingesting was not being digested. Each bite slid down her esophagus and flopped into her belly like a rock. A foreign object inside her. A conscious effort was required to dissolve each lump into nothingness as she swallowed it. Not especially difficult, but it was a bother.

They mostly made small talk over the meal, the sort which always occurs between mother and daughter after a long separation. Elizabeth was trying to avoid to say anything consequential about herself and her current existence, and thus she found herself listening to stories about relatives and childhood friends and neighbors she hadn't given a thought about for five years. A sudden thought struck at her, "Mother, you haven't told any of your friends about, well, what I am now, have you?"

"I haven't had a moment's chance to even see anybody I know today. But why shouldn't I? You don't expect me to keep something as wonderful and exciting as this all pent up inside?"

"I just don't know if it'd be right. I mean, you've been very nice and understanding, and I'm very grateful for that, if I haven't let you know by now, but I wonder if other people might be a little less tolerant, maybe."

"Do you think you're something I shouldn't talk about? Something I ought to be ashamed of? Like a drug user or a criminal or some kind of deviate?"

"Now, I'm not saying that. Don't twist my words around like that. Like you used to."

"I'm not. That's exactly what you're saying. You're telling me that I ought to be too embarrassed to tell anyone that you're a vampire. And I think I'm hurt that you think I'd do something like that. They'd just nod and smile at me and say nice things, and then they'd go out and call a loony-wagon on me. And I'm starting to wonder maybe I should be the one calling a loony-wagon to come get you!"

"What? You don't believe me?" Elizabeth shot up. "You old bag of rotten blood! If you weren't so withered and worn out, I could really show you a few things, and then you'd know better!" She glared down at the old woman, still in the chair below her. With each word, she was appearing to shrink up, as if she was about to wither away just as Elizabeth was describing her. Elizabeth whirled away to keep herself from doing something she'd regret. "Oh, dear God, what am I saying! It's happening, isn't it? Just like Jonathan and the Master and all the others said. I'm losing my grip on myself! I'm going to become one of the wild mindless ones!" She knelt down on the floor and curled up into a ball.

After a minute wrapped up in herself, Elizabeth felt a quick, hot touch. Scorching. She jumped, and her mother backed away. "I'm sorry," she said. "I'm sorry that I touched you. I'm sorry about the dinner. I'm sorry about everything I've done, whatever it is, that's making you unhappy."

"And I'm sorry, momma. I'm sorry that I snapped at you like that. It was just something I couldn't hold back."

"You're so cold, Elizabeth. Colder than anybody I've ever touched before. That's because of the way you are?"

"Yes. Yes. And you're so hot that you almost burned me." And she went over to the couch, and gestured for her mother to join her.

At last Elizabeth told her mother everything. All about her resurrection, all about the Master, all about Jonathan and Deborah and Diana and the one who wasn't Daniel. As she spoke she cried little red tears, which, along with her cold flesh, were what finally convinced her mother of the truth her daughter told. But no, Elizabeth still couldn't speak all the details of all her kills, all the destruction of which she was the source. She figured that her mother would be able to piece together anything which wasn't spoken out loud.

"So you see," Elizabeth concluded, "what I was worrying about when I asked if you told anyone, was the thing the Master told me, that it's the fact that humans don't really believe in the vampires that gives us our strength over them. If they really knew the truth, we would become helpless before them. And if you talked to your friends, even if they thought you were crazy, it'd put a little seed in their minds, and in the collective mind of all the humans in the city. And that'd start the vampires down the road to our destruction."

"And what you were saying when you were breaking down? You were afraid you were reverting to a savage state, the way your Master warned you?"

"Yes, yes, and that's the thing which is becoming more terrifying to me with every moment. He said that every vampire who broke away and tried to exist independently, sooner or later, always went wild. Jonathan seemed to be confirming that. There are some things, recent things which I haven't been telling you about, which make me afraid that it's beginning to happen to me."

"Well," her mother replied, assuming that demeanor which Elizabeth recalled she usually reserved for solicitors and repairmen, "you said that this Master fellow, who certainly sounds like an interesting person to meet, and I'd bet that he couldn't railroad me the way he seems to do everyone else, anyway he said that no one could survive and not go insane without him. This Jonathan man, who's another one I'd like to get a look at someday, says that everyone who stays with your Master cracks up, and the only way to survive is to stay in his stable. Well, I think that they're both blowing a lot of hot air. Each of them was just saying whatever he thought he had to in order to keep you in line. Jonathan and his group disprove what your Master claimed, and I'd warrant that if they'd have left this new guy alone long enough, you might see him disprove Jonathan's story, too."

Her reassuring words went a long way towards calming Elizabeth down. Still, she was uncertain. "It's all such a risk. And a risk to you as well as to myself. Who's to say that, if I go wild, I might not keep enough of my intelligence to come and kill you, or go and wipe out my brothers and their families? I'm just afraid that, if I stay on my own, that's going to be a constant danger."

"Hmm. It sounds like you're finding yourself between a rock and a hard place. You don't want to go back to those slave-drivers, and you can't bear the thought of going it alone." She paused for thought. "Well, I can think of only one solution. You needn't try to live by yourself. You can come back here to live with me."

At any other moment in Elizabeth's past eight years of life, and past few months of undeath, she would have rejected that idea completely out of hand, maybe with a laugh, but more often than not, with anger. This was her one moment of weakness. Every reason was on her mother's side. This was her home, the safest of safe refuges, the place which Deborah's spell had duplicated as the dearest place in her heart. If there was anyplace on earth where she should be able to keep her sanity, this was it. She laughed a sigh of relief, and accepted.

Later, after they had talked and talked until nearly dawn, Elizabeth lay herself down on her old bed. The new bedsheets smelled funny, and the depressions in the mattress no longer fit her changed body, which was a disturbance to her, but the springs still creaked in the same old way, welcoming her. It finally occurred to her, as the crack of dawn was upon her, that the whole evening had very likely been planned out by her mother in order to reach this conclusion. She did not mind, not very much.

8.

Existence, Elizabeth concluded, was principally a matter of habitual behavior. A person found himself going through the same patterns night after night for an extended period of time, until they were ingrained. This could go on for years, decades. But then there would be a sudden and shocking change, and none of the former assumptions would be valid any longer. The key to survival, both in life and in the state of non-life, was the ability to recognize the changes as they were about to be forced upon oneself, and to make a swift and pain free adjustment. Hardship and heartbreak were not always going to be avoided, but this method would help to minimize the time of difficulty, and speed the resumption of the normal period of habit.

Putting this theory into practice, Elizabeth tried hard to adjust herself quickly to residing with her mother again. Some aspects were not as difficult as they had been during adolescence. There were fewer hormones coursing their way through her body, for one thing. No worries regarding school and studies. No hassle about sex.

On the other hand, there was one difficulty which greatly exceeded what she remembered: money. As a grown daughter, she thought as a matter of course she was expected to contribute financially towards the household. She decided early on that it would be desirable not to let her mother know the extent of her abilities to create anything she needed. A temptation of which it was better to avoid the occasion. But when she came home one night with a pocketful of cash which she had conjured up out of nothing, her mother howled with anger, "I'm trying not to think about what you're doing out there in the evening, but I don't want any of the dirty money which you're taking off those poor dead corpses!"

Elizabeth didn't try to explain, she didn't try to create any more dollars again, but the problem persisted. She knew her mother would prefer that she obtained gainful employment. Elizabeth thought that she had better things to do with eternity than putting herself under that millstone again. Besides, she couldn't figure out any legal financial arrangement she could make which would not require her to make some sort of daytime appearance, and how could she pay taxes if she was not recognized as being alive? Her mother would not think it ethical for her to blur minds or falsify records. So, finally, they jointly agreed to ignore the problem. She wasn't causing any expenses to her mother anyway, she told herself.

She was anxious that the cats might molest her when she was helpless in her room during the day, but that fear never materialized. After a day or two of curiosity and investigation, they too settled themselves to the new routine. Often the first thing she was aware of when she recovered consciousness was the feel of their weight curled tightly against her legs, or a thin raspy tongue licking her hands. Felix, the larger, dark-haired one, was getting a little old, but he was still vigorous, and she'd usually create some small apparition to tease and amuse him. Dana, a white female she'd found once in a parking lot and brought home, was very shy and withdrawn, and required a lot of affection to bring her to overcome her timidity, but her affections were lavish once that barrier was overcome. For just a few minutes she felt free to play with them, until the hunger began to rise in her, and she had to get up. She couldn't bear the thought of being tempted to attack them.

During this period, she didn't take very much care about her hunting, just so long as it took place well away from home. She looked only for the forlorn and lonely, in order to bring them relief. She was too mellow in her mood to commit any act which would cause sadness to even a mere mortal. After that, it was back home again to share a few hours together with her mother, talking for the most part.

The second night of her stay her mother decided to watch television, but when the set was on Elizabeth could see nothing except a tiny light tracking across the screen. After a moment, she figured out that her senses were so sharp and fast that they were no longer fooled by the illusion of the cathode ray tube. She was capable of seeing the electron beam, which moved across the screen so quickly that humans saw it as a full picture. She blinked and stared, and tried to will her sight to slow down enough to perceive what her mother was laughing about, but she couldn't do it. She could hear the sound, of course, but the lack of a picture was a bother, and after a couple of minutes, the beam became an irritant to her eyes. So, after that night, her mother cut back her viewing to only a handful of shows she couldn't bear to miss, and Elizabeth stayed out a little bit later on those nights. "I spend too much time glued to that damn box, as it is," as her mother observed.

She tried to stay awake as long as she could, but her mother had to be in to work early in the morning; so, sooner or later, she would have to go up to bed. This was the bad time for Elizabeth: hour after hour with no outlet. Stores and libraries were closed. The vast majority of the mortals were safe in their homes. This was the time when the vampires would have their talks, she recalled. After the hectic chase and feeding, when the city was calm and the first glistens of dawn were not yet in the sky. She sometimes allowed herself to wallow in remorse and self-pity.

Elizabeth thought. She thought over every scrap of memory she retained, of her mortal life, of her experiences in undeath, or what she had absorbed from her unnumbered victims. A thousand voices shouting and echoing in the corridors of her mind. She felt as if her brain was going to burst, when she realized how much she had absorbed in such a short time. Eternity was in front of her. Perhaps vampires went wild when they'd taken too many victims, and the voices of the dead came to overwhelm their own mental processes.

Inevitably her thoughts would drift on to contemplate him, Not-Daniel. She argued with herself that she had allowed the whole thing to snowball all out of proportion. This sort of thing might happen all the time. For all she knew for sure, one of the vampires other than the Master had taken her own life: the figure had been so shadowy it might have been anyone. Did that one, whoever he or she might be, have this sort of feeling of anger and rejection over losing her? Of course not.

After that, Elizabeth was ready to get away, away from her interior toil. Taking long walks. Flying over the vistas of the city. Floating effortlessly and allowing the winds to carry her where they would. And still the thoughts followed her. Where was he at this moment? Stalking below where she floated? On the next block over from where she was walking? And with whom?

Then, at long last, dirty streaks of light began to appear in the east, and she made her weary way home. Back to the safe room. Back to the peaceful womb.

One night, when she couldn't bear the thought of another lonely vigil uncomforted, she sought solace by letting it all out in front of her mother. How the thoughts of him were continuing to obsess her. Wondering why that one figure kept coming back inside her, again and again, despite all the others she had taken and was happy to let go. Her mother shrugged with a greater degree of casualness than Elizabeth thought appropriate, and her reply held a touch of flippancy in its tone, "Well, I can't claim to have any kind of expertise about you vampires and your ways. But if you were a young woman who happened to still be alive, I might think that you were suffering from a *crush* on him."

For an instant she felt a blistering of rage inside her, but a moment later she had to battle a violent urge to laugh out loud. "Don't be ridiculous, Mother. He's the very last person I can imagine I'd ever want to see again, either vampire or mortal."

9.

The very next night Elizabeth found herself once again standing and waiting outside that certain building, the dwelling of the vampires. She had wanted to get there as early as possible, so that she could intercept him whenever he came out, but, when she got up that evening, she had heinous trouble getting herself going. First Dana was more than usually cuddlesome, and required more than the usual amount of affection. Then, for some reason, she had trouble deciding on what she should do about her appearance. She was scrupulous to maintain her basic features and size, to keep her mother from getting too worked up about that, but she was puzzled about what sort of garment to create for herself. Formal or casual? This is ridiculous, she thought. It was as if she had gone back in a time warp, trying to decide what to wear on a first date... It's not like she was trying to make herself appealing to him, or anything like that. She just wanted to get things talked out between them, just to try to get herself over this unrelenting fixation.

Next, somehow or other, she got into a squabble with her mother. She couldn't even remember what it had been about. Her mother had apparently had a rough day at work, and Elizabeth was testy enough already, and they found themselves fighting before they even had a chance to realize it. And so there was yet a further delay while they got the argument settled, after which Elizabeth could explain that she'd be late coming home and for her not to wait up.

And then, Elizabeth discovered that she wasn't content to follow her usual pattern of hunting. Usually that pattern got her a plodding businessman coming home or a dowdy housewife out grocery shopping late. The vampiric equivalent of a burger and fries. But she was feeling a little more ambitious now. And since it was too late to catch him before he got out for the night now, she figured that she had time to kill.

In between her neighborhood and the building of the undead lay a wide stretch of decayed territory, another place where the humans had once worked and lived and thrived, abandoned due to the changing tides of economic growth and decline. How strange that cycle now appeared to Elizabeth, from her vantage point overlooking the unending vista of the future, to see the wreak and decay a few brief decades brought to the mortals and their plans.

At any rate, in her mood of the moment, Elizabeth was depressed by that bleak waste of boarded windows and lightless rooms. She alighted on one typical corner. Not a single light visible. Even the homeless had abandoned these shells, and she touched no human consciousness within many blocks. She pulled herself into a compact form and summoned her power.

She razed a line of rowhouses, and in their place she erected a fairy palace. Glimmering spires towering over walls of gold and jewels, surrounded by a foaming moat filled with quicksilver and crossed by a single bridge of diamonds. Inside, the great halls were decorated in jade and crystal, mirrors reflecting back the images repeating into infinity. An invisible orchestra played a waltz. Elizabeth did not wish to bring a thousand broken humans to the gates, so she placed a massive glamour over the whole thing, casting it into invisibility for all mortals, save those who would be called to it. The few whose blood willed to be hers tonight.

And they were two.

One was a woman who walked the streets in her madness, seeing threats and mysteries behind every face that looked down on her in pity and disdain. The city was never other than a phantasm of horror and death to her perception, and thus the glamour was powerless to blur her sight. She looked up to the towers with a grin of innocent delight. At last, she thought, after seventy years, the magic was descending down upon her, the fantasy she had sought since infancy, and she was ready to taste the fruit of bliss and drink of the fountain of youth and beauty.

And the other was a young tough, not a quarter of the woman's age. In his eyes also the city's shadows held only peril, concealing the forms of rivals with eager thirsting knives, and the poison kisses of women ready to betray him for the price of a vial. He stood stunned when he saw the palace, unable to believe that it could be real. But when it didn't go away, ten years of the street fell off his shoulders, and he ran to it with the joy of a child seeing a roomful of toys.

They saw each other when they reached the bridge, and Elizabeth's enchantment flowed forth to receive them. No longer a bag lady, but a princess young and pure. Not a street hustler, but a hero with glowing eyes and cleft chin. It was automatic for him to take her arm, and escort her over the moat and inside the gate.

The music grew louder and faster in pace, and they danced, with a hundred phantom couples surrounding them. They paid no heed to the apparitions around them, however: their eyes were caught in each other's gaze. As the swirling of the dance drew to a close, they slowed, and came closer together in one another's arms. And at last their lips met.

A hundred battles he had waged, all for the honor of her name. A thousand suitors she had rejected, all to await his arrival. This was the night when sorrow was to be put aside, when warfare and long waiting was ended. They were together, triumphant over coy fate and the crossing of the stars, and no power on earth or in heaven was to separate them again.

Solemn ceremonies formalized their bonding with the blessings of God and society. Now the time was come at last, when the tittering phantom maids brought her to the boudoir. They seated her at her toilette, and gracefully withdrew to allow her to comport herself, and make ready for his coming. Hearty good-natured jokes were told as the ghostly lords cheered him on with the final toast of the evening. He was nervous, he who had never faced a foeman without the steely glint of confidence in his sword arm. He quickly licked his lips as he opened the final doorway. They saw each other then, and they smiled, letting down their guards of fear and uncertainty. They were alone now.

But not alone. Elizabeth was there, concealed, within the weaving of the room and the hall, and knitting the very form of their countenances. She empowered their fantasy, throwing down their mental fortifications of doubt, casting aside their reserve. Plunging them deep into their own wishes. She smiled in her invisibility as they drew together, falling with hurried and eager vigor down upon the pillows. Not yet, not yet, she thought, although she was hot with the desire for their blood. Allow them to finish the tapestry. Swift motions were concealed beneath the sheets. Cries of excitement that sounded almost like anguish. Finally, surcease. Then it was, and only then, that Elizabeth crept forward and softly reached for them.

10.

That was a good thing, the taste of their blood and their memories, sweet to pull them inside and store them along with all the others. She felt their shock and their horror at what she was doing to them, but also their gratitude, that she had given them those precious moments of fulfillment, the dream that had actually come true. The pleasure had quickly worn off again, just as it always did. The pain was inside her again, urging her to pick herself up from her hiding place, and devour once more. She fought it. There wasn't enough time, she told it, not enough time to go off and find some other human and get back to weave the spells of concealment around her, here beside the vampires' condo. Like any human urge, it paid no heed to intellectual reasoning. It wanted quenching and it wanted it now. She shifted uncomfortably.

It was getting late. Frost formed on the window of the parked car in which she was secreted. She didn't bother to clear it off, because sight was much less important a sense than her radar net of awareness. She wished she believed enough in God to pray that she had learned Diana's spell for suppression of her undead essence well enough to fool the others.

Then they started to come back. Gregory was first, bloated as he always was, full of gore to pour into his pool. Then Una, also filled, filled with self-righteousness over some new blow struck for freedom. They were both very much absorbed in themselves, and she could tell they weren't even looking for any strangers. Maybe she would be lucky, she thought.

More floated past her, alone or in small groups. Stephen looking eager to return to his private creation. Deborah like a storm cloud, brooding over her eternal guilt. Alicia came back in the company of Claire, which made Elizabeth frown. She didn't like the idea of Alicia getting along with anyone else. Then the others came in quick order, except for Charles and Jonathan. They wouldn't be back until the very break of dawn, returning from their nightly game of hunter and hunted. No one appeared to notice her. She fidgeted again. What was keeping him?

At last. At last. She felt him coming, flowing with the quickening breeze. There wasn't much time. She'd have to be fast. He was settling down on the sidewalk, taking on his solid form. He was within a few meters. Now was the time to allow her spell to fade, to enable him to detect her. And she laughed then, to see how he jumped with the sudden realization that he was not alone.

He whirled about. "Who's that?" His voice echoed off the front of the building hauntingly.

She was beginning to enjoy this. Remaining hidden inside the car, she projected her voice to whisper in his ear, "Not so loud, not so loud. You're going to wake up all the others, and we don't want that, do we?"

"I don't know about that. Anybody who means well wouldn't stay hidden this way."

"All right. I'm coming out." And when she opened the door, he suddenly grinned, and began to run toward her. "It's you. At last. I've been looking everywhere and waiting for you."

That caught her aback. She held up her hand to stop him. "Why? What do you want with me? I thought I was the one who was looking for you."

He stopped short. There was an expression on his face of hurt puzzlement, as if he was expecting her to feel the same unabashed thrill at finding him, as he was feeling to discover her. "Well, I remember seeing you that night when everybody came to save me from the Master. But then suddenly you went away, and nobody seemed to pay any attention. I asked about you, and either they wouldn't say anything, or they'd only say things that weren't all that nice about you. Some of the vampires don't like you, and others thought that you did wrong to turn on them when they went to so much trouble to help you. At least that's the way they talk about you. And you were the one..." He halted.

"The one what?"

"I don't know. There was just something about you that I could feel was *different*. The others, they're all different from each other, with all the strange things they think and do, but you were something else, something unique. There's something untamed about you, something I can feel rather than see. Like the difference between seeing animals in the zoo and going out in the jungle to meet them."

Elizabeth didn't know what his game was or the motivations behind it, but if he was trying to win her over, he was saying exactly the right words. Yes, she thought as he was saying them, that's just the way it is. She didn't want to be inside Jonathan's petting zoo. "Is that something you like?" she asked. "Something you want to be a little bit more like, yourself?"

"Yes. I think I do."

She walked slowly and thoughtfully around him, sizing him up. He hadn't changed his body a bit, not since they took him from the Master, not since she first saw him laid out on the bed of pain.

Slender. No, lithe was the word. Lithe. But looking very unconfident in himself, and mistrustful of her. "Well, I guess I can try. It couldn't hurt. But it's getting very late. It's going to be dawn too soon. It'll have to wait until tomorrow." She began to fade away.

"No, wait! Um, it might take a long time for us to get back together. I feel like we've wasted so much time already, weeks when we could've. I don't know, when you could've taught me what you want to teach me. Already." He laughed nervously. "I'm not usually this tongue-tied. Sorry about this."

She laughed along with him. "It's all right. I'm not going to hurt you. Just tell me what you want from me."

"Well, maybe, if you don't think I'm being too forward here, maybe you could come in and stay in my apartment for the day."

She frowned now. "I don't want the others to know that I'm around."

"Or maybe I could go and stay with you?"

"No, no, I don't think I want that. Let me see. Damn, look how light it's getting already! Charles and Jonathan are going to be here any moment. Well there really isn't any time for me to get anywhere else safe now. I'll have to accept your offer. But look here. I think I know a way to hide myself, to suppress my aura. But it won't work by itself when I'm going to be so near the others all day. I'll need your help. Come here. Closer. Now, put your arm around me, and let me slide your own aura around me. You can be my cloak. Can you feel how I'm hiding myself under you now? It'd be hard for anyone else to notice I'm here now, wouldn't it? Okay, now let's go inside."

Elizabeth was enjoying herself again. Being with him felt good, better than it ought to, she suspected. The pain was diminished to a fraction. It was another way of merging, putting her self just a little bit into his being, but not enough to lose any of her own awareness. A cozy sensation. The feeling she got when she was a girl and her father picked her up to take her to bed. She hadn't realized that she missed that sensation. A sensation of being cared for, of being cuddled. Like being loved.

11.

Elizabeth awakened disoriented. Then she remembered, first with a shock, and then with a smile. Oh, if her mother only knew, she thought. She had been sleeping in the same room with a *man*. How sinful. She would have liked to stay there lounging, but peril threatened. She got up and went over to jostle the vampire who called himself Daniel. A pity to stir him. He looked so innocent, so carefree. She wondered if that's the way she had looked when she had first gotten her freedom from the Master, and why didn't she feel like she could look that guileless any more....

He started to speak, but she didn't allow him to make a sound. Instead, she enveloped him over herself again, and silently directed him to form a window. Out they floated, and she waited until they were far away before she allowed him to free himself. Then they both laughed, loudly and heartily. "That felt just like being back in college," he said, "sneaking dates in and out of the room under the head resident's nose." He chuckled again, but then grew more serious. "But was it that bad? What are you afraid might've happened if Jonathan or one of the others had found you there?"

She had to admit that she didn't know. "But it was something I didn't want to risk. I left there when I suddenly discovered that the vampires there don't have more than a fraction of the freedom which they claim they have." She looked at him in sudden suspicion. "Have you been to visit everyone there? I mean, have you gone to see Jonathan yet?"

"No, Jonathan was the last. I was planning on going to see him tonight. Before I met you, that is."

"Good God, I was just in time...."

"Why? Jonathan seems to be such a nice guy. What could be wrong with him?"

"Oh, well, it's all pretty complicated. I guess that it's nothing I could really explain in a way that'd make it clear why I couldn't stand it anymore, after the night I went to Jonathan. I'm sorry. I just can't talk about it."

"All right. So, what do we do now?"

"Well, I'm certainly hungry now. I feel like I have a better appetite than I've had in months. How about you?"

"I'm always feeling the pain. But I don't know if I feel right giving it the complement of calling it *hunger*, considering what we have to do."

"Well, whatever we're going to call it, let's go find a big group."

And they did.

Afterwards, in the pleasant glow of the satisfaction of their need, they sat in a small all-night cafe, invisible to the bustling waiters circling about. Elizabeth was starting to get concerned. This was not going at all in the way she had planned it. She had wanted a quick confrontation to make him answer a couple of questions about who he was and what he wanted from her. Then she wanted a quicker goodbye, never having to see him again, only now she was enjoying just being around him, seeing an undead face which was new and fresh to her, without hiding depths of unspoken thought. His was the face of a friend. So she was upset, that she planned to destroy this friendship while it was still a bud.

"You know," she said in as casual a manner as she could attain, "you notice that I haven't addressed you by name a single time. I'm having a hard time deciding even what to call you."

"Well, I feel the same way about you. But I figured that you'd tell me your name when you were ready. Why not call me Daniel? It's what the Master said was my name."

"But that's just it! It's what the Master told you. What do *you* say? What name sinks into your being and says that it's *right*, the name you ought to have, the name you had back when you were a living person?"

He got a look of embarrassment, holding his head down. "I don't know."

"What?"

"I don't know! How should I know? I don't know anything at all about the way I was back then. Only one or two things the Master said, along with his other teachings."

"And that's the strangest thing," she said. "When he brought me back from the grave, I couldn't remember a thing about my old life, but then he just grabbed a hold of me, looked into my eyes, and everything flooded back. From him, into me." Her eyes started getting wide then, as she began to have an intimation of the truth.

He didn't appear to notice this. "Well, he didn't do that to me. I don't know why. I asked some of the others, but they all seemed to remember everything about their mortal life. I was hurt. But there was one thing the Master did tell me, and I could never understand it." He finally noticed her increasing agitation. "What's the matter now? You look like you're ready to jump out the window. Am I doing something wrong?"

"No. Don't mind me. Just tell me, what did the Master say to you?"

"Well, I remember his eyes. You remember them, too, don't you, the way they stared right through the center of your skull, and seemed to be laughing with cruelty as they saw what you had inside? That's the first thing I remember when he brought me back. I was so empty, and I wanted to fill myself up, with a yearning like nothing else in the universe.

"And he told me, and I can remember exactly the words he used, it seemed so strange to me, 'Take a look in my eyes, and you'll learn many things. But there's one thing you can't get from me: your name and your memory. Come with me, and I'll show you where you have to look to find what you want most.'

"He gave me some kind of small animal to bite and drain, to give me a little bit of strength, and then he took me and made me fly with him, over to another cemetery. We alighted, and he pointed down to one stone, and said, 'Look down, this is where your name is hidden. No, not carved on the rock, but carved in the heart and soul of the person who has *this name*. Until you find her, you can be called anything you may want, but you won't ever find the name and the being you really need. For myself, I'm going to call you Daniel.' And so, that's where I've gone, every night I've had the chance, to that gravestone, trying to figure out the puzzle, looking for that person who calls herself *Elizabeth*," he concluded, with a very significant look at her.

Elizabeth dropped her head into her hands. Then she stood up, and her words were hard. "And so I was right all along. You're just another snare. He took half of you away from me, and now he wants me to give you the rest like a free present! Why can't he let me go? What does he want from me? Everywhere I turn, all I try to do is look for an open face, but I never get anything but more lies and cheats and mazes!" She rushed away, smashing through the window and into the air.

He tried to pursue, but she was full of anger and anguish, and it powered her flight. He called out to her, "Wait! Don't go! Don't leave me, Elizabeth!" She didn't pause. One last cry he sent towards her, before falling away in his despair:

"Can't you even tell me my name?"

12.

It didn't take long for Elizabeth to calm down. She landed on a quiet street and found a corner to settle down in. So, she thought. Here I am again. Hurt and forlorn and alone, again. Running away, again.

She ran from Jonathan and his group. Before that, she ran from the Master, with a little help from the others. Most of the ways she had reacted during the course of her lifetime had been cases of running away in some form or other, as she now looked back upon them. She was just keeping up an honored tradition in her existence.

Somewhere, she had gotten sold a shoddy set of goods. They told her that God would save her from running away. They told her that love and sex would save her from running away. They told her that sisterhood would save her from running away. And both Jonathan and the Master had told her that undeath meant that she no longer would have to run away. Apparently, there wasn't anyone or anything, living or not, who was going to tell her the truth.

Not fair. She was expected to stand up for herself and be strong, be pure. But everything was conspiring against her, to keep on knocking her down, to prevent her from ever getting the opportunity to learn to stand straight. So, why believe any of it any longer? Why keep on believing that she had to stand up?

A very tempting idea, that. To try to go back to the grave again. Stop fighting it. Give it all up to the burning and cleansing of the Sun. Wouldn't that be just what he'd deserve, the not-Daniel, to let his name and memory be burnt up? Just stay right here and wait a few short hours. Take a couple of steps out into the open, and then all her troubles would be over.

As she sat and pondered, Elizabeth thoughtlessly allowed all of her protective spells and glamours to slip away, and her web of sensitivity to dull. No matter, but therefore she had no awareness of the presence which was approaching her, slowly and tentatively. Unobtrusive bands of mist began to surround her, gradually contracting. A dim consciousness of them intruded on her ruminations, but she brusquely pushed it aside. The bands collapsed suddenly inward to form chains around her limbs, and Elizabeth had no choice but to notice them, then.

She was yanked to her feet, and turned around. In front of her coalesced a body; she saw its sexless skeletal shape, flesh dripping down from sunken cheeks, empty eye-sockets and open viscera, and she knew at last that she was confronting a feral vampire. One of the ones who had surrendered all semblance of consciousness. Dead in soul but driven by the hungry pain to mindless animation.

Instinctively she struggled, but after a moment she made herself stop. After all, death was death, one way of another, and she had resigned herself to it. This was perhaps even more appropriate than the Sun, she reflected: symbolic of the way in which everyone had used her and abused her and then discarded her. The bonds tightened more, generating a sensation of pain she didn't bother to suppress. They dragged her towards the figure. Sucker-mouths with sharp piercing tongues appeared on the chains, battening themselves upon her. The great ragged maw of the vampire opened wide, wide, far wider than was possible on the human form, round and toothed like the mouth of a lamprey, a chasm which could swallow her whole.

As it made contact with her, Elizabeth perceived the essence of its emptiness: a vacuum where mind and personality had imploded. A black hole that walked. A dank opening in the fabric of reality, propelled by habit to seek and stalk all life, and undeath as well, as if anything could possibly refill it. But the vacuum was an infinity, and all the blood and memory that might enter its chasm was lost, lost, poured out to make a stain that would color the void for just a moment with its flavorings, but then dissipate, lost beyond recall. Empty and vile nirvana, union with a cold and unknowing infinite blackness. Elizabeth was like a beacon to it: a bright and airy lure with the thousand stolen souls jostling around inside her ready to overflow. It whined in its want of her like a beaten dog, and set its terrible sucking mouth on her.

In a flash Elizabeth knew she could not surrender to it. The feral vampire pulled at the structure of her being, annihilating everything it touched. She remembered the blistering touch of the Sun on her hand, but that had been an act of cleansing, removing her own corruption from the peaceful face of Earth. This was pollution, evil. Each moment of its continuing existence was a cry denying the reality of any thought and emotion and dream. She had to fight it.

But could she fight it, could she escape? Already it had bled away from her a score of memories from the myriad lives that were within her: a picnic where a boy had tasted his first kiss; a vision of bliss arising out of religious fervor; a scream of a woman coming at the sight of Elizabeth's onrushing mouth; and with each second the drain was increasing. She was sliding on a steep sandy slope. Trying to halt her tumble just loosened the surrounding gravel and speeded the fall. The vast mouth drew nearer still.

She could not defend herself against it. So she attacked. She formed herself into a thin and sharp needle-shape. She cast herself from the slope and launched right into the maw, jagged, piercing. Through the mouth and into the reeking flesh behind it. Tearing and severing the empty brain. It grasped at her as she shot through it, but she was smooth and metallic, allowing no purchase on her clean form.

She was through it. Free. It thrashed on the ground below where she was standing, its spinal cord cut, helpless until it could reorganize its form by instinct. But Elizabeth didn't wait for it. She instantly formed herself into a bird-shape and fled. No, not fled. She wasn't running away, not this time. She was leaving the battlefield after winning the victory. She cried out in triumph.

But she was hurt, hurt. Her elation wore off as she realized the extent of her injuries. Not physical hurts, that was an impossibility for her, but it had ruptured segments of her mind, torn away pieces of her spirit. Even as she was flying, she could feel memories continuing to ooze out of her like a hemorrhage. They poured down over the city streets, draping onto the sleeping humans and slipping into their dreams. She started to lose altitude as her wings grew shaky. But she soon saw sight of her goal, and slid down to a bumpy landing in front of her mother's house.

13.

Elizabeth picked herself up off the ground, returning to her human shape. *Pull together now,* she commanded herself. Don't want her to see what I've been going through tonight. Staunch the flow of memories with a spiritual bandage; she'd see about healing it later when she had more time. Up the walk, smoothing her hair and clothes. Everything's completely normal, just another night on the town.

"So, the prodigal returns at last," came her mother's caustic words as she unlocked the door. Elizabeth attempted a warm yet concerned look. "Isn't it pretty late for you to be waiting up for me?"

"No, it's Saturday night. I never work on Sundays, as you know."

"I'm sorry, I didn't even realize it. It's so easy to lose track of the way, hum, people count the days."

"Well, come on in, close the door. You may not feel it, but I do. And I'm the one who's paying the heating bill."

Elizabeth came in and sat down on the couch with a flop, displacing Felix but picking him up and putting him in her lap. Her mother could sense the heaviness of that act and got her concerned look. "You look like you haven't slept in a week. And that's bad. I know how much you can control your appearance, although you don't like to admit it. Anything you can talk about?"

She heaved a sigh. "I don't think so. It feels like more than a week since I left last night. I've learned a few things, some things I don't think I wanted to learn about. But I've also learned something about myself that I do feel happy to know."

"Sure you don't want to tell me? That's what I'm here for."

"Not right now. But I can tell you that I know a bit better what it's like to surrender to the wild urges, and I know now that I am not going to ever allow myself to do that."

"Well, that's certainly a relief."

Elizabeth rankled at the sarcasm she detected in that reply, and started to respond angrily, but she thought better of it. She needed friendship and affection at this time, not more rancor. She shrugged and forced a smile. Finally, she managed to relax a little. She sighed again and leaned back on the couch, allowing the purr of the cat to sink soothingly into her brain, as she turned her attention inward, to start the process of healing her hurts. As long as I have this, she thought, I can handle the world. This last refuge, where I'll always be welcome, no matter what I've done and what I've gone through. She finished the healing process, and turned her senses back outward, to radiate from her body and through the walls to feel the surrounding slumber of the city.

And she felt the horror drawing nearer.

"Oh, no," she murmured. "Oh dear God."

"What did you say, dear?" asked her mother lightly, hardly looking up from her needlepoint.

She was an ass, an imbecile. She was an idiot. She hadn't killed it, she couldn't kill it. But it had touched her, had tasted her, and it wouldn't let her go. There was a link between them now, an umbilical cord which stretched over the long kilometers, and it followed, reeling her in like a hooked fish. The memories she had shed as she flew over the city, it lapped up eagerly like a cat over spilled milk, and it craved more, more. It craved the source. It would follow her, all night, every night. It would hide in the nearest crack if daylight struck, and each evening, as soon as the Sun was hidden, it would arise to confront her anew.

And she had led it here, to her last sanctuary. It wanted her, but when it had taken and drained the last dregs, it would turn and suck up her mother, the cats, as a freshening and delightful desert. She had betrayed them.

"Are you listening to me? Are you feeling all right? You're shaking. You look like you're seeing a ghost."

Elizabeth made herself speak, and terror was riding in her voice: "Momma. Don't try to help me. Don't ask me to explain. Just listen to me. There's something coming. I want you to go hide. Go down in the basement. Turn off all the lights. Go sit down in the corner in the back, down between the freezer and dryer. Try not to make any sound. Try not to even think if you can. It might be able to sense your very thoughts. Take the cats and try to keep them quiet. And don't come up, no matter what it sounds like is happening up here. Stay down there, until you hear me tell you it's safe, or it's dawn. Don't come up. No matter what."

"But I don't understand!"

"Get down there! *Now!*" And there was such naked fear in her voice that her mother obeyed without further complaint.

There was no time, no time. No time for traps. No time for strategy. If she ran, it still might attack her mother. She had to stay. To fight.

She mustered her power. She had done so much already this night, how could she find the strength to go on? Concentration. She raised her arms, and created obstacles. A wall of stone. A chasm filled with jagged spikes. Nothing could stop it. It had no mind, but instinctively it could alter its form to penetrate each defense she raised.

Spells of glamour poured out of her body. An illusion of desert. No life. Nothing to attract a thirsty vampire. But the spells required a consciousness to see them and be deceived. It had no mind, and it knew that its goal was still there.

It had arrived.

The tentacles snaked out from its dark and seething core. The walls didn't stop them. She created cleavers and guillotines which cut them off as each one penetrated into the room, and they fell to the floor and writhed like snakes, still crawling towards her. She conjured stomping boots with sharp spikes, and crushed them. They squashed and emitted obscene odors.

This continued for several minutes, and Elizabeth began to harbor hope, that it was unintelligent enough to keep on using the same strategy until Sunrise. But then there was a pause. It perceived in its inanimate fashion that the one method was not succeeding. Elizabeth waited for what it would try next.

It began to expand. Larger and larger, and Elizabeth almost screamed to see how its vacuum didn't attenuate, no matter how vast it grew. Infinite emptiness, and it continued to grow. And then it began to move forward.

It encompassed the entirety of the house, and then it began to squeeze.

The foundations trembled. Elizabeth desperately strengthened the structure, pouring herself into the plaster and the joints, fighting the relentless and growing pressure. The windows shattered, and she rushed to fill them with mortar, before any of it could get inside. She was stretching herself to her limits, plastering each crack, reinforcing each brick. At last, when she felt like she couldn't hold it back for another moment, the attack ended. She had won again.

It was mindless, but it possessed a thousand shreds of intelligence, tattered fragments of what were once human and undead brains, which still clung limply to the serrated insides of its being; these shreds still had some remnants of mind. It was capable of using these tatters, when it had great need. It could remember things that hurt it, and learn.

Without warning, it formed a hundred needles, just like the one which Elizabeth had made of herself, and shot them into the house. She couldn't stop them: they were too sharp, they were too fast. They pierced the walls and the ceiling. And when they had entered, they lodged in the holes and dissolved, leaving a hundred openings, and it flowed inside.

It was in the room.

Like deadly gas hissing through the holes, its black vaporous bands poured into the room, and fell like a liquid to collect on the floor. Elizabeth finally emitted a scream. She levitated, to keep it from touching her. But it was rising, and it launched an arm like a pseudopod toward her. It couldn't be defeated. She couldn't escape it. It would stalk her forever, until she faltered and was destroyed. With a cry of total despair, she felt herself reverting to a more primitive level herself: becoming a beast to combat that which was lower than a beast.

She bared her long sharp teeth and attacked.

She grabbed at its viscous substance, tearing at it with long sharp talons. She ripped strands from it and threw them against spikes she made protrude from the walls. Bite it, tear it, fight it. Make it hurt. Make it scream the way she was screaming now. Make it flee. Make it die!

There was silence. Elizabeth's mother had followed her instructions, holding the cats tight against her chest. It wasn't hard. She could feel the thing coming, even with her dull human sensitivity, she could feel the uncleanliness penetrating the walls of her home. She felt an unwholesome sensation like hairiness pressing down upon her face. The feel of sweat. The lank flavor of sputum. The cats huddled against her, shivering. That one scream almost made her lose her guard, almost made her cast her own safety aside, and run to her suicide for her daughter's sake.

And then came the sounds. Savage, bestial noises. Tearing, rending. Growling. She fell into despair, certain that she was hearing the sound of the thing tearing her Elizabeth apart. She prepared herself for her own imminent death.

Nothing came. No sound. The loathsome vileness passed. But Elizabeth didn't call to her. She couldn't take the silence. It still wasn't dawn, it was becoming a never-ending night! Finally she braved the steps and opened the door to a slow creak.

She found Elizabeth alone, curled on the floor in a fetal position, crying her bloody tears.

Elizabeth heard her enter and slowly looked up. "There wasn't any other way," she said. "It had my scent. It was going to follow me forever until it destroyed me. There was nothing I could do to stop it. I couldn't make it go away."

She stood shaking slightly, so her mother led her to the couch. After a moment, she continued, "It was so hungry. It wanted to drink me with such a longing that it was making me want to drink myself too. The only way I could defeat it, the only way, was for me to, to do to it, what it wanted to do to me.

"I absorbed it. I grabbed its empty vacuum, and I took it inside me. It's there now. I can feel it. It's still hungry, it'll always be a spot of hungry despair inside me. But it's safe now. It's small and powerless, tucked away in my mind, in my soul. Just like everything else I've ever killed. And it's going to be there forever."

14.

Elizabeth awakened in an unfamiliar haze. She panicked for a moment, fearing that somehow the feral vampire had gotten control over her during the day; she reassured herself that such a thing was impossible. The fact that she was conscious and still aware of her own existence proved that.

But what was wrong? She was in her room, nestled in her comfortable bed. Night was peacefully falling. Everything was normal. Were the undead subject to some kind of infection she didn't know about? She tried to rise and couldn't.

It was then that she noticed the huge tomato stake hammered through her chest. And after that she realized that her head had been severed from her body, and an entire bottle of powdered garlic had been poured in her opened mouth. Three plastic rosaries were strung around her neck and arms, and crucifixes were put up on all four walls of the room surrounding her bed.

She tried to give forth a little laugh, but with no air coming up through her throat, she couldn't, and the motion of her mouth made more of the garlic slide unpleasantly down her windpipe.

It was easy enough to dissolve the stake and reconnect the cut flesh. Less easy to make the decision to open the door and head down the hallway. There was more garlic strewn at the doorway and all the way down the hall. Her steps made footprints in it. There was another cross nailed on the door. She took it down and carried it with her.

Her mother was downstairs ripping out an error in her cross-stitch. Elizabeth purposefully made a little noise as she reached the steps. Her mother gave no indication of surprise, but swallowed as she looked up calmly.

"Good evening, mother." She came over and sat down on the sofa, right next to the woman, who didn't flinch. Elizabeth did see that her hands shook a little as they continued to rip out the yarn.

Finally, her mother spoke in a near-whisper, "I'm sorry, Elizabeth."

She tried to smile and look nonchalant. "Well, this is good in a way because it proves to you once and for all that I'm what I've been telling you I am."

"Yes, it does that."

"But you've been watching too many bad movies. That's not the way you can get rid of me. You can't kill me, not at all, not without my willing it." This wasn't strictly true. Her mother could very easily destroy her by dragging her inert body outside into the Sunlight. But Elizabeth certainly wasn't going to tell her that at this point.

Her mother finally gave up on the pattern and threw it down. "I've been really proud of myself, you know," she said. "I've been keeping it all inside for all these weeks, when I've felt like I was going to burst apart. I did all right at night, when you were here with me and talking. I could tell myself that it was all just a big trick you were playing on me. A game, just like when you were a little girl playing sick to stay home from school... But then, during the day, I'd come into your room and see you, see how you put shutters on the windows to make it completely dark, and the way you were just lying there. And I couldn't wake you up, no matter how I shook you. You didn't breathe. You were a corpse.

"And then I have to run and hide. But I was keeping it in, keeping it from showing, I thought. Until what happened last night. That told me in a way I couldn't deny any longer, that it's no game. You are what you are."

"I am a vampire."

"Yes, yes. You're a vampire. A killer. Undead. Anyhow, God in Heaven knows that I wasn't going to get any sleep after that. There were too many things going around and around in my head. Mostly, I was remembering how afraid you were, the night you first came here, that you weren't going to be able to keep yourself from going wild some day. Like that *thing*. And then I thought about how the only way you could beat it was to become more like it, and make it a part of yourself...

"Well, I finally got up, and I got dressed and went to early Mass. And the reading was the one where Jesus says to cut off your right hand if it was going to lead you into sin. Better to go to Heaven with one hand, than to Hell with both. And the priest talked about the way we humans let the evil collect inside us and all around us, until it's so thick that we can't cut it away. That's when I decided to do what I had to do."

There was a silence for a long time. Elizabeth sat and allowed her mother's words to sink slowly into the deepest portions of her mind. Her mother seemed expectant, even impatient. Finally, she blurted out, "Well, I'm as ready as I'm ever going to be. You might as well do it, and get it over with."

"Do what?"

"You're going to have to bite me and kill me now, aren't you? You can't trust me any longer. You know that if I tried to kill you once, I'll have to try again. I'm ready to take responsibility for my failure. You're doing it entirely for your own safety."

Elizabeth snorted. "Don't be ridiculous. I'm not going to kill you, mother."

To her surprise, the woman got a somewhat hurt expression. "Oh. I guess I just assumed that's what you'd do now."

"But you're my mother. I wouldn't ever do anything to hurt you."

Another long pause. Elizabeth knew that her mother was fighting to say something more, and waited for it. At last, she spoke, "Not even I wanted you to?"

Elizabeth was beginning to understand; she knew she had to follow form and indicate shock. Then her mother could go on and say, "I've had a long, full life. I've raised three children, and they're all grown up now. Even before your death, I hadn't heard anything from you for months and months. I'm so alone. You can't imagine how lonely, not with all those minds and souls you have churning around inside you. With me, with humans, it's different. And I know that I'm not going to be around very much longer. After your father died, then I knew that there wasn't anything keeping me on this Earth any longer. And a person knows when her body is starting to run down, even if there's nothing wrong with her that a doctor could find.

"I've tried to be a good woman, a God-fearing woman. I believe in what the Church tells me, I really do. But I'm so afraid, so afraid of that one moment of darkness, before I'd know whether it was really true or not... I guess that means I'm not all that good a Christian after all, am I?

"But you came back. You know what it's like. You've been through that moment, the moment of death, and past it. I wanted you to make me like you, make me a vampire like you, until you told me you didn't know how. Well, that's all right, I realized. I don't think I'd like to spend an eternity without ever seeing the Sun again. But then you also told me how you hold on to a little bit of everyone you've ever bitten and killed. They're dead, but they're still present, a part of you. And if you live forever, then they're going to be forever, too, in some way. So, now that I'm dying, I want you to take me. Take me, so that I can stay with you for all time in whatever way it is that you still hold your victims." Another pause. "Please?"

"You're not going to die for a long, long time, mother."

"There's some things a person knows, and I know that I've been dying for years now."

"Not any more." There was such certainty in Elizabeth's voice that her mother ceased her protests. Elizabeth sighed. No more secrets were to be kept after tonight. "Look," she said, pointed to the cross-stitch. With a gesture, she made the frayed and knotted strands right themselves, falling into perfect order. "I knew that you weren't healthy from the moment I first saw you in the cemetery. A vampire can detect that sort of thing from a long distance. And I couldn't help myself, for what I did. It was an automatic reaction on my part to correct the problems I could feel. Have you had any of your headaches since I moved in? Stomach problems? Have your legs been giving you any more pain?"

Her mother shook her head to each question.

"I guess you might have figured that your problems were all in your head, and that they went away when you got me as a guest, as someone you could think about instead of yourself and your pains. But your pains were real. You had the beginning of an aneurism in your brain that could've led to a stroke. You had a partial duodenal blockage that's been disturbing your digestion for years. Varicose veins in your legs. And what you couldn't detect, what wasn't causing you any pain yet, was a pretty severe case of arteriosclerosis. There was a very good chance that you really might not have lived more than two or three years.

"But I fixed it all. You're probably the healthiest woman of your age on the face of the Earth today. Barring accidents, you ought to easily live past a hundred now."

Her mother looked down, and her expression was one of relief but mixed with a certain degree of dismay. "I see. Thank you, I think."

Elizabeth smiled. "And you can't hide what you're feeling now, either. You're feeling resentful that I'd so something like that without even telling you. I understand that. You have every right to feel that way. I know what it's like, the helplessness of having somebody else controlling your body's nature. That sense of violation. I've treated your body like it was an inanimate object, altering it any way I might choose. And I'm sorry I did it. But, like I said, it's something I couldn't help doing. Because even though I'm no longer alive, even though I'm not a human being at all anymore, I still love you, and I had to do what I thought would help you."

Her mother finally began to weep as Elizabeth was saying this, at long last letting down the guards she had been erecting all these weeks to hold in her complicated and contradictory emotions. "All right," she said between sobs, "all right, I'll forgive you if you'll forgive me. We're two grown people. We can do it. But I can't change myself as easily as you seem to be able to change me. It's going to take me some time to really accept all these things you're saying. Unless you can alter the thoughts and feelings I have at will, too."

"Now that's something I'll never do. I promise it. I'll swear to it. I swear by the hard burning light of the Sun. That's about the only thing a vampire can swear by, the only thing that we're powerless against."

"And I guess I'll have to accept that. There is one thing that I'd like you to promise me. Will you do it? You say I'm going to live for many more years, but even that's going to end some day, and I'm sure that it's not going to feel like a long time at all when the time comes. So when the end is near, whenever it may be, will you come back for me then? Will you take me then, so I can finally be one with you, forever?"

Elizabeth's face darkened. "You don't know what you're asking me to do. I've told you that I have everybody I've ever killed here inside me, but you don't know anything about what's it's like. You don't want to be like that. Believe me. They're dead, really and totally dead, in a way nothing like the state I'm in. They're changeless. They can't ever grow into anything else. They're like photographs or record albums. Their every thought and every reaction is always going to be the same. When I allow them to be aware inside my mind, it's like turning on or off a switch. They can't be really happy like that, no matter what they act like when I turn them on. I'm the one who's in control. I'm the only one who benefits from having them in me. They're nothing but facets of my own ego, my own self now," she concluded, and she got a thoughtful look as she was saying this.

Her mother wasn't deterred. "But at least it's something! Something to count on. Something to let me know that there's going to be more than that endless darkness, after I go. I still want you to make me that promise."

"Well, I'm not going to promise it. I'm not going to commit the both of us to a course which we might later regret. But here's what I do promise to do for you: I will come to you, when the time of your death is at hand, and I'll offer you that choice. But I want you to be totally certain. Because it's something that can't be undone."

Her mother was finally happy with that. Elizabeth, however, stood up, and took a determined step toward the door. Her mother grabbed at her arm, "But where are you going now? I thought we were finally settled, and that we could spend a nice quiet evening together for a change. Don't hurt my feelings by going away again."

Elizabeth looked down at her mother sitting there, feeling waves of guilt washing over her for what she was doing; yet she also felt a certain contempt, as if her mother were a lower form of life reaching out its disgustingly moist and hot hand to grasp at her. "I'm sorry, mother, but the things we've just been talking about have only just hit home for me. I've finally realized something that I should have known a long time ago. Don't ask me to explain it. It's all too complicated, and too close to me right now, for me to discuss it. Don't wait up for me. I don't know what's going to happen next, if I'm going to be back tonight, or next week, or not for the rest of your lifetime. But I'll remember that promise, mother. Look for me, when the darkness is deepest around you, and your every hope is lost."

And she was gone.

15.

Elizabeth found him exactly where she expected him to be, standing morosely in front of her empty grave. The night was cloudy and wet, but hinting at the coming arrival of spring. When he detected her approach, he couldn't hold back a broad puppy-like grin, although he quickly restored his self-control. "I'm so glad you came back. I was afraid that you weren't going to, and I didn't know what I was going to do if you didn't." He held out a hand, and she took it in friendship, appreciating the smooth dry coolness of his flesh. This was where she belonged, she decided, here among her own kind. She had been demonstrating weakness by falling back to her mother and all the attending props of her mortal life. She resolved that she wouldn't show such weakness again. "Come on, let's get out of here. There's nothing here for us."

They floated up into the air. The man, the not-Daniel maintained enough of his form to ask a question, "But where should we go? I know so little about this city: only the Master's places, and the places where the others go. I don't want to be around them tonight."

"No, we need to find a place where we can be alone. I think I know where."

She led him back to the empty factory. Since she left it, her spells of avoidance had faded, and it had begun to attract the usual quota of vagrants and other homeless mortals. This was good, because Elizabeth still hadn't fed herself this night, and her appetite was painfully strong. The other had fed, but he wondered if he might be needing extra strength, and so he joined with her in the meal. Elizabeth was enjoying being in his presence again. So many of his mannerisms, the words he chose and the movements he made, were instinctive, and were delightfully familiar to what her memories communicated to her about him. But he was so terribly shy around her! Careful never to get too close to her, and apologetic for anything he said that he could imagine to be offensive. She would help him learn to overcome this.

After their hunger was sated, and any other humans in the vicinity were frightened away by their glamours, they settled themselves in a quiet inner office. He smiled shyly. "I hope you don't mind if I ask this, but I was wondering just why did you come back? I realize that, although I'm wanting something which only you can give me, there really isn't anything I can give you in return. I don't know that I'd want to be nothing but a charity case for you, someone you're helping just out of the goodness of your heart."

Elizabeth replied: "No, I think the urge for charity is one of the things which we vampires gave up when we rose from the dead. It's only been one night since I went away, but it feels like a year has passed. And I've come to understand that I don't have and never had the right to hold on to your memory. It was all just for my own egotistic satisfaction, to have you as a belonging in my soul at my beck and call. I preferred to hold on to a ghost that was never going to grow or change, rather than give it back to you. I was acting like a child. At any rate, I've learned now that it's better to give your self back to you, and to give you the chance to exist as a complete person, even if it means risking my losing that piece of you that I was holding on to. It's worth it. For the sake of friendship." He didn't say anything in reply, but the warmth of his smile as he took her hand again was enough of an answer.

"Well," she said, pulling away from him and standing up. "I guess it's time to go ahead and get started at it."

"What do you want me to do?" he asked.

She shrugged. "That's the problem. I don't know exactly how to do it. I mean, the Master just looked into my eyes, and all my life just seemed to pour out of him and into me. But I don't know what he did."

"Let's give that a try." He stood up beside her, adjusting the height of his body so as to be level with her. And she tried. She concentrated, drawing up every scrap of his being she could locate and tried to force it across the distance between their faces by willpower.

Nothing.

He couldn't hide a flood of exasperation. "Now what? Are you sure that's all he did? Is there anything he might have said which might unlock things?"

"Um, now that I'm thinking back about it, he did. When he stood me up to meet his gaze, he gave out in that big booming voice of his, 'Your name is Elizabeth,' and then it all just erupted. Maybe we could try that." She felt a certain reluctance at this point. His name was one of the closest and deepest secrets she had kept of him, and she was resentful, now that she had to finally give it back. She steeled herself, and looked back into his face, and intoned: "Your name, your real name, is Carlos."

Carlos... There. She had done it. She had given him his true identity at last. He looked eager for a second after he heard it, and then he concentrated, plumbing his depths for any association which might arise out of that name. Elizabeth didn't try to force the memories from herself to him this time. She tried to make them slide out softly, gently, naturally. But once more, there was no result.

"Carlos," he muttered, and shook his head. "There's this tiny flicker in the deepest part of my soul, and it's saying that that's the right name... But I can't get anything else."

"Damn and double damn!" Elizabeth exclaimed, kicking over a chair. "I finally get myself ready to give you up, and then I can't even figure out how to do it! It's just not fair!" She sat on another chair and sulked.

16.

Carlos stood over Elizabeth, watching her sob with a concerned expression. He was still running that name through the currents of his mind, still trying to make its acquaintance. He allowed the name to slide in and out and around the membranes of his brain in the same way that one slides a delicacy around one's tongue. It was difficult for him to appreciate her anguish at this moment, when he was savoring his own discovery. But an idea kept coming back to him, time and again, despite his every effort to resist it.

Elizabeth pulled herself together. "Well, I've tried my best," she said. "I've given you all I can. I suppose that you're just going to have to make do with it. I know it'll be hard for you, but just think, with all the endless centuries in front of you, you're certain to find a million new memories."

"I know that. But somehow, it isn't the same. It feels like I'm having to be like an adult, without ever having had the experiences of childhood."

"But I've tried! Don't pester me! I haven't heard you making any useful suggestions!"

Carlos frowned as his anger welled up. "I've thought of another way. But I wasn't going to even bring it up. I was going to forget it, just for your sake."

"For God's sake, tell me then!"

"All right, I will, because you insist. You've been harping on and on about the way the Master gave you your memories. We've seen how that won't work for us. I suppose that we can conclude that it's a special ability that only he has, like the ability to bring us to life at all. But you know that's not the only way for us to share memories."

He paused dramatically, and she impatiently urged him to continue.

"I can take the memories from you in the same way you took them from me, in the first place."

Elizabeth looked blank for only a moment, until she began to realize exactly what was his meaning. Her eyes widened. "No, I won't do that for you. I won't sacrifice my entire existence just for your sake. You can't ask me to do that much. It'd make you no better than me."

"I haven't asked you to destroy yourself for me. It was only something that occurred to me, and you insisted on me telling you about it."

There was a pause as they both weighed what had been said, and the consequences. Elizabeth's mind was reeling at his suggestion. The very fact that it would occur to him was a source of alarm. She almost subconsciously began to construct internal fortifications, in case he tried to attack her. She could feel him doing the same in response. If it came to open hostilities, she was certain that she was the stronger, and could defeat him. Destroy him again. But Heaven help her if she was forced to kill her only friend....

"I wouldn't try what you're thinking of doing..." she warned.

"I don't see why you have any more right to my memories than I," he replied with a growl, and took a short step in her direction.

No escape. Again. Again she was being forced to destroy, to consume, when that was the last thing she desired. The way of the undead: eternal violence, destruction without cessation. Charity was an act for humans and for humans alone....

And then Elizabeth stopped and laughed.

Carlos looked puzzled, suspicious for a moment that she was attempting some subterfuge. But there was no rancor, no trick to her mirth. She laughed on and on, falling into a chair. She was helpless. He could take her without a struggle at this moment, if he wished. But he didn't wish that. He wanted to know what she was finding so funny.

"I know it," she said in gasps between spasms of renewed mirth. "I know the answer! And it's so easy! It's terrible, a crime, the way the Master has perverted us, the way we've perverted ourselves. When the solution is staring us right in the face!"

"I don't get it."

She cleared her throat to calm herself down. "We've been programmed. All the vampires have been. The first thing we always think of is to take, to destroy, to satisfy ourselves first. Even the ones who think that they're doing something for someone else are fooling themselves. Una, Diana, Jonathan: they talk about trying to help one another, or the world at large, but their actions are still nothing but take, take, consume, consume.

"Yes, I drained you dry. I took your memories and your soul, and I still have them. And you can attack me to try to steal them back by force. But you don't have to. We are both vampires. We can share. You take of my blood, and I take of your blood, at the same time. Together. We'll mingle the memory. share each other's soul. We can become like one being." And she reached out, and gently caressed his hand.

He grasped that hand and held it tight. "Yes, yes," he murmured, allowing a flood of affection and rightfulness to roll through his heart. "It's the only way. We'll show them all. We'll become something new, something that hasn't ever been seen before in the world of the vampires. A new being. Better than the others. We'll be stronger. But that's not the important thing. Better, because we're rising above the bloodshed, turning away from death. We'll be, it'll be as if we were *alive* again." He took her hand, and drew it up to his mouth, and softly he kissed it.

And his mouth pressed against her undead flesh, harder and harder, and then lovingly he bit into it.

She reached for him, bringing his neck close to her face, and she too bit.

Her blood entered into his body, and simultaneously his entered into hers. They stepped closer, so that each could bite into each other's throat. Carlos reeled in the discovery of himself, and more: he was also feeding on the memories of every human she had consumed, making them one with himself in the same way they were one with her. And more: softly and serenely, her own soul was pouring into his, blending, merging, interweaving. He tasted the entirety of Elizabeth, and she tasted the whole of Carlos. And they were jointly surprised, to find unfamiliar reactions beginning to happen, a frantic excitement which grew between them, feeding off one another and reflecting back on itself. An excitement unlike anything they had known as vampires.

Sex had never been a vitally important aspect of Elizabeth's being while she was a living creature. She had obtained a degree of pleasure now and again, and it had served as another of her many methods of escaping from her life-long ennui; she had always found it too messy, both in the physical act itself and in the emotional complications which inevitably arose in the aftermath. Enjoyable, but too convoluted to devote more than a token of her time and energy.

Elizabeth had been almost glad to discover that the vampires were largely asexual beings: they possessed the appearance of male and female, but little of their behavior was derived from this distinction. Claire had played at seduction, but the goal was blood, not passion. Deborah mourned the loss of her child, but the destruction of her Rebecca had become a symbol of her self-immolation, not an indication of her withered fertility. Phil's machismo was nothing but braggadocio; the sex act was no longer a possibility for the undead. The Master alone still possessed more than the trapping of sexuality. He was dominant in every relationship. His was the fertile bite, the touch which brought them forth from the grave. He was the eternal chauvinistic masculine which rendered all the others, whether male or female in appearance, feminine in relation to him.

But for Carlos, sex was a mystery, among all the other mysteries of his mortal life. As he felt the lack of all the other aspects of himself, he felt his masculinity like the phantom pain of a severed limb. Now, he struggled with an overwhelming rush of sensations, flooding his mind and his soul. Together, they dissolved the constraints of clothing, and their hands reached out for each other.

They stepped closer. Carlos allowed his teeth to withdraw from her, and Elizabeth likewise pulled back from his throat. He grinned in embarrassment at his deepening physical reaction, and she felt a deep-seated thrill to see the glistening blood on his teeth: her blood, entering into his body for his nourishment. She kissed him hard, and her mouth filled with the taste of herself, a taste of iron and her own memories reflecting back from him to her.

They stepped closer yet. His blood was in her, spreading warmth to her cold body, her sleek thighs, her small lithe breasts. His hands spread the warmth to each spot they caressed. Her blood was in him, bringing vigor, a surging, a swelling.

She ran her lips down his torso, his expansive chest, his muscular flank. Each kiss was a fiery new bite, setting the flame to his flesh. Blood spewing out to meet her tongue. The blood returned to him with his own nuzzling of her body. The sharp nails of his hands raked the skin of her back as he brought her even closer into his embrace.

Teeth penetrated simultaneously with flesh. Motion against each other. Their bodies dissolved back and forth, into mist and returning into solid form, faster and faster with their rhythm. With the rising tide of excitement.

One being, in spirit as well as body. Like the merging with the other vampires which Elizabeth had experienced before (and which Carlos was now experiencing within the crucible of her memories, in a much more than vicarious fashion, sharing and knowing all of her being, thought and soul), but infinitely better: not a subjugation of self to common purpose, but a transcendence of self to encompass all the world. Waves of their ecstatic synergy radiated out over the city. A million mortals stirred in their restless slumber and plunged joyfully into dreams of bliss and serenity. The scattered active minds of the vampires in their individual pursuits paused in bafflement to feel this new sensation, not unlike their union but unique to their knowledge. Diana took a deep breath of desert air to taste fully of the sweet jubilation far beyond the possibilities of her austerity. Gregory gnashed his teeth to resist the tide of selflessness that threatened his egocentric equanimity. Deborah cried in consternation to experience a moment of forgiveness, and Stephen cried with joy to feel a second of completion. And somewhere, in some hidden corner, the Master felt the touch of their pleasure, and smiled an enigmatic smile.

The ecstacy was rushing forward to a peak, a crescendo, spiralling inward into a tighter and tighter ball of hot excitement. A glowing Sun searing inside their panting bodies yet bringing renewal and not destruction. Red blood surging. Uncontrollable. Teeth piercing to the heart of flesh to rend the inner linings of their souls. Faster. Tighter. Thrusting. Blood pouring out and inward again. Eruption....

Awareness returning to their bodies, pouring with crimson sweat. They smiled, and they were one.

17.

Elizabeth was the first to recover from their passion, and softly she disentangled arms and teeth and minds and mist. She stood up, stretching her body, this flesh which finally knew the purpose of its resurrection. She giggled a little, seeing the room in disarray around them.

And then she paused as a light filled her eyes. She looked up through the window to see the Moon, nearly full, emerging from behind the clouds as it approached its setting. Vast and lovely. She could appreciate the power it had held over the primitive minds of the mortals throughout their history, their glorification of it as the symbol of the feminine principle. She bowed her head to it in acknowledgement.

And then it was that she realized that the pain was gone.

"Carlos! Carlos!" she shouted as she shook him from his reverie. "Can you feel it?"

"What?" he replied in a daze. "I don't feel anything."

"That's it! That's just it! The pain! The hunger! It's gone! As if it never was."

He hesitated, plumbing into the depths of his being to see for himself. At last, he said slowly and triumphantly, "Yes... Yes, you're right!" He reached out to embrace her again.

"We've done it," she said, smiling out at the world. "We've won. We've conquered the beast inside us, once and for all."

"We've shown the way for all the others. We've found the fruit of immortality without destruction."

Elizabeth pulled away from his arms again, to look out at the skyscrapers of the city. The city that slept on, unaware of their triumph, the birth of this new and transcendent being that had come into existence in its midst. But she didn't feel rancor. She felt no anger. They had outgrown the negative principle. They had defeated the Master and Jonathan and that final inevitable choice, of death or mindlessness.

They were free.

NOCTIS IRAE

1.

The world was a magical place. Infinite possibilities lay in every moment, and they could never fully explore every potential which might occur to them. Each word, each action was a new adventure, since it was to be shared between them, shared in their exciting new, spiritual way which was infinitely deeper and more exquisite than that which was known by mortal lovers.

Elizabeth and Carlos set spells to radiate outward from their refuge in the old abandoned factory, but the glamours were unlike the illusions of terror and destruction which the other vampires used to protect themselves from unwanted human intruders. Instead, they created spells of enchantment, which lured those who fell under them in the contemplation of the beauty of the spider web in front of them, or the grandeur of the decaying buildings, or the subtle wonder of the fugitive blades of grass thrusting tenuously along the cracked concrete. These spells were a delight for the mortals, but too intense for any of them to experience more than once, and thus the lovers maintained their privacy without having to resort to fear.

The effects of their spell spread over a widening area of the city as each day passed, bringing calm and good fellowship among the mortals, to a degree which hadn't existed in the city for decades. Those among the mortals who made their livelihood by observing their social and political developments were astonished, and generated mountains of commentary about this unusual spring of contentment. Tempers were long, crimes of violence and anger were far less in number than was normal. The one fact which didn't seem to jibe with the rest was the abnormally high numbers of deaths by accident and disease which were reported. The true cause of this, unknown to the mortals of course, was the activity of other members of the undead community. They also felt the peculiar lightness and happiness in the air, and were disturbed by it. To alleviate their discomfort they were increasing the number of humans they took.

Carlos and Elizabeth were little aware of this. They felt very far in distance from their old methods of maintaining their existence. They were a perpetual motion machine unto themselves, requiring no energy from outside. They felt no hurry to inform the others of their wonderful discovery. They had too many other interests.

As close as they had become, very nearly a single being, (although they kept their individual forms and personalities) they still had occasional disagreements, which as often as not led to quarrels. This was the strangest thing they discovered: within minutes of the beginning of their anger, the pain gradually, but inevitably, returned. If the fight lasted more than an hour, they found themselves compelled by the old drive, to go out and find blood. This in itself tended to cut short any dispute. But once they were reconciled, and shared their spiritual intimacy once more, they returned again to their state of grace.

And ah, those reconciliations... The taste of each other's blood never palled on them, their appetite was voracious, their imagination infinite. Having absolute control over physical forms, they explored any possibility which was conceivable to either of them. With their sharing of one another's soul, there were no secrets hidden. Carlos knew every fantasy which had ever come to Elizabeth, and she knew every wish he had ever made. The sexual act had infinite expression, infinite variation as long as the blood flowed between them. Elizabeth proved to be the one who was insatiable in her curiosity, eager to explore greater degrees of originality and peculiarity in their amusements. Never having experienced a satisfactory sexual relationship during her tenure as a human, she was delighted to discover the astonishing range of expressions which were now possible to them in their intimacies. Carlos, on the other hand, relished simplicity, the directness of communion which they shared in passion devoid of complex gymnastic maneuvers and questionable techniques. Yet the union of spirit which they had together was such that he too could delight in the ecstasy of the unusual, and she too could cherish the vigor of the commonplace. They were happy together.

One night Carlos began to speculate about their new nature. "You know, it seems to me," he said to Elizabeth, cradled in his arms, "since we're no longer vampires in the strict sense of the word, we shouldn't have any of the restrictions which the vampires have. I wonder if we have the power to control the flow of water now, or go out into the light of the Sun."

Elizabeth came awake with a shock, stiffening in his grip. "What? The Sun?" A deep fear struck through her.

He smiled reassuringly. "Why not? We aren't under the power of the Moon any longer. It doesn't hurt us any more. And Moonlight is nothing but the reflection of the Sunlight. So, I can't think of any logical reason for the Sun to be any more harmful than the Moon is to us now."

She frowned a little in reply. "Not very much of undeath has anything to do with logic. I'm trying to remember what the Master used to say about the Sun."

"I recall him telling us some sort of mystical mumbo-jumbo about the Sun trying to burn and destroy us in retribution for the harm we did on Earth by killing the mortals. But if we don't hurt the humans anymore, there wouldn't be any reason for the Sun to hate us. So, either way, by logic or non-logic, we should be safe in the daytime. I'm very seriously tempted to give my theory a try this very morning."

Carlos, who all along had been speaking somewhat flippantly, was surprised by the hysterical edge in Elizabeth's voice as she replied, "No! Promise me that you won't do it! I won't let you! By everything we mean to one another, I swear that I won't let you take that risk. You might be wrong. I don't think I could bear it, if you destroyed yourself. Stay in the night. Stay where it's safe. Here with me." And she drew him close to her, biting lovingly into his shoulder, so that he soon had no desire to be anywhere else in the world.

2.

The next evening, Elizabeth sprang up from the bed with a start. "Good God, how could I have forgotten?" Carlos opened one bleary eye. "Forgotten what?"

She rubbed his hair. "Carlos, honey, would you like to do something especially for me tonight?"

"Oh, oh. What am I in for this time?"

"Now have I ever asked you to do anything bad? At least, since we've gotten close to each other? Of course not. I'm hitting myself on the side of the head because of this. I don't know what's come over me. Ever since I met you, I can't seem to keep anything in my mind straight."

"My confidence is steadily growing less and less with each word you say without getting to the point."

"All right, all right. I just remembered my mother. I just got up and walked out on her, without a word of explanation. I meant to get our business over with for once and for all, and then I was going to go back, at least to tell her what happened. Goodness knows what she thinks must've happened to me... She must be worrying herself into the grave."

"Which is exactly what she wanted, if I recall your memories correctly."

"Don't be a smartass. This is serious. I have to go back. I feel responsible for her, ever since I found her at my grave. Even though she is just a human."

"It seems that you tend to adopt any old thing you happen to find mooning over your grave. OK, OK, I'll go with you!" he exclaimed, as she pinched a certain sensitive portion of his anatomy to help to convince him.

Later Carlos found himself having second thoughts. It was a fine night. Every night of this spring was fine, as their radiating waves of delight introduced moderating factors into the air flow of the city, but he was feeling increasing trepidation.

"I'm still not convinced that this is the right thing," he commented to Elizabeth, who was willfully swimming through the air, dragging him along behind. "I thought we had an understanding that we ought to keep our relationship to ourselves. I mean, I know she's your mother and all, and that, as a mortal, she isn't likely to be able to do anything which could threaten what we have together, but I just don't like the principle of the thing."

Elizabeth grimaced back at him, fighting to keep her good humor. The last thing she needed tonight of all nights was a fight. She needed to prove to her mother how good things were between them. "I'm not going to keep arguing about it. The decision is made. I'll take responsibility for anything that might happen, OK?"

"Well, I guess I have to come right out and say it, then. You ought to know it by now, since you have all my memories. I just don't get along with family very well. I've never been able to hit if off with the parents of anybody I've dated or lived with, and I'm just feeling a little nervous about this time, too."

Elizabeth paused to look back with concern. It was true, this was something she had learned along with all the contents of his mind and soul, but she hadn't given it a thought up to now. Too wrapped up in herself again, she thought deprecatingly. "Well, this is a bit different," she answered. "When we were alive, we had a much stronger connection with our parents. Usually, they were the ones who were supporting us, or at least they were there for us to fall back on if we needed them. But it isn't the same situation anymore. We're totally independent now. And even if my mother objects (which is something I can't really imagine her doing, myself), there's not a thing she can do to stop us."

"I understand what you're trying to say. I'm sorry that I didn't consider it before now. Still, this is something that's very important for me. I have to do it. And I'd feel a lot better if you came along with me. If you were there standing by me."

They landed and coalesced. "Are you sure that I have to come in with you?" Carlos asked. "Don't you think it might be better if I waited outside, maybe, just for a couple of minutes? Just until you're sure that she's in her best mood. I don't think a stranger ought to barge in when she might be eating dinner, or taking a bath, or whatever it is that the humans do when they're alone."

Elizabeth looked exasperated and sighed. "Oh, all right. If you insist. I guess we need to have you at your best, as well. You stay out here on the porch, while I go inside and talk to her for awhile. I'll come get you when I decide the time is right. Is that satisfactory to His Majesty?"

"Very much so, Your Ladyship," he nodded with a smile, and gave her a kiss of gratitude.

So Elizabeth knocked and went in, leaving Carlos outside. He sighed, shaking his shoulders to relieve the tension. The night air was sweet to his senses, thick with the odor of opening buds. Elizabeth's mother had a deadly touch with plants, but it didn't halt her from trying. The yard showed signs of many years of attempted cultivation, with little success. Carlos looked through the screen, at all the half-dead and dying trees and shrubbery, features which he had never seen personally, but which were real and dear to him, for they were important landmarks in Elizabeth's life. He saw an old and nearly-dead rosebush, where Elizabeth had cut her finger when she was five years old (the first shedding of her blood which she could remember, and thus an occurrence with great significance for her undead being). He saw the old knotty pine which she had first triumphantly climbed at seven, and the grassy yard where she had played badminton and croquet with her friends. Warm waves of nostalgia washed over him.

There was one element out of place. On the street in front of the house there was a fire hydrant. It was old and beat-up in appearance, with flaking paint. There was no such hydrant resident in Elizabeth's memory. It couldn't be new, not from its appearance. Carlos had a feeling that he shouldn't be doing this, but he couldn't resist the temptation to investigate further. The discrepancy troubled him. It'd only take a minute to walk out and take a closer look, and Elizabeth need never know.

He strode up to it, gave it a little kick. It was solid enough... He bent down to take a closer look. His brow furrowed. There was absolutely nothing out of the ordinary about it, except only for the fact of its presence in a location where it shouldn't be. He shrugged, decided that it was so unimportant to Elizabeth that she had never bothered to fashion any memory about it.

And then the cap popped off the hydrant, and, before he could react, an arm reached out, grabbed him, and drew him inside.

It was dark and cramped and stuffy. Carlos blindly lashed out at whatever was holding him, first with his fists, and them with his mind. No reaction.

Then a small glow appeared, revealing that he was bundled up in a cubicle, shrunken against his will into a tiny form which could fit inside the hydrant. He recognized his captor, spitting out his name in anger:

"Jonathan!"

"Hush, not so loud, my friend! Don't let them know we're here."

"I don't care who or what hears! All I want to know is what do you think you're trying to do! You don't know what you're letting yourself in for, trying to hold me captive like this! What's going on here? For that matter, how on Earth did you even know where to find me?"

"Please, please, I know that you're very close now to our common friend Elizabeth, and she and I have had our little disagreements in the past. Let me assure you, I'm doing this from the best possible motives. I wouldn't dare to presume on you and your relationship with her if it wasn't an absolute emergency!"

Carlos growled, but after a moment, he conjured up a chair and sat himself gruffly down in it. "All right, I'm listening. You have thirty seconds to talk, before I start getting violent. This had better be good."

"I think you might be surprised at the lack of results should you assay an attempt at breaking out of this place. I am older and stronger than you, friend Daniel."

"My name's not Daniel any more. I'm Carlos. Elizabeth told me that, among many other things. Your seconds are ticking away."

"Carlos, very good. Well, then to be brief, I had to grab you off the street as soon as I realized your identity, because you are in terrible danger. Both you and Elizabeth."

"My impression is that the only danger which either of us could face would be from the other vampires. Which means, since you're their admitted leader, then the only danger is you."

"Ah, you're hitting it almost right on the head. Yes, it's the others. They're canvassing the entire city, all night and every night, looking everywhere for the two of you. You've done a superb job of hiding yourselves, I must admit. We can feel the impulses flowing from your sexual pleasure. Don't look at me like that, it's obvious, they're flowing all over the city, we just couldn't identify the location from which they radiate. The others have turned on me. They knew that I was aware of almost everything that happened throughout the city. They tried to compel me to give them any sort of information which might aid them.

"That's when I rebelled. I fled. I hid. Because I knew the information they sought. I knew that Elizabeth came here to live with her mother, and I was certain that sooner or later she would bring you back here with her. So I made this tiny refuge, with every scrap of skill which I possess, to be small and unnoticeable, so they wouldn't find me, but discordant with Elizabeth's memory, hoping that one or the other of you would notice. It's been a *vile* time for me. I'm afraid to leave here. All the blood I've had, for some nights now, is that of the stray dogs I've been able to lure here to me."

Jonathan was starting to shake, and his usually suave and calm voice was beginning to waver, "You know all about Guillaume, don't you? Of course you must, she's told you everything. My only care, my own darling one, my little Guillaume... They broke into my rooms. They took him. They have him now. They've been sending out threats, broadcast mentally all over the city. They say the terrible things they're doing to him, and the worse things they're going to do, if I don't go back to them. If I don't help them. But I can't. I won't go back, no matter what they do."

Carlos was puzzled. Jonathan was the first vampire who had befriended him. But Elizabeth had instilled a distrust in him now. Could he believe anything which he was being told now? "But why, what's going on? Why do they want us, why are they going to such lengths to catch us? What's going to happen if they do?"

"It's the *end*. The end of everything. But don't misunderstand me. It's not Elizabeth that they want. It's all part of the plan, his plan, to have her free and hunting and enraged. It's you they're after. You're the key, you're the last one he made, and you're the one who..." He stopped short, and his face was engulfed in terror. "Oh, by all the powers that still exist! I see it now! How could I have been so blind! They let me go, but put a hidden tracer on me, knowing that I'd lead them to you! They're coming! You must run! You must hide! Now!"

And as sudden as thought, Jonathan vanished, along with his refuge, and Carlos found himself squatting uncomfortably on the sidewalk in front of Elizabeth's mother's house. He jumped up in alarm, looking around for the attack.

And faster than thought, there zoomed toward him a tiny form like an insect. The form of Alicia, in her compact shape which could penetrate and take control of any other being. She shot to him, and into his flesh.

3.

Elizabeth entered her mother's house.

Her mother was sewing and watching television. She leapt up, startled. "Oh, Elizabeth! You've come back!" Elizabeth felt herself melt with affection. "Yes, mother, I'm back. For just a little while."

"Oh, nonsense. My girl is back again, back from all her traipsing and running around, back to rest here where she knows she's going to be safe." She gave Elizabeth a friendly hug, but Elizabeth could detect tension in her arms.

She pushed her gently away. "Sit down, mother, sit back down. There's an awful lot to talk about."

"Yes, of course. To start with, you can tell me why you had to run away without so much as a goodbye that last night. If I didn't know better, I'd have thought you were trying to put me into my grave."

Elizabeth felt abashed. "Well, I guess I have to apologize for my behavior that night. I was just so excited by the decision I had made. But I don't apologize for going away, because that was the best and the most intelligent decision I've ever made in my existence."

"Go on."

But she wasn't sure of how to go on. How do mothers do this? she wondered to herself. She had prepared a speech to make, but with a couple of words, her mother had reduced her back to the condition of a stuttering teenager again. "The best way to start, I suppose, is to tell you that you were right all along. About him. The one who was calling himself Daniel back then. What I was doing was suppressing my true feelings for him. I thought I was angry and hurt at him, but I know now that I was really feeling: *attraction* for him."

Her mother nodded again, but with an increasingly severe expression.

"So what I had to run off and do in such a hurry, was to go find him. To talk to him, at last. To figure out what we were going to mean to each other. And that's what we've done. We're together now. We're happy. But why are you frowning like that?"

"Oh, it's not anything important. I was just thinking about the things that are going on in between the words you're saying. I suppose you vampires don't have any concern for the way old women like me think about morals and values and suchlike. For what's right and what's wrong for men and women together, even if they don't happen to be alive anymore."

Elizabeth felt outrage bubbling up inside her. "Now what's the matter with you now? You were the one who was encouraging me to go see him from the start!"

"Going to see him isn't the same thing as going to bed with him, in my book."

"You don't understand anything, or you would know better than to say such stupid things! We've found something wonderful together, something more real and important than anything else in the world, and you're trying to make it sound like it's something filthy!"

"Nothing ever changes, dear. I can remember hearing the same sort of talk when I was a youngster. I didn't grow up in a convent, you know. There was more than one boy who filled up my ears with talk about doing something more real and important than anything in the world, while his hands were saying all sorts of other things. I could see through that. I'm sorry if I failed to raise you with the same sort of sense."

"I'm not going to let myself get mad! I don't want to ruin this night of all nights!" Elizabeth forced herself to take several deep breaths. "OK, I think I understand where you're coming from. I know what it must sound like, the things I'm talking about. All right. But there's just one thing you're forgetting, mother. I know that I look like and sound like any normal young woman, but *I am not human*. You can't judge me by the rules that are there for mortals. Your morality falls apart, when you try to apply it to me."

Her mother also took a long breath. "I'm trying. It's just something else that's completely new, something that's coming up on me totally unexpected. I think that I might have anticipated almost anything else than this from you, by now. I've just always thought so highly about you, that you were such a perfect lady, that you would never go out and do something like this."

"I've got a little bit of news for you, mother. This sort of thing wasn't all that strange for me even back when I was alive. But that's all long ago in the past for me now. The relationships I had when I lived are like shadows compared to this. Like a mouthful of sand compared to a bloody, I mean juicy, piece of steak. That's because it's not something physical. Well, there's a physical aspect to it, but with us vampires, we share more than just the body. We exchange everything we have inside us. We know all of each other's memories, all our dreams, all our thoughts, all our entire existence. Carlos, that's his real name, incidentally, Carlos, knows me better than anybody on

Earth, now. He knows you better than any of your friends, because he knows every single thing I know."

"Everything?"

"Yes, mother."

"Hmm. I'm beginning to think that I might've preferred a more normal sort of relationship for my daughter, after all."

Elizabeth smiled. "Too bad. That's the way it is."

And her mother laughed, although a little bit stiffly, maybe. "But I don't suppose you could give a mother her greatest wish, to see her only daughter in a wedding gown, could you?"

"Well, if you really, really want it, we might manage something. But I'm going to have to wear a blood-red dress."

"I believe I might be having second thoughts, then. Well, I figure you must have him cooling his heels outside to have gone through all this rigmarole. Might as well bring this Carlos on in. He's not, um, a person of, er, *different nationality*, is he? I mean, with that name...."

"Frankly mother, I honestly don't know, and I couldn't care in the least if he was."

As she accompanied Elizabeth to the door, her mother paused and gestured for her to come close to listen. "You know," she said nearly in a whisper, "I think this might be better than the thing I was really afraid of, after all. I remember what you said to me, on the night you left. You said that you'd come back when my time was finished. So when I saw you come in the door, that's what I was more than half afraid of. So I'm glad. I know I wanted you to come and take me before the end, but not yet. I've realized that I want to hold on to this life for a little while longer."

Elizabeth patted her hand. "It's going to be all right now, mother. I'm not here to destroy you. This is going to be a time for happiness, for celebration." She stepped to the door. "Carlos? Honey? You can come in now. Carlos?"

No reply.

Elizabeth's immediate reaction was irritation. "All right, Carlos, a joke's a joke. But I want you to come in now," she said. "I know you were feeling a little reluctant to come meet my mother, but that's no excuse for acting like a child." But there was still no answer.

Then she began to experience the first sinews of fear. "Carlos? Aren't you there? Where have you gone? Can't you hear me?"

Her mother's voice was sarcastic. "I wonder if maybe the two of you weren't quite as close as you've been leading me to expect."

"Don't you dare say that! I can't imagine where he might have gone! What could have been so important? Carlos?" She looked around the yard for any kind of sign or message. Nothing.

"Elizabeth, maybe you ought to just come inside..."

"Shh! Let me think! I have to concentrate!" She began to focus herself. She and Carlos were one in body; her blood was his, and his blood was hers. They should therefore be able to detect traces of each other's presence for an extended period of time, Elizabeth reasoned. She plunged deeply into the portion of him which she contained. Touching his essence. Seeking to duplicate the path he would have taken.

She felt the traces. She felt the manner in which he stood on the porch, waiting just as she told him to do, before he was drawn away by something. She couldn't feel what. He had walked across the yard, just like this. She followed the trail like a hunting dog. Like a bloodhound: following his blood which called to her.

He had gone to the street. Then he stood again, for awhile. And then nothing. It was as if he had ceased to exist. At least exist as a part of her.

Now Elizabeth had to increase her concentration still further, probing even deeper. Piercing any spell of hiding, all glamours of deception.

Yes. There was the faintest reek of the undead. One, two. Two different vampires. Two vampires had met him, and then taken him away. Away from her.

And now the rage came over her, rising like a storm cloud out of her inner depths, consuming all care, all caution, from her being. Two vampires, and that meant the others. They were jealous of the two of them, envious of the love and splendor which they had attained together. But she would show them now. They would feel the bite of the vampire scorned.

She had just kept control enough of herself to call back to her mother, as she began to rise into the air, "They've taken him away! You'd better get inside, mother! It might not be safe to be outside in the city tonight, when I catch up with them!" And she shot into the air, sleek, jet-powered, slicing across the city in a thought.

The vampire condominium. She beheld it in her mind's eye, like a target sighted between the crosshairs. She was strong, stronger than the lot of them put together. She was a missile, hurling through the skies of the city on target. She'd tear their building apart, if they tried to keep him from her.

She arrived in a moment and then stopped short, mindful of traps or safeguards. She reigned in her anger for just a few more seconds, to probe the building and its inhabitants.

It was empty.

They were gone. They had taken her darling, her Carlos, and, fearful of her just and unstoppable vengeance, they had hidden themselves, hidden in some dank hole like worms. Like vampires hiding from her angry and purifying Sunlight. Sunlight. The Sun was inside her now, the Sun which she and Carlos had kindled together, flared into hot fury now, and flew out of her mouth like dragon-fire, smashing through all the sorcerous protection surrounding the building, irresistible, reducing it to ruins. And she tore into the building, with hands and with spirit, ripping it apart brick from brick, looking in every rat hole, for the slightest traces. But she found nothing, no hint that the undead had ever even resided there. Even Guillaume was gone, the one whom traitorous Jonathan sought to hide and protect. She had failed.

Elizabeth sat in the rubble of the condominium, oblivious to the bleating cries of outraged and fearful mortals beginning to gather, and the sound of approaching sirens. She contemplated the city with its thousands of buildings, tens of thousand of hide-holes. How could she find them? How could she ever get Carlos back again? Even assuming they were still in the city at all... She shook, and there appeared the first of her red tears.

The Moon appeared from behind the clouds, and the hunger set in.

The hunger, the pain, the force of undeath. The lust which was never still, save only for a moment in the rush of living blood. The hunger which she and Carlos had banished, but only by being together and sharing their love and passion. Now he was gone and the hunger was back, like an old lover returning to claim her as soon as her new love was absent.

Elizabeth arose, in the form of mist, spreading over the ruined building, and over the curious crowd, and further, without diffusing; she spread her substance over the entirety of the block, the neighborhood, and finally over the whole city. The hunger demanded an offering. She had to answer it.

She gathered her anger, and feeding it to the hungry pain, allowed it to be unleashed over the city. The aura of peace and tranquility which she had broadcast along with Carlos shattered like a pane of glass. A million mortals suddenly perceived the worthlessness of their living days. Automobiles were consciously crashed into walls. Buildings were set afire. Knives and bullets pierced flesh, the flesh of those who wielded them, and the flesh of those around them. Wealthy businessmen wrecked their offices. Men of God took razors to their wrists. The streets filled with raging humans, marching, rioting, without any reason or sense of purpose, smashing windows, looting and attacking one another at random. Mortal authority ceased to exist, for their representatives were among the leaders of the mobs. Above the city, a dense, raging cloud developed, the physical manifestation of Elizabeth's seething agony. She sought to seal the Moon behind it, to keep it away from her with its unclean radiations; to no effect. She knew it was still there, riding high in the heavens unaffected by her petty rage, and that knowledge only increased the anger and the hunger all the more.

Within the cloud, but more than the cloud, within the city, but more than the city, within the fires of rage and despair, but more than the rage and despair and hunger and pain, Elizabeth flowed through and transcended all in her elemental fury. She fed on it all, on all the city's rage, all the city's lives pouring out as a libation to her hurtfulness. She was now the city in its entirety, and she as the city was crying out in her loneliness. Yet still, nowhere could she touch the essence of Carlos, or any of the other vampires who existed in the city. They were invisible.

Then a voice spoke to her as she brooded stormily over the city, a familiar voice which rang out in titanic ringing tones in her mind rather than actual sounds, saying, "Very good, Elizabeth. You're very much my child, and I'm well-pleased. Look down now, and you'll find what you're looking for."

And it was as if a veil was drawn away before her, opening a portion of the city below where she levitated. There, in an open park, she could see the tiny figures standing, looking back up at her. And in the position of honor and leadership among them, she beheld the form of the Master.

4.

Elizabeth slowly and cautiously descended from her perch above the city, bringing herself into a solid frame. She felt herself to be travelling down a grooved path through the air, a path which led her to a position in front of the Master, as he sat triumphantly upon an elevated throne. Once she landed, she wasted no time on thought, but launched her will viciously at him, concentrating her strength in the manner in which she had reduced his form to ashes, all those months ago. But the Master brushed her effort off with barely any effort, and his mouth stretched to emit his laughter. "You attacked me once, Elizabeth, and you managed to crush me. My plans weren't entirely ready yet, and I was holding back my strength, to keep any of you from suspecting the truth. This night everything is ready, everything I've thought about and dreamed about for more centuries than you can even count. You aren't going to defeat me, never again. You really thought that you could overcome me with your tiny little spells and your measly little will? Didn't it ever occur to you that I was only *playing* with you, like an adult makes believe his children have him pinned down? Look around, see how all the others have finally given up their silly rebellion against me: look at how they adore me. They realize now, all of them except only for Jonathan, and there'll be time to deal with him later. They know there is nothing to being a vampire, nothing outside of *myself*, only what I graciously decide to share with you. The sooner you figure the same thing out, Elizabeth, the sooner you can all accomplish your assignment."

The Master gestured, and Elizabeth's gaze followed, to see those who stood gathered behind him. At his right hand was Philip, with a heavy keyring at his waist, and she felt disgust to see the blind adulation that was in his eyes as he stared up at the Master. Behind and below him, she saw the others, looking not entirely worshipful maybe, but compelled to follow his will: Gregory and Deborah and Diana; Stephen and Claire and Charles. Missing were Una, Alicia and Jonathan. Elizabeth wondered briefly about those absences. But behind the vampires whom she knew, Elizabeth saw a horde a figures which were strange to her, hundreds at least: blank faces with eyes betraying emptiness. The vacuum which Elizabeth had absorbed called out to them in fellowship, and she knew that the Master now controlled even the mindless vampires, and she quailed to discover their vast number.

Again the Master laughed, seeing her discomfort and growing fear. Above them, the clouds which Elizabeth had stirred continued to roil and threaten. "So, you've finally decided to be reasonable. You realize, of course, that with a snap of my fingers, I could unleash the horde of the mindless, savage vampires behind me, and allow them to tear you to shreds. I see you blushing, and yes, I know about your secret little battle with one of my children, and how he's now carefully tucked away in a little pocket in your soul. Do you now truly understand the extent of my might, that I have *millions* of the feral ones completely under my command, holding them at bay at this very moment? They're my army. These other vampires, the ones who still hold on to their minds and their souls, they're my honor guard. This one who calls himself Philip, at my right hand, is my sergeant-at-arms, and my jailor; he's taking the place of the one who would have held that honor, before he rebelled against me, the one who names himself Jonathan." He almost spat out the name in his disdain.

But Elizabeth still resisted him. "But where's Carlos? I know that you must have him. Let him go, and I'll do whatever you demand of me."

For a third time the Master boomed his laughter. "Even despite all this power and glory I'm flashing before your face, your spirit is still undaunted. You please me, child; because I'm not looking for another broken-down slave kneeling at my feet... You're ready, ready for the purpose for which I created you, which I programmed into your heart the night I brought you back from the dead. You are the special vessel, the instrument of my final purpose. Let the one she wants be brought forth!" he barked in commandment. Philip immediately reached into his garment, and withdrew a small box. He opened it, and it expanded to become a barred doorway, to which Philip possessed the key. Then, Carlos slowly emerged from the dark cell behind the door. Elizabeth almost cried out and rushed to him, but she paused when she saw that his eyes were dull and powerless; she recognized that his mind was possessed by Alicia, ridden like a broken nag.

"He's still in good health, I assure you of that," the Master spoke, although without any hint of compassion. "My servant Alicia is in control of him. And you will remember the nature of her power, how she keeps control of her victims by means of their own blood. If he should struggle or resist, she consumes a little bit of his essence, which is also your own essence. It's only with great difficulty that we are restraining her from eagerly consuming him down to the last dregs, in her seething hatred for the two of you. I therefore recommend that you not attempt any foolish actions."

Elizabeth felt herself deflate, and her voice was weak and wearied, "All right, you've won. What is it that you want me to do?"

"Why, the only thing I want is for you to do precisely what you are already doing."

5.

In answer to her look of puzzlement, the Master continued to speak in magnanimous fashion, "I see that you still don't understand.

Climb up on the dais, and stand here with me, and I'll finally let you see everything which has been kept hidden up to now."

Elizabeth struggled to climb the stairs. She seemed to be losing vitality with every step she took towards him. His vampiric power drew all strength into him, leaving all others empty and desolate. Obeying his command, she halted in front of his throne. The Master stood, and turned her head so that it faced outward. "Look at them," he bade her, pointing down at the undead host which was gathering around them. "You see the work I've been slaving at for centuries gathered all together for the first time. I've created every one of these vampires who mill around us, and every one is now under my authority. There's enough hungry pain here to empty every mortal in this city. And you need to know now, that this very scene is being duplicated in every human city on the night side of the Earth. Didn't it ever occur to you how strange the coincidence that I, the all-powerful Master of all vampires, would so honor you with my glorious presence in this city for so many years? You see, I am *myriad*. There are a thousand Masters standing in front of a thousand hosts all across this entire hemisphere, and a thousand others are waiting only for nightfall on the other side of the globe, to summon another thousand armies to them. And in each of these two thousand places, we have chosen out of the horde one *special* vampire, one who will be the instrument, the one who will execute the great plan of wrath and vengeance."

Elizabeth looked back at him in surprise, and he continued with a smile. "Oh yes, you too are not unique, you most precious of all my children. When I knew the time was approaching, I in my many bodies each picked out one individual, whom I revived in the usual fashion, but in each I placed a seed, a seed of discontent. You were fated to reject me, and then to reject all the other vampires, Elizabeth. Nothing on Earth was to provide you with contentment, except for the *second* chosen one. It was fun; I made a hundred variations on the relationship which was to be your destiny. You found the thing the mortals call love, while others have encountered greed, or of envy, or of self-immolation, or any other behavior which happened to strike my fancy. And at last, in this past couple of nights, I began to tie the strings together: all over the world I acted to separate you, and all of your brothers and sisters elsewhere, from your chosen ones. To cause you hurt. To force you to brim over with rage. To make you stir up thick clouds of anger to hang heavily over all the cities of the world. And now you're primed to be the channel for the next step."

He turned to the crowd, and called out, "Let the one named Stephen come to me!" Stephen did so, and Elizabeth felt sorry to see the nakedness of the terror in his eyes. He was ready to surrender his memory, to become a mindless one in an instant, if the Master hadn't been holding on to his will. Instead, he made an awkward bow, and his voice broke in nervousness as he said, "I'm sorry, Master, for whatever I've done to offend you. I know I've said and thought some things maybe I shouldn't have. My project, my library and my special little world, maybe they were silly little ideas, but it was something that made me happy. You can understand that, can't you, Master? I suppose it's unseemly for me to grovel and beg for my life like this..."

"Nonsense," said the Master firmly, and took Stephen's hand. "I'm certainly not angry or disappointed in you. You have done *well*, Stephen. You too did my bidding, never realizing that you were doing so. It was my secret instruction to you, hidden in your mind when I brought you forth from the grave, to absorb every fact of this world you could find, to make a perfect collection and a flawless copy of the planet. You too had others in your quest, in every city. Be proud, because your performance has earned you a place of great honor." Stephen's face lit up like a star as he heard these words, until he looked as if he was ready to float away in total bliss. "But now your goal is achieved. Your collection is complete, as of this night. Stand here," and he positioned him on Elizabeth's left, placing her hand around his shoulder. "and spread your arms in front of you, and create for us all one final time your small world of wonder and contentment."

As Stephen did his bidding, the Master looked at Philip. "Now bring forth the withdrawn one." Philip took out another box, and opened it into a door, and from it he pulled out the floating form of Guillaume. The Master reached for him to give a caress, and spoke soothingly to the childlike body, "And here is the next piece of the puzzle. Jonathan spent so many decades caring for you, filling you with all knowledge of the undead. How he wept in his puzzlement, when you withdrew into this embryonic form! If he hadn't betrayed me, Jonathan would have learned tonight that you too were merely following your instructions. You and your brothers in all the other cities now contain a perfect copy of the vampiric world, just as Stephen and the other collectors contain the mortal world." By his will the Master guided the floating form to a position on Elizabeth's right, with her hand placed upon its flesh.

The Master returned his attention to Elizabeth, taking a stand behind her and reaching his arms to contact hers as they stretched between Guillaume and Stephen. She felt his cold breath on the nape of her neck, and his rolling voice was loud in her ears. "you, you are the *conduit*, Elizabeth. You extend now between the worlds of the mortals and of the undead. Touch them now, Elizabeth, touch them in the way you learned from your lover Carlos, the manner in which I secretly educated you on the night you came out of the grave." He put his power into her, and he forced her body to open gaping wound-like mouths in the palm of each hand, thrusting out like beaks, with sharp slavering fangs. She cried out in agony at his molding of her body, but he did not relent. He pressed her hands forward, causing them to bite into the throats of the others, Stephen on the left and Guillaume on the right. Stephen shivered sensually, pushing himself to make her bite deeper; Guillaume thrashed like a fish on a hook. She felt their essences flowing into her, a one-way path of thought and sensation entering in, but with no outlet back into them. Her soul distended with the unwanted memories. She was helpless to fight it, and the Master chuckled behind her head, knowing what she was feeling and enjoying it.

He spoke again, "Yes, it's good. They fill you up nearly to the bursting point, but not quite, not quite. You're sucking in their strength, and with every moment it makes you stronger and stronger. Still, it isn't enough." He looked once more to Philip. "Bring out the last prisoner."

He complied, and dragged forth Una. She was sullen and kept her eyes down to avoid the Master's gaze. He said sternly, "I don't feel the slightest trace of anger for you. You were only doing what you thought was intelligent. In doing that, your words were an attack on my royal prerogative. You were ultimately correct all along, knowing the night would come when I would return to claim you all. But you challenged my right of rule over the vampires; even now I can feel the smoldering hatred and rebellion you feel against me. In your tiny, microscopic fashion, you're a threat. So you are the first one who must be sacrificed now."

He brusquely pushed her against Elizabeth, saying, "Go on, here's more food for you." Una looked up just once into Elizabeth's eyes, begging for a moment's more existence, but Elizabeth was powerless under the Master's control. She bit her with her natural mouth. Yet even this wasn't enough for the Master's purpose, for he grasped Una's quivering body, and stretched it out like putty, to allow Guillaume and Stephen to bite into it also, which they did avidly, seeking blood and thought to replace what they were losing to Elizabeth.

It was a sacrilegious parody of the passionate merging Elizabeth had known with Carlos. She and Una and Guillaume and Stephen were forcibly brought into one, but it was the merger of the maggot with decaying flesh. Una melted into the three others, and they fought over her spirit like jackals, tearing it apart and leaving nothing behind. But even the portions which the others were taking was ultimately flowing back into Elizabeth, and she was swelling, swelling. Her mind was hemorrhaging. She couldn't hold in so much blood... The fabric of her being was coming apart at the seams....

"Yes!" the Master cried. "Now!"

She ruptured. A silvery red light poured out from the front of her being, the content of her soul and the beings of Una, Stephen and Guillaume, mingled together into a spongy shining mass, the raw material of their dreams. Ecstatic, the Master jumped in front of her, expanding his body into a giant form, so that he could take up this material in his hands.

He rose in the air with it, leaving only a thin umbilical cord behind stretching back to Elizabeth and the others. Above the glowering clouds he rose, into the bitter light of the mocking Moon, and higher still. At the same moment there his thousand other selves rose up, each bearing a similar mass of decanted blood and souls from every city of mortal lives. They began to merge, forming a greater and mightier being still, the Master at long last revealing his gargantuan and unimaginably potent true being. He was free of the atmosphere now, shaping the mass around himself as a spacesuit, with the trailing lines reaching back to the Earth to provide him with blood. Keeping in the shadow of the Earth's sphere to avoid the deadly touch of the Sun, he traversed the vacuum.

Thus he came to the Moon. How his hatred brooded over its cratered and pitted form. For a billion years it had floated over his head, curdling the stolen blood in his belly, denying him his rightful mastery over the night. A laughing dead face scorning his quest to purge the world of the filth of life. He had grown at long last the mightier, and his contemptuous spittle flew across the empty void to scorch and sizzle on its barren surface. With a flick of a hand, he could send it forth into deep space, never to trouble the undead night again.

But no, for powerful as he had become, there was still another object in the cosmos which was the mightier, and the Master needed the corpse of the Moon to aid him in his goal to defeat it. He did not cast the Moon away; instead, he took the dream-stuff and formed from it a vast net, which he looped around the globe of the Moon. The surface seared and consumed much of the net, but enough withstood the contact, enough for his needs.

And he began to drag the Moon inward.

Slow, slow, slow was the progress. The Earth turned, exposing cities to dawn, and drawing others into the darkness. This hour revealed the Master's purpose for drawing Elizabeth into anger, for the deep cloud cover remained, caught up in his titanic world-spanning spell. He would not allow the vampires respite through the day, although they felt the Sun tearing agonizingly at their bodies from above the clouds. His will impelled them, keeping them gathered in the open, where the heat roasted their flesh and the brightness melted their eyeballs. They were not even allowed to go out and seek blood to replenish themselves. Only Deborah prospered during the day, glorying in the sensation of a suffering more sublime than she could have ever imagined, and she danced a dance of jerking motions in front of the Master's empty throne.

And for Elizabeth, the agony was immeasurably heightened, as her being continued to flow, streaming outward and upward, up the umbilical cord into the sky. She had passed beyond consciousness of self and surroundings. She was nothing but a sucking wound that never lessened, never healed.

Outside the barrier of glamour, the world of the mortals came to a stop. The thickness of the clouds, and the glamour he cast over the humans' satellites, prevented them from the sight of the Master above the world, sparing them that vision which would have rent their minds into unending madness. But they knew that the unnatural had broken into their ordered and quiet lives. Prayers were raised. Wars slowed to a pause. Mortal souls looked within themselves for answers; they were denied. Had any of them been capable of guessing the unclean truth, their living wills might have been able still to halt the Master's course, but he was beyond their most horrendous imaginings.

The being of Una was soon utterly consumed, before the first day was passed. So next the command of the Master sent Charles forward, to proffer his throat before Elizabeth. He had retreated totally into his memories of beasthood, and had little consciousness to be drained. He lasted only a few hours. So third was Gregory. He resisted fruitlessly for a moment. He was large and fat, replete with a distended bellyful of lives, and he lasted for the rest of that day, and all of the second night. Next, Claire gave only a few minutes' sustenance, the hollowness of her dreams of the forgotten past providing little for Elizabeth and Stephen and Guillaume to devour.

Fifth was Diana. The remaining vampires cried out when they saw her begin her approach to the dais. She had been their glory, their crown: the one who had come closest to transcendence. And her reserves were strong. Her being lasted on and on, longer than any might have suspected, through the second night and all the second day, and still she continued to survive under Elizabeth's teeth into the third night. The final night.

Closer and closer the Moon was spiralling in towards the surface of the world, and those vampires who yet possessed minds would have vaporized if they could have seen it, two times, three times, four times its accustomed size in the heavens. Even in the darkness they could feel it, and they recoiled in their fear. What could the Master be doing? Why was he prolonging and increasing their agony? Did he want that accursed sphere to crash down upon their very heads?

But that was not the Master's goal. A fact there is of cosmology, that one world cannot smash intact into the body of another; gravity does not allow such a catastrophe. When a certain limit is reached, the smaller mass *fragments*. Like a crystal ball hit by a hammer, the Moon shattered, silent in the depth of the vacuum.

The fragments fell upon the Earth with destruction and fire, levelling the cities in an unstoppable apocalypse. Where they fell, the flames rose up to consume mortal flesh. Out of the fires there arose great smokes lifting into the upper airs, a dense mass, choking and poisonous. And thick.

Thick enough to wholly screen the radiations of the Sun.

The Master suddenly manifested himself before the surviving vampires as they lay weak and miserable on the ground. His might had protected them from direct hits by the fragments of the Moon, but the conflagration burned in the surrounding city, lighting the underside of the great cloud in gold and crimson. He was haggard, nigh to being drained of his own bottomless depth of strength by his three days of labor, but he boomed in triumph:

"Yes, yes, look! The plan is a success! The Moon, the most ancient enemy of us all, has been destroyed, and its remnants have been used to form a shield for us! The Sun will never sear the face of the Earth again!

"Now, at last, now is the moment of all our dreams! The humans are helpless, hiding in their deepest holes, but there's nowhere for them to escape from us now. There will never be another dawn to save them from us! The prophecy has been fulfilled! This is the eternal night! *The Night of Wrath is now!*"

6.

Carlos slowly tried to pick himself up off the ground, but he lacked the strength. So he crawled. Alicia had finally pulled her fungi-like tendrils out of his being, to join in the grand celebration of the triumph of the undead, but she had taken much; many memories were now lost beyond recovery. He crawled up the dais, to where Elizabeth lay.

She was dead. The last moments of the Master's spell had required an ultimate surge of power, and had totally consumed the dregs of what had been the beings of Diana, Stephen and Guillaume. And also of Elizabeth. Carlos bowed his head. He hadn't any liquid left within his body to create tears.

Refusing to give up, he leaned his head forward, put his throat against Elizabeth's mouth, and forced his skin against her teeth. They broke, but there were sharp edges enough to open his flesh, and a slow, weary trickle entered her mouth.

Her frame gave a spasm, and she bucked, trying to throw him away from her. He controlled his dead weight and stayed on top of her. Soon she had enough blood to regain consciousness, and she croaked bitterly, "God damn you, why couldn't you let me just finally die?"

It took him a moment to summon the strength to answer her. "But I love you."

"No, no. It's not love. It was never love. Didn't you hear a single word of what he told us? He was just manipulating us all along. He put the seed in my soul to find you, and the seed in you to find me. We weren't ever anything but breeding stock."

He shook his head a little bit, then paused until the dizziness went away. "I don't believe that. The little bit of your blood that's still in me doesn't believe it either. Sure, he's the one who made us come together, but we're the ones who brought our love into being. He's nothing but death. We made something that was alive. We were more than him, and we still are. If he's finished with us we can go and make something that can still be beyond him. We can't give up and let him conquer everything."

Elizabeth turned away to look at the dancing reflections of the fires in the skies. "But what can we do? He's won. He is in control of everything already. The entire Earth belongs to him now. He can step on us like insects."

"Think, love, the other vampires are still under his control. Every human they take is feeding him. Isn't there somebody, anybody, out there whom you'd want to save from his touch?"

Elizabeth managed an ugly grimace. "You had to find the one reason I can't refuse, you bastard. Yes. Yes, there is, and you know it."

7.

Neither Carlos nor Elizabeth possessed the strength for flight, but with each other's support they managed to pull themselves to their feet and stagger on their way. When they broke through the barrier created by the Master's power, they were appalled at the silence. Not silence as a lack of physical noise. The volume of brute sound was stunning: fires explosively igniting office buildings in chain reactions, discharges of lightning echoing thunderously among the clouds, hurricane winds roaring around broadcast towers whipped by the hungry firestorm. But there was no human sound. Their senses, which could detect the padding of kitten's feet across the length of the city, could hear no shriek of pain, no cry of fear, not even a murmured prayer of desperation. The city was empty of mortal life. Those who could flee had done so, seeking the hopeless dream of escape in the countryside. But the old, the infirm, those who were unable to flee, they too were gone. The Master had unleashed his legion of the feral ones, and the streets were thick with the fear emanating from them as they trod their random paths. Nothing living could evade them, not even the rats or insects. Elizabeth and Carlos were in considerable fear that they would themselves be attacked, but they in their shattered and fragmentary state were insufficient to attract attention. Their souls were like microbes. Even as they walked, however, they could feel the terror attenuating, the fear spreading thinner as it encompassed a wider circle. The mindless vampires were starting to move outward from the city.

Carlos whispered aloud his thought that their journey might already be futile. "We don't have any way of knowing if one of them might have found her. Or maybe she might have left. Or one of the falling rocks could have landed on her."

"No," Elizabeth replied with determination. "No, she's there. She's waiting, waiting for us. I know it. Don't you see, everything that's happened to either of us, ever since we were resurrected, has been foreordained. Predestined by the Master. We're still not really free, we're never going to be free. He's still the puppet-master, and we're still not doing anything other than what he programmed us to do. This is the next step he has set for us to follow. So I know that she has to be there, still alive for us."

As she was speaking a great flare shot upward in the distance behind them, and the ground convulsed. All remaining lights in the city went out. They climbed back to their feet and looked up to see a glowing cloud rising to join the other choking vapors. The fires had reached the nuclear plant to the east of the city, triggering an explosive meltdown. Yet another nail in the coffin of humanity.

The darkness closed in on them as they went on, both darkness in the physical sense as they passed further from the raging flames, and also in a more personal fashion, as their sense-net began to fade away. They were weakening. Probably several days had passed since they had begun their footsore journey, but with no Sun, no Moon, no stars, there was no timepiece by which they could judge. The Master had slain time, another victim of his slavering thirst for destruction. Carlos and Elizabeth shuffled through piles of leaves and petals rendered colorless by the shadows. The grass was withering and the trees were losing their springtime buds. Without the Sun, plant life was dying. Or maybe the mindless ones had grown so strong in their power that they were now suctioning off their sappy vitality.

At long last they arrived at the street and saw the house standing undamaged at the end of the block. The only house in which their flickering senses could detect the pulse of life remaining. Elizabeth smiled without any humor. "Just think," she said through cracked lips, "all of this, this whole thing, happened because we decided to come to this house. So few days ago. We two are the ones responsible for everything that's happened."

Carlos denied it, "No. They were looking for us everywhere. They would have found us, sooner or later. Probably it would've only been a few hours delayed. But it's like you said, this is the way everything had to be."

They made their way up the sidewalk to the porch, and Elizabeth halted. "I think I should go in by myself. She's never met you. This is going to be difficult enough as it is, and having you with me would probably make it worse."

Carlos nodded, but his face was concerned.

She brushed her hand softly against his cheek. "I know, I know what you're afraid of. I'm feeling the same way too. It feels like we're challenging fate again to have you stay out here. But I want you to promise me that you'll stay here, no matter what may come. I'll be back out as soon as I'm through, and then we'll have what we need to restore our strength."

He tried to laugh but the sound emerged sounding more like a choke. "Don't worry, I'm not going anywhere. I don't think I could even crawl across the yard by myself now. Go on. I'll be as safe here as anywhere else on Earth, now."

So Elizabeth opened the door and entered. Dark. Silent. Several days's worth of dust on the furniture. That was a bad sign. With an effort that made her wince, she concentrated her senses one more time, to look for her goal. In the basement. Of course.

She opened that door without a sound, and got down two steps. But she forgot about the creak in the third one. There was a hysterical cry from below, "Who's there?" and a weak battery light flashed into Elizabeth's face.

"Oh,' said her mother wearily, "it's you. At last. I've been expecting you." The light vanished and there was the sound of matches, and a couple of candles were lit, revealing her mother huddled under a tent of mattresses and cardboard boxes. Once more she had strewn the floor with her powdered garlic, and hung her crucifixes on the surrounding walls. But Elizabeth experienced no difficulties from the symbols. Her mother's faith was dead. "Come on down," she said emotionlessly.

Elizabeth came forward, to kneel in front of her mother. There was a pungent odor. A couple of little cries rang out, and the two cats peered suspiciously from behind the woman; seeing who the intruder was, they lost their fear and came forward to rub against Elizabeth. She was silent, fighting back tears as she listened to her mother's rambling words. "Come closer, let me get a good look at you. You look like living sin. Your hair's a rat's nest, and you look like you haven't had a bite to eat in a week. Isn't that man of yours treating you all right? I'd have thought the two of you were having the time of your lives, or whatever it is you'd call it, with the things that've been going on. I'd offer you some tea or a piece of cake, but I seem to have run short."

She didn't appear to be in a state of full consciousness as she continued to speak emotionlessly. "You never really knew your grandmother, my mother. Her name was Elizabeth, we named you after her. She passed away when you were just a baby. People didn't live as long back then as they do now. You look so much like pictures of her when she was young it's uncanny. When I was a little girl, she used to always read me to sleep with the lives of the saints. How I loved those stories. The signs and miracles and prophecies. I used to tell her that I was going to grow up to be a saint just like them, and she'd smile and tell me there was no reason why I couldn't. When I got older, those sorts of things just seemed to drop away from me without my even realizing it. I believed, oh yes I assure you that I still had my faith, but when I got to be an adult I just couldn't feel the miracles in my heart, the way I could when I was little. Now it's funny. A prophecy has come true, right here in my own life. You told me how you'd come back to me in the darkness. I didn't know what the darkness would be like, how literal the fulfillment would become. But you've come to fulfill it now, haven't you, Elizabeth."

"Yes." One word, brutal and emotionless.

Her mother gave an almost imperceptible shiver. "Prophecies and miracles. The stories she read me were true, all of them. It's just they aren't quite as pretty when they really start to happen. I'm looking back over the things that've happened in the past year, and I see that my life has been a whole string of miracles. The way you came back to me. The way you healed me. And that, that's where I made my mistake. When you told me of how you cured me of all my pains, all the crosses I had been given to bear. I started to think that I was in one of the pretty stories. I thought that I was going to live such a full and happy life, then, and when you came to me again, I would be old and withered up, and happy to see you come to take me away with you. That was wrong. I was only setting myself up for a fall. I see that now."

Elizabeth stirred uncomfortably. Her mother's monotonous whisper didn't even seem to be addressed to her, but was a monologue running on from herself to herself. Trying to reassure herself that she was still there. But she wasn't. She was a shell, broken, empty. Elizabeth feared that she might be so empty that she wouldn't get any nourishment from her at all.

"Mother," she said quietly, reaching out to touch her hand. The old woman stopped. Her rheumy eyes seemed to hold no comprehension.

Elizabeth spoke again: "Mother, this is the bad time. The worst of all the times you've ever known. The worst time that has ever been. That ever could be. Humanity is finished. Everything you mortals have ever looked up to, ever worshipped, has been conquered. The Moon has been destroyed. The Sun is powerless behind clouds that aren't ever going to break, not for thousands of years. The green of life is withering. The power of storm and fire has been enslaved. Time no longer has any meaning." She swallowed, and her voice lowered. "If there ever was a God, I think that even He must be under the Master's thumb now, too.

"And Death. Death has ceased to be a menace. Look at me, look at Carlos and the Master and all the others. We laugh at Death. We've died and passed through it to come back to life again. Death is destroyed for us and for you mortals, too. You see, you're all dead now, dead minds and hearts and souls. There's just a few of you who are still walking around and don't realize it yet. Do you understand any of what I'm trying to say?"

Her mother blinked in puzzlement at the question, but then nodded slowly, "I am dead."

"Yes. So what I'm going to do now is not an act of killing. You're already dead, so how can I kill you? What I'm going to do is actually going to bring you back from death. Not into full undeath the way I am. But it will be better, better than the way you are now. No more mourning. No more pain. And we'll be together, always."

As Elizabeth was speaking, her mother's hand reached reflexively to one of the crosses on the wall, about to pull it to her breast; then she looked down at it, and cast it aside. She got up, and raised Elizabeth up with surprising strength, and said, "I'm ready. Go on and do what you have to do. And thank you, thank you for this gift."

"Thank you, mother. I'll always love you."

It didn't take long. Her mother didn't have much vitality left in her. Elizabeth wiped her mouth reflectively and almost turned to go, before she remembered the cats. She knelt again to take them into her arms. They purred, trusting to the end, suspecting no evil from her. Elizabeth's heart sank. She at least could talk and reason with her mother. But these were more difficult: how could she make them understand that she was bringing them into herself, saving them from the cold destruction of the mindless ones? She steeled herself with that thought, and went ahead and did what she had to do.

Afterward, Elizabeth walked calmly up the stairs and across the room. She breathed deeply and refreshingly of the murky air. A vampire needs to be strong; to gain that strength she must have blood, she thought. No matter the source, no matter the good or bad of it. She was eager to rejoin Carlos, to share this new strength with him and renew their love. Maybe they could make some more certain plans now, try to find some refuge where they'd be beyond the Master's reach... "Carlos?" she called.

Of course, once again, he was gone.

8.

Back to the park. No other ideas. At least Elizabeth was able to move with speed this time, flowing quickly along the raging winds. Back into the fires, and she caused them to brush aside for her passage.

She was surprised to find the Master present there in bodily form. He sat in splendor and glory on his throne, and, although there was no detectable change in his physical appearance, he seemed even fuller, even more triumphant, even more certain of his conquest and rule over the Earth, than when he brought the Moon down. He looked up at her approach, and his eyes pierced her, seeing everything she had done and thought. She shook when she saw him, fighting hard against the urge to attack him again in her anger. *Stay in control*, she told herself. He had probably drunk the blood of a thousand humans, compared to her one. He could wipe her off the face of the Earth with a glance.

She alighted, and was surprised a second time, to see that the others were there, those who were still in existence: Philip, Deborah and Alicia. They were sleek and filled, and looked disdainfully upon her ragged appearance. The Master smiled broadly as he spoke: "Good to see you, sweetest of my tools! I'm positively delighted you too have decided to come join the grand festival this one final time. Maybe less sated than some of the others have been in this endless night, but I'd bet that the one who filled you was sweet on your lips and nourishing to your soul.

"But where is your darling companion? Is it possible that the blossom of young love has already begun to wither?"

Elizabeth kept her voice even. "You should know better about that than I."

"I don't understand."

"I'm just sick and tired of all this running around, so just drop it, all right? What do you want from me this time? Why have you taken him away from me again?"

The Master allowed his face to show a brief frown. "It wasn't done by my orders. The both of you have finished every service I required of you. You're free to walk the darkened world as you wish, taking your fill of the mortals in any way you should desire. You may not believe me, but I solemnly declare to you that I didn't take your Carlos away from you this time, and whatever might have happened to him was not by my will."

"Well, who did it then? Somebody must have done something to him. You're claiming to be the ruler of the world? Well, I'm here as one of your loyal subjects, to demand justice of you. Or maybe you aren't quite as high and mighty as you think you are."

"I think it might be possible to have a little debate about your claims to loyalty, but I like to think of myself as a magnanimous ruler, and so I choose not to pursue the question at this time. Furthermore, I won't allow it to be said that one of my subjects, who has performed a valid service with which I am well pleased, made a claim on me and didn't receive satisfaction. I promise you, therefore, that your claim shall receive all due consideration and investigation, when the time is appropriate.

"But for now, there's other business of much more pressing importance. For behold, subjects, our labor in this city and the other cities of the world is complete! There's nothing left alive in any of them. They have been sterilized, through the action of my armies of mindless vampires under my control. They have moved now beyond the city limits, and are beginning to ravage the open countryside. I recommend that you join them in that effort, leaving this city behind as a nameless corpse, a memorial to the folly of the humans. They thought that they would make themselves immortal by the building of their structures. Let us, the true immortals, laugh in our disdain as we abandon it.

"And so, I declare a festival! Let there be a celebration of my glorious conquests and in anticipation of those still to come! I bid you dance, dance before me and show me your happiness!" And the last three vampires left, Deborah, Philip and Alicia, gave themselves over to the wild gyrations which Deborah had made before him as the Moon crashed. Elizabeth felt his will heavy on her, urging her to join them, but, by concentrating all her power, she resisted it. A minuscule victory, but she took heart from it.

It was, she realized, too easy a victory. She had received help. She whipped around, and saw coalesce behind her the form of Jonathan, with Carlos beside him. She rushed up to him, "What happened? Where did you go? Why did you leave me again like that?" Carlos tried to calm her down, taking her quickly into his arms and whispering, "Jonathan came to me, just like he did before, and gave me energy, and told me things which made it vitally important that I go with him. I'm sorry that I couldn't stay, or wait until you came out. It was just too sudden, too necessary that I go with him. I hoped that we could get here and do what we had to do before you got here in order too spare you the danger."

"But I don't understand..."

"There's no time to explain! No time! Just wait a couple of minutes, and listen to what Jonathan has to say. Then be ready with me to help him, when he needs us."

As they were speaking, Jonathan was striding boldly up to the front of the Master's throne. The Master obviously was aware of his presence, but studiously avoided looking down at him, concentrating instead on the dance of the vampires. Jonathan held up his hand and called out, "Hail to you, Master! Behold, the one who was your most loyal servant for many centuries has come once more before you!"

The Master feigned not to notice for a few moments longer, and then languidly cast his gaze downward. "Could I be hearing a vague buzzing like that of some irritating insect? I admit to a bit of surprise that any insects have survived the great extermination brought about by my *true* servants."

"I am come to beg pardon for my offenses, and to discover the manner in which I might return into the grace of your favor."

"A king who has been once crossed by his slave feels a little reluctance to admit him back into service. What can you do to show me that I should be welcoming you back? Do you wish to sacrifice your vitality to me now? Or were you planning on offering me the taste of the scarcely more valuable soul of that Carlos, the single vampire whom I've never had the opportunity to savor? I certainly can't think of anything else at this point which might entice me enough to take you back."

The other vampires had halted in their dance, and they stood around Jonathan with expressions of mockery on their faces. Jonathan paid them no attention. "I didn't come here to negotiate with you, Master, but, if that is the manner in which you wish to deal with me, I am prepared to answer in like fashion. Therefore, I declare to you that I have certain information which you might find desirable to possess."

The Master scoffed. "I know everything on Earth now. I, or those mindless vampires under my control, have devoured every scholar in the world. There is no data you could possibly provide me that I don't know already. But go on, tell me this secret knowledge you claim to have. If I'm sufficiently amused by what you have to say, I might yet show enough mercy to employ you as my clown."

"Thank you, Master. I wouldn't have the temerity to suggest that you are lacking in any knowledge that the humans might have obtained in their history. But I might make the polite suggestion that you might not have paid quite enough attention to some of their findings in the sphere of physics. In particular, I refer to that principle which the mortals have called the Second Law of Thermodynamics."

"It's not unfamiliar to me."

"Ah, but has it not occurred to you that it might have some possible application even to us, the undead?"

The Master didn't speak, but his frown was deepening.

Jonathan began to talk more quickly. "You have conquered the world, Master, and no one can deny your primacy and might. It's not possible to make any accurate estimations at this point, but I'd guess that at least two-thirds of the human race has been exterminated already. Considering the current level of depredations caused by the mindless horde, as well as starvation, disease and other sources of mortality, I'd hazard that the remaining mortal population is unlikely to survive any more than the period which they used to call a week, back when time could be determined. Would you consider my estimates accurate, based on your greater knowledge?"

The Master slowly nodded.

"Very good. The problem I foresee is, *what will happen then?* After the last human is consumed, and then the last particle of animal life, and all remaining plants, and even the vitality of the microbes and bacteria? The empty lust of the mindless ones is well-known to all of us, and it will certainly not be quenched even after all life has been exterminated. What then?"

"The mindless ones are under my control. When their task is finished, I can easily return them to their graves."

"Yes, that might be a satisfactory solution to that problem. But what about the rest of us? We too need to feed. We need blood, and memories, and dreams to devour. But what will happen to us after the last human is consumed? How are we to continue to exist and thrive, in this endless world of glorious darkness, to continue to serve your pleasure?"

The Master meditated on his statements for a minute, and then arose. "You have failed. I do not accept this information you're trying to give to me. I don't need to be told it, because you haven't said anything I didn't know already... Your theory is correct. When all life has finally been destroyed, you vampires will no longer have any form of sustenance. And that is of no concern to me."

There was a stir among the others. "What's he saying?" "What's going to happen to us then?"

Jonathan laughed bitterly. "I can tell you what Master is hinting to us. When mortal life is no more, he won't have any more use for you. He will then consume you, and then there will be nothing in existence but himself and his massive ego. We are all going to die, to feed him, and it's too late to stop him now. When he came to us to tell us of his great plan to conquer the world, I realized this secret meaning of all his honeyed words. That's when I ran away. And that's the true conclusion of your plan, isn't it Master? We were nothing more than tools which were useful for a little while, and then we were to become nothing more than food for you?"

The Master's mouth moved into the shape of a cruel smile, and he said simply, "Yes."

His laughter echoed hollowly among the dead trees: "You blind fools, so absorbed in your own little thoughts! You've been playing for all these centuries at being the great hunters, and you've amused yourselves wasting all the wonderful powers which I so magnanimously loaned to you from my infinite might; never for a moment did a single one of you ever stop to think through the *true meaning* of what you were, and of what the Night of Wrath would really result in. Short-sighted cretins! All of this, each moment of it, was arranged by my prophetic Plan ages ago, when the first stupid apes were dropping from the trees and picking up stones for themselves. Even then, my majestic Design for their distantly foreseen but inevitable destruction was being arranged. You haven't been anything but implements, and nothing more. Just a few weeks, as time used to be reckoned, and all life will have been snuffed out from the Earth, completely and irrevocably, and the clouds will prevent any sprouting of hidden seeds and the renewal of life, and then, I'll fall back into the cold stone of the Earth, there to contemplate the eternal pleasure of my own starvation.

"Why are you looking askance now, trying to edge away from me, you miserable little insects and vermin? There's no escape. The whole Earth is in the palm of my hand. Try to flee this particular manifestation of my being, and you'll find me hidden inside every cold rock. Sudden fire will flare at your steps to melt your flesh and crack your bones. Every dusty stretch of ground shall yawn open to engulf you. Be still, and appreciate the singular honor which I am paying you by deigning to extinguish you with my own mouth!"

He began to expand that mouth along with his entire frame, to a massive form like a bloated whale unnaturally walking on the dry land, but with long claw-like arms stretching out toward the quailing vampires. They backed away, except for Philip, who fell upon the ground to worship him as a god, and was thus the first to be taken up in his claws.

But Jonathan did not flee. Carlos, standing behind him, called out to Elizabeth, "Help us now! It's the last stand! Give him every bit of energy you can spare!" They joined hands, and unleashed the strength of their love, a might that was untainted by the Master's foul hand, and they fed it into Jonathan's body. Jonathan marshalled that power, and suddenly sent it forth as a bolt of force that seared away the gloom of the endless night and withered all despair.

But the bolt did not strike at the Master. Instead, it sailed over the top of his head and shot upwards, into the clouds, and vanished. The Master started to laugh at this wasted attack, but then he paused, dropping Philip from his lips, sensing an incipient change to the environment, the nature of which he could not yet perceive. "What was that bolt for?" he demanded.

Now it was Jonathan's turn to laugh. "It did nothing, except to bring about more swiftly what would have happened by itself, soon enough," he replied. "You've been planning and scheming for all these millions of years, at least if you're finally telling us the full truth. And all of your goals have had one single end, to remove the power of the Sun. But you've underestimated life one more time, Master. You've forgotten that there's another power in the world, another force which is united with the power of light to form life. Another power before which you're helpless. The thing that would be almost comical, if the destruction you've wrought wasn't so tragic, is that you have brought about yourself the very conditions which are going to cause your destruction."

He pointed upward to the thick cloud cover, and as he did so the first drops of rain fell.

"You're the fool, Jonathan. Water may impede me, but it cannot destroy me."

"This is no ordinary water, Master. It is filled with the energy of Carlos and Elizabeth's love, and the love of all living things."

In moments the rainfall passed from a trickle to a shower, then to a downpour and a torrent. Heedless of the damage the water was doing to his own form, Jonathan continued to stand, pointing gleefully upwards at the waters as they cascaded down. The Master, trapped in his gargantuan form, thrashed in agony as the liquid worked its way around and through his body.

He thundered, "No! It's too late! I won't let it happen! I can't be defeated. Not again!" But in a moment he was no longer able to give voice, as his face was melting into a fatty liquid. He sought to erect a structure around himself, to protect and save him, but the fury of the sudden holy storm was too mighty, and Jonathan, Carlos and

Elizabeth combined their energies to help it wash away his every attempt. Great chunks of his form were cut free by the purifying rain, and they rolled off the dais and lay smoking on the ground. A great and vile smoke of burning arose into the clouds, providing more seed for precipitation.

The Master's vast distorted bones became visible, but still the vampires could sense his will, twisted but inchoate, writhing through them in his continuing agony.

Then, slowly and almost imperceptibly, even that remnant faded away from their detection, save only for a tiny beating impression of pain, pain that had endured from the beginning of the world, and which would never know cessation until its end.

The Master was dead.

9.

The last five beings on Earth huddled miserably on the basement floor of a ruined building, seeking but not finding some space which was still dry.

After the destruction of the Master, Elizabeth pulled the nearly dissolved form of Jonathan away to the insufficient shelter she and Carlos had found under a gazebo, and to which they had already dragged the unconscious shapes of Alicia and Deborah. Carlos had tried to save Philip, but he refused any aid as he knelt desolate in front of the depression where the Master had lain. As Philip's body wore away, he had formed his arm into a great sword, and cut his own throat, to pour out his remaining blood into the empty space, praying that would be enough to reanimate his fallen Master. But it was not, and thus Philip destroyed himself.

When they had reached shelter, they tried to heal themselves, but found their flesh resisting their wills. As the Master faded away, so too they were losing their powers, which had all derived ultimately from his. Every time they moved from structure to structure, their healing was slower and required more effort. At last, after they made it to this shell of a mortal building, they were afraid to try to go any further. And thus there they remained.

As the rain fell, the air turned colder, and soon the precipitation turned to snow. It wasn't the soft and delightful snow that Elizabeth had experienced during the first winter of her undeath; it fell a heavy, sticky and cloying substance, that got on their bodies and wouldn't fade away until it had burned all the way down to the bone. It also stuck to the ground, and built up into drifts reaching higher and higher, as it fell on and on, day after day. Soon enough they were trapped in the basement, with the door blocked by deep drifts, unable to move elsewhere now even if they had tried.

As the precipitation continued to fall, the clouds slowly began to lessen. After several weeks the band of friends could dimly perceive the passage of days, a faint period of vague light as opposed to the pitch blackness of the night. With the return of the cycle of day and night they experienced the return of their hungry pain, as the Sun in its spite hounded their weak frames.

They were the last vampires still in existence. They desperately sent out calls with all the strength of their united minds, while that strength lasted, seeking for any reply that might come from any corner of the world. But there was no answer. Any of the other undead who possessed minds had been summoned to the great dance of triumph before the Master, in his myriad of bodies across the Earth. All had been destroyed in the sudden onslaught of the rain, unleashed all over the planet by the energy shot into the clouds by Jonathan. They assumed that all the mindless ones had perished as well, literally not knowing enough to stay out of the rain. They were alone. The last beings on Earth.

They were starving together. There was nothing living within reach, nothing they could bite and drain and use for their revitalization. Carlos and Elizabeth were capable of circumventing this, of course, but after merging themselves one time in the sexual act, they felt ashamed and guilty, as they saw the jealous and mournful faces of the others who could not partake with them. So they too forwent their special sustenance, and joined the others in their slow fading into nothingness. There was nothing worth continuing their existence for.

The others found scarce amusements. Periodically the rage of her guilt would overtake Deborah, and she would fling herself into the snowdrift at the open door, trying to dissolve herself. But her inner fear of death was more powerful, and it would cause her to pull back. Her body was ragged and horribly scarred, no longer able to bring about any healing. No fingers or toes, almost no visible face remaining, she lay in a semi-conscious trance on the floor at other times, giving forth moans of misery.

Alicia took her insect form with her remaining strength and wove a spider-like web in a ceiling corner. Being compact, she was able to horde a greater amount of strength than the others, but she had sacrificed her human brain and the power of speech, and so spent most of the endless days in silent contemplation of the others on the floor. At other times, raging in her jealous hatred for Elizabeth and

Carlos, she repeatedly attacked Jonathan, forcing him into bouts of sexual acrobatics, trying to achieve the state of higher being with him. But since the act arose out of self-interest rather than love, she always failed. Often she sat and glared at Deborah, kicking the prone body with her chitinous legs when its cries grew too irritating.

In between Alicia's attacks Jonathan sat meditatively in a corner, never speaking. Elizabeth feared at times that he was already dead, but when he responded almost reflexively to Alicia's advances she knew that his body must have still contained some vitality.

Finally, there was a burning day of dread and despair. When evening fell, it was apparent that the end was near. Alicia had fallen from her web, and lay in a tiny ball with her legs sticking up in the air. Deborah was nothing more than a large mass of gelatin-like material that gave forth random pulsings of movement, causing a noxious odor to arise. Jonathan lay dissolute on the floor, unable to stir. He managed to beckon to Elizabeth and Carlos, who still had the ability for slow movement, and they crawled over to him. They held their heads close to hear his ragged whispers.

"This is the last night for me. I can feel it. You may last a few days longer, but you're doomed too, unless one final hope is realized."

Elizabeth ran her hand over his feverish forehead to try to give him some comfort. "Don't try to talk," she said. "Save what strength you still have."

"No, I have to talk. I have to tell you all the things I've been thinking over. It's vital: the very last chance for any life to return to the world. You have to listen, and listen carefully." But his voice cracked, and he was racked by a coughing fit for several minutes, choking on and spitting up wads of the bloody substance of his lungs.

"That's a little bit better," he wheezed after a time. "But I can't talk for long. You have to help me. I've thought and thought and thought about every word I ever heard Master say, in all the years, the centuries, in which I knew him. There's only one thing he ever said, ever, that might help us. Do you remember, Carlos, Elizabeth, that one sentence he spoke, when Carlos and I appeared before him on the night he was destroyed? The sentence he uttered describing Carlos?"

They concentrated. So much had happened so quickly, and such suffering had occurred since then. Suddenly Carlos said, "I think I remember it! It was something that sounded very strange at the time and puzzled me. Something like saying I was the only vampire who was foreign to him...."

"The only vampire he hadn't savored'," Elizabeth added. "I felt a deep stabbing in my heart when I heard those words, but I don't know why."

Jonathan only nodded.

Elizabeth frowned. "That's it? That's something that gives you hope? What could it mean?"

Jonathan whispered, "Think back, back to when you were young in undeath; think with your heart as well as your mind."

Elizabeth struggled to plunge back into her memory. But Carlos looked increasingly confused and exasperated. "I don't understand. The Master said more than once that he couldn't give me any of my memories. That's why I had to go looking for Elizabeth. What's so strange about what he said that last night?"

Jonathan managed to speak once more, "The Master said he was the one who brought us all out of death. But how could he have done that for you, if he didn't *know* you?"

Elizabeth replied with a cold certainty, "Because the Master never touched Carlos. I remember it now. That night, in the hospital. I was the one, I was the one who took your blood. He never tasted a drop of you, and so he never learned any part of your being. And that means, that means..."

"It means that you were the one who brought me back: the one who made me a vampire!"

Jonathan smiled. "Yes," he sighed. "Somehow, somehow, it was Elizabeth who returned you out of the grave. An act of love and devotion for you even then, when she first saw you. She was moved by her pity, and you were revived. Somehow she lost that memory. Master lied again. He wasn't the only one who could return us from death. Elizabeth can do it, too."

Elizabeth turned away. Her words were hurtful, but possessed a hidden element of fear. "But I don't see how this could help us. You say I can raise up vampires. So what? It's too late. Everything is dead already. I don't have any power anymore. I can't raise up anything now."

Jonathan choked out a single sentence, *"Are you sure?"*

"I don't know what you mean."

"Yes, you do."

Carlos interrupted, "Well, I don't. What going on? What are you trying to do to her?"

Jonathan tried to calm him down with a feeble wave. "Don't get angry. I'm not trying to do anything to hurt her. Elizabeth, you were the channel, the focus point through which Master passed all the power which brought down the Moon."

"Yes," she replied tersely.

"And you were also the focus through which Master ran the souls of Stephen and my little Guillaume."

"I'm not going to listen to you any longer!" she cried out, climbing to her feet. "If you say another word, I'm going to jump right into the snowbank and destroy myself, and you won't be able to put me through any more torture! I won't go back there! I won't let you drag me back! Everything's gone, all gone. The Master destroyed me along with all the others. The only memories I have left are what Carlos gave me. I won't go back there again."

Jonathan tried to rise and follow her. But the strain was too much, and he fell back to the ground, hacking and wheezing again.

Carlos jumped up when Elizabeth did so, running to her, but she pushed him away with such strength that he fell back down, right next to Jonathan. Jonathan reached out for him, forcing out the words, "It's the end. I'm about to die. She won't listen to me, so you're going to have to make her do it."

"What? How? I don't understand what's going on?"

Jonathan reached up to grasp his head, and pulled it down to his own throat. "You must take me. My strength, my knowledge will be your guide."

Carlos tried to pull back, but Jonathan's grip was tightening with the beginning of the rictus of death, and the odor of his coagulating blood was thick in Carlos' nostrils as he lay upon him, until he could no longer resist. He bit, and drained him.

Then Jonathan's mind entered into communion with Carlos, teaching him, telling him what must be done. He turned to Elizabeth, and she screamed to see the presence of Jonathan in his eyes. "It's all right," he said reassuringly. "It's still me. But Jonathan's just here to help me. To help all of us."

"No, I can't do it! It's like I said! There's nothing left! I can't go back there, or I'll get lost. I'll fall into that great jagged wound, and there isn't anybody to come save me now!"

Carlos took a step toward her, and she backed a step away. "But it's the last hope. The only hope for the world. You were united with Stephen and Guillaume. Between them they held the contents of the entire world. Maybe, just maybe, if any piece of your soul survived that ordeal, they might have survived too. And since we've discovered that you have the power of raising the dead, by the power of your love and pity we might together be able to bring everything back, back into existence!"

"This is just Jonathan talking. He just wants to try to get his little baby boy back. He's absorbed you, not the other way around."

Carlos took a second step forward, and this time she remained where she was. "No. I can feel him, and yes, he tells me that he would be lying if there wasn't a personal desire in the thing he needs us to do. But it's the whole world that's at stake. If you refuse, you're condemning uncounted billions to destruction. All the mortals, and all the undead, and every form of animal and plant and insect. You've got to give them the chance."

"But if that's true the Master's back there too. If we bring back the world, we're liable to bring him back as well, and then we'll be right back in the mess we started from."

Carlos took a third step, and enveloped her in his arms. "That's the chance we're going to have to take."

She was trembling. "I'm so afraid. All I can remember is the pain, a pain like icepicks running through my body, the feeling of myself pouring out, on and on with nothing coming back in to fill me up again. I don't want to have to remember it. I don't want to feel that feeling again."

He replied, "But we're going to do it together, this time." And he tenderly raised her mouth to his neck, and turned his own face to hers.

They entered into communion. As it happened, Carlos was shocked and amazed to discover the levels which Elizabeth had managed to conceal from him up to now: a huge expanse of mental scar tissue, like the pocked surface of an airless and dead planet. She wasn't holding anything back from him this time; she bared everything, communicating to him that this was what Jonathan wanted to plunge her back into. The depths which they would have to survey, if they were looking for Stephen and Guillaume. Then Jonathan brought his own consciousness out from the interior of Carlos, a Virgil for their journey into the Inferno. He leapt boldly into the depths of the scar tissue, seeking, calling out for Guillaume. In the long centuries of their togetherness, they too had achieved a level of special communion, not perhaps with the same sexual intensity and self-sufficiency which had been achieved by Elizabeth and Carlos, but caring and affectionate in its own way. Jonathan was seeking for any fragment of this love which might yet be extant. He sank deeper into the damaged tissues, until he was lost to the perceptions of the two of them.

They waited, with the spiritual equivalent of breathlessness.

And they heard a sound, soft and almost undetectable, like the distant crying of a baby. It was Guillaume, who had regressed himself to a state of infancy. And if Guillaume survived, then certainly Stephen must be trapped somewhere down there as well....

There was an upwelling of excitement as Elizabeth and Carlos realized that their goal might yet be achieved, and the ragged spiritual landscape quavered. That quaking was enough, just enough to cause a rupture in the massive psychic scar tissue below them, a rupture out of which poured a purifying light. And the light arose, eating away at more and more of the scar, and shone around them. The light of the Sun, Stephen's Sun, which smiled placidly over the fortunes of the undead, and they felt no pain. They felt no pain, even as it assailed them with its brightness, assaulted them and broke them to pieces. They faded away into dissolution, and knew no more.

POSTLUDE

They awoke in each other's arms, with a soft flow of blood still moving between their bodies. Opening their eyes they saw that they were back in their safe refuge, in the abandoned factory. Elizabeth laughed; of course, the world which was contained by the souls of Stephen and Guillaume was complete only to the night in which the Master had captured them all.

Carlos looked around. "I'm all confused again," he said. "It's, it's like it was all a dream. Did any of it really happen?"

"Vampires don't dream," she replied. "Or at least that was what I was told. But I don't know. There are so many things that are so strange, so much of what happened that's all dark and confused to me."

Elizabeth arose, and pulled aside the drape to look out the window, at the great and grave night, dark yet clear, with stars glimmering over the outlines of buildings. She sent forth her senses, detecting the hum of human activity: a horde of unthinking and unknowing mortals, totally unsuspecting that their world had been destroyed in fire and blood, and then brought back into being again, poured forth from her own substance. Like a medal of honor in the sky, there was the full Moon setting behind the silhouetted city, unshattered, pristine like a jewel. She cried out to it in her heart like meeting a long-lost friend again.

Or was Carlos right, and none of it had been so? She seemed to detect subtle *differences* in the world, as if reality had been pulled through a wringer, enlivened, re-animated, painted anew in fresher colors. Which made a certain degree of sense to her, as the world which Stephen had contained was one of fantasy and romance, the world as envisioned by art rather than the humdrum inanity of true existence. Yet on the other hand, this sensation of renewal could very well have been produced from the reaffirmation of her own existence, pardoned from the death-sentence of cold and miserable starvation.

For a moment, there came a stab of fear into her being, thinking that this too was nothing but another trick, another programming of her behavior by the Master, to take away the world and then bring it back into reality again, for some unguessable
esoteric purpose of his own. Could she never set this fear behind her? At what point does a natural skeptical distrust cross the border into

paranoia, and to a madness which would lead ultimately to a surrender of her essence to the call of mindlessness?

And a second telling fear came to her, of the realization that the Master was in fact still a part of this world, active and malevolent. "Carlos," she said in a concerned voice, "They'll be looking for us tonight, the other vampires, under his command. What are we going to do? If he catches us, then the exact same course of events will happen all over again."

"But there's one important difference," he replied from behind her. "This time we know what he's up to, and we can make plans. The Master told us too much. We know now how his plans work, and that he can be resisted and destroyed. We won't let the others catch us unawares again. Even more, we know now that there are other intelligent vampires in other cities, all over the world. As long as we resist, his plan can't be accomplished, and we have a chance now to find them all and organize our resistance."

A great desire began to emerge in her being, to set out into this exciting new world, to explore its nooks and crannies, to see in just what ways it was new, and how much of the old had been spared, a voyage of discovery which would take them to other cities, other places of undead mystery and enchantment, to seek the other vampires, to see and learn even more fantastic and exotic ways in which they had chosen to spend their eternal existence, and to see in what ways their undead state was influenced and controlled by the Master.

But then she hit herself on the side of the head, and cried out yet again, "I've done it again! I've forgotten about my mother! She still hasn't gotten the chance to meet you yet, Carlos. I won't let you set off on all this journeying until the two of you finally get together. I've been looking forward to showing you off to her for so long now. I'm not going to let another chance pass by again."

"All right," he replied with a laugh, still standing behind her where she couldn't see him. "I think, after everything we've gone through lately, I've finally developed the courage to face anything, even your mother. But there's something I want you to do for me, first."

He turned her around, and she saw that, while she had been staring out the one window at the setting Moon, Carlos had opened up another window, the one facing in the other direction, revealing the rapidly spreading light of the Sun about to rise.

"If I'm going to have to face your mother, I want you to stand here with me first and face the Sun. We're more than vampires now. I know it, all the strange things that happened have proved it to me. I know now that the Sun will no longer do us any harm. So you're going to have to stand here, right beside me, and greet the Sun, as a brother and a friend. Who knows, maybe we can even give your mother a bigger surprise than she expected; we can go see her this very morning."

Elizabeth felt the old fear coming back one more time. What if they were wrong? What if this world they were beholding was only an illusion brought of their twisted imaginings? What if the world had been skewed by its passage through the souls of Stephen and Elizabeth herself, so that the whole thing would shrivel and burn under the coming of the Sun? At this moment, more than at any time in the entirety of both her life and her undeath, she didn't want to be destroyed.

"Don't be afraid," Carlos reassured her. "We're strong. We're together. And we have the whole of eternity before us, to laugh and love, both night and day, for ever. Together."

Together. She took a deep breath, and reached out to hold his hand. Together they stood, and prepared, for good or for ill, to face the kiss of the Sun.

HUMOR/HORROR FOR A DYING PLANET

from III Publishing

THE LAST DAYS OF CHRIST THE VAMPIRE
by J.G. Eccarius $7.00
Did Christ really rise from the dead? Is he still alive? Can some outcasts and teenagers defeat his plan for Armageddon?
"A book of stunning originality, full of surrealistic shocks and haunting images."   - Robert Anton Wilson
"One of the most wildly blasphemous books we have seen since the classics of sacrilege." - Fifth Estate

THIS'LL KILL YA
by Harry Wilson $6.00
Who's killing the town's censorship committee? Could it be Satan, or their own evil hearts?
"[An] entertaining and thought provoking book." - Writers' Workshop
"Apocalyptic Global vision with robust down-home wit."
- Gene H. Bell-Villada

WE SHOULD HAVE KILLED THE KING
by J.G. Eccarius $5.00
"A picaresque novel for the Baby Bust Generation. The book opens in England in 1381 when Jack Straw and Watt Tyler were hung for leading a rebellion of the serfs ... and casts forward a bit into the future to describe what an anarchist society might look like and what kinds of problems it may face." - Flatland
"... anywayz, i really thought this was a kool book, i was freaked out after I finished it. Be sure & read this!" - Iron Feather Journal
"All in all, an interesting, chewy, different book." - Factsheet Five

@ SAMPLES $2.00
edited by Bill Meyers
A collection of current day anarchist writings on the environment, literature, and community defense.

Send cash, check or money order to III Publishing, P.O. Box 170363, San Francisco, CA 94117-0363. Please include $1.00 for shipping the first book, and $.50 for each additional book.